NEW CONCEPT ENGLISH

环球英语全能新概念丛书

词汇进阶

环球雅思学校

新概念英语学习推荐用书

（第四册）

梁琦 张艳 编著

中国水利水电出版社
www.waterpub.com.cn

内 容 提 要

本书通过例句、英文释义、词根词缀分析等多角度讲解，突出了《新概念英语》(第四册)的高频词汇，让理解与记忆同步，能切实帮助读者提高英语水平。本书适用于学习《新概念英语》(第四册)的读者。

图书在版编目(CIP)数据

词汇进阶．第4册/梁琦，张艳编著．—北京：中国水利水电出版社，2008

(环球英语全能新概念丛书)

ISBN 978-7-5084-5184-8

Ⅰ．词… Ⅱ．①梁…②张… Ⅲ．英语－词汇－自学参考资料 Ⅳ．H313

中国版本图书馆CIP数据核字(2007)第194180号

书　　名	环球英语全能新概念丛书 **词汇进阶(第四册)**
作　　者	梁琦　张艳　编著
出版　发行	中国水利水电出版社(北京市三里河路6号　100044) 网址：www.waterpub.com.cn E-mail：sales@waterpub.com.cn 电话：(010)63202266(总机)、68331835(营销中心)
经　　售	北京科水图书销售中心(零售) 电话：(010)88383994、63202643 全国各地新华书店和相关出版物销售网点
排　　版	北京中科洁卡科技有限公司
印　　刷	北京市地矿印刷厂
规　　格	880mm×1230mm　32开本　9.5印张　294千字
版　　次	2008年1月第1版　2008年1月第1次印刷
印　　数	0001—4000册
定　　价	**18.00**元

目　录

Unit 1

Unit 2

Unit 3

Unit 4

Unit 5

Unit 6

Unit 1

Lesson 1

fossil man [ˈfɔsl] ***n.*** 化石人

♥ There is fossil man being exhibited in that museum.
那家博物馆有化石人展出。

♥ The fossil man may be ten thousand years old.
这个化石人可能有1万年了。

实际应用
fossil 化石
fossils of early reptiles 早期爬行动物的化石
living fossil 活化石

recount [riˈkaunt] ***v. formal* to tell someone a story or describe a series of events** 叙述

♥ The old men recounted how the village developed.
老人们讲述了村庄是怎么发展起来的。

♥ The boy recounted how he survived the disaster.
那个男孩讲述了如何在灾难中幸存下来。

相关表达
narrate *v.* 叙述，讲述；recite *v.* 叙述，背诵

记忆点拨
re(又，再）＋count(唱）

saga [ˈsɑːgə] ***n.* a long and complicated series of events, or a description of this** 英雄故事

♥ The book is a saga of four generations of the Coleman family.
这本书讲述科尔曼家族四代人的传奇故事。

♥ She told me the saga of her family problems.
她没完没了地跟我讲她家里的事。

相关表达
epic *n.* 史诗；story *n.* 故事

legend ['ledʒənd] *n.* **an old, well-known story, often about brave people, adventures, or magical events** 传说，传奇

♥ He enjoys reading ancient Greek legends.
他喜欢读古代希腊传说。

♥ Yao Ming is a marvellous basketball player who was a legend in his country.
姚明是一个非凡的篮球运动员，他在他的祖国是个传奇人物。

相关表达 **fable** *n.* 神话；**myth** *n.* 神话

记忆点拨 leg(读) ＋end(结尾) things to be read(供阅读的东西)

migration [maiˈgreiʃən] *n.* 迁徙，移居

①**when large numbers of people go to live in another area or country, especially in order to find work** 移居

♥ America is one of the most popular countries for migration.
美国是最受欢迎的移民国家之一。

②**when birds or animals travel regularly from one part of the world to another** 迁徙

♥ Scientists have studied the migration of these birds.
科学家们已经研究了这些鸟的迁徙。

相关表达 **migrate** *v.* 迁徙；移民
immigrate *v.* 移入
emigrate *v.* 移出

记忆点拨 migr(移动) ＋ate(动词后缀)

anthropologist [ˌænθrəˈpɔlədʒist] *n.* 人类学家

♥ It is rare for an anthropologist to spend more than 15 percent of his career outside the university setting.
一个人类学家把15%以上的工作时间花在大学科研以外是很罕见的。

♥ An anthropologist spends a lot of time writing, editing, doing field work, teaching, consulting with other professionals.
人类学家花费大量的时间用于写作、编辑、调查工作、教学以及与其他专业人员交换意见。

相关表达 **anthropology** *n.* 人类学

记忆点拨 anthropo(人) ＋log(y)(学科) ＋ist(人)

archaeologist [ˌɑːkiˈɔlədʒist] *n.* 考古学家

♥ The archaeologists found a lot of fossil insects near the village.
考古学家在村子附近发现了许多化石昆虫。

♥ Archaeologists excavate, preserve, study, and classify artifacts of the near and distant past in order to develop a picture of how people lived in earlier cultures and societies.
为了描绘人类在早期文明和社会中的生活景象，考古学家挖掘、保护、研究并且将近代和古代器物分类。

相关表达 **archaeology** *n.* 考古学

记忆点拨 archaeo（古老的，原始的）＋log(y)(学科) ＋ist (人)

ancestor [ˈænsistə] *n.* **a member of your family who lived a long time ago** 祖先

♥ It is an island once owned by his ancestors.
这是一座曾经属于他的先辈的岛屿。

♥ My ancestors came from Spain.
我的祖先是西班牙人。

记忆点拨 an(前) ＋ces(走) ＋tor(名词后缀)（走在前面的人）

相关表达 ancestry *n.* 祖先；血统；descendant *n.* 后代

Polynesian [ˌpɔliˈniːziən] ***adj.*** 波利尼西亚（中太平洋之一群岛）的

♥ We were attracted by the amazing performance of the Polynesian dancers.
我们被波利尼西亚舞蹈演员精彩的表演所吸引。

♥ My professor was researching how Polynesian seafarers discovered and settled nearly every inhabitable island in the Pacific Ocean.
我的教授正在研究波利尼西亚航海者如何发现并定居在太平洋几乎每一个可以居住的岛上。

相关表达 Polynesia *n.* 波利尼西亚

记忆点拨 Polynesia（波利尼西亚）＋ n(……的，……人)

Indonesia [ˌindəuˈniːzjə] ***n.*** 印度尼西亚

♥ Indonesia was dominated by the Dutch East Indias Company from 1602 to 1798.
1602～1798 年，荷兰东印度公司控制了印度尼西亚。

♥ Jakarta is the capital and the largest city of Indonesia.
雅加达是印度尼西亚的首都也是最大的城市。

flint [flint] ***n.*** 燧石

① [uncountable] **a type of smooth hard stone that makes a small flame when you hit it with steel** 燧石；火石

② [countable] **a piece of this stone or a small piece of metal that makes a small flame when you hit it with steel** 打火石

♥ Flints can be used to light fire.
打火石可以用来点火。

♥ A piece of flint was used as a tool by primitive human beings.
一块火石曾经被原始人作为工具。

词组拓展　a heart of flint 铁石心肠
flint-hearted ***adj.*** 冷酷无情的

rot　[rɔt] ***v.*** **to decay by a gradual natural process, or to make something do this** 烂掉

♥ The ripe fruit began to rot when no one came to pick it.
没有人来摘这些成熟的水果，它们已经开始烂了。

♥ The beams had rotted away.
横梁已经腐朽了。

相关表达　rotten *adj.* 烂的

Lesson 2

beast [biːst] *n.* *written* **an animal, especially a large or dangerous one** 野兽

♥ The residents told the travelers there are savage beasts in the forest.

当地居民告诉旅游者森林里有猛兽。

♥ Cindy's brother was a real beast.

辛迪的哥哥简直是个畜生。

相关表达 feast *n.* 盛宴

census [ˈsensəs] *n.* **an official process of counting a country's population and finding out about the people**（人口）统计数字

an official process of counting something for government planning（政府计划）统计数字

♥ The census enumerated twenty-one persons over one hundred years old in this district.

根据人口调查这一地区共有 21 位百岁老人。

实际应用 population census 人口普查

acre [ˈeikə] *n.* **a unit for measuring area, equal to 4840 square yards or 4047 square metres** 英亩

♥ The farmland covers an area of 200 acres.

这个农场占地 200 英亩。

♥ The Browns own 100 acres of wood.

布朗一家拥有 100 英亩树林。

词组拓展 acres of space 大片空地

content [kən'tent] ***adj.*** **happy and satisfied** 满足的

- Mary is a good wife, he is clearly very content.
  玛丽是一个好妻子，他明显很满意。
- Many people in Beijing are not content with their housing conditions.
  在北京，很多人对住房状况不是很满意。

相关表达 **contents** 内装物品

记忆点拨 con（合起来，聚拢地）＋ tent（帐篷）

Lesson 3

Matterhorn [ˈmætəːhɔːn] *n.* 马特霍恩峰（阿尔卑斯山峰之一，在意大利和瑞士边境）

♥ The Matterhorn is one of the world's most famous mountains, located in Switzerland.
马特霍恩峰是世界最著名的山峰之一，位于瑞士境内。

♥ Matterhorn in Switzerland is one of the most popular mountains by climbers.
瑞士的马特霍恩峰是最受登山者欢迎的山峰之一。

alpinist [ˈælpinist] *n.* **a mountain climber** 登山运动员

♥ An alpinist always specializes difficult climbs.
登山运动员总是专攻高难度的攀登。

♥ The alpinist club in my university is famous.
我们大学的登山社团很出名。

相关表达 mountaineer *n.* 山地人；登山运动员

记忆点拨 alpin(e)（高山的）＋ ist（人）

pioneer [ˌpaiəˈniə] *n.* **someone who is important in the early development of something, and whose work or ideas are later developed by other people** 先锋，开辟者

♥ Dr. Li is a pioneer in cancer research.
李医生是癌症研究的先锋。

♥ They have found a pioneer treatment for cancer.
他们已经发现了对付癌症的开拓性治疗方法。

记忆点拨 pion ＋ eer（实干家）

词组拓展　the pioneer spirit 拓荒精神

summit　[ˈsʌmit] *n.* **an important meeting or set of meetings between the leaders of several governments** 顶峰；最高会议

♥ He has reached the summit of this mountain.
他曾经登上这座山的顶峰。

♥ A four-nation summit meeting will be held in spring.
四国首脑会议将于春天举行。

记忆点拨　sum(总) ＋mit

相关表达　**summary** *n.* 总结；**sum** *v.* 总计

词义辨析　summit peak climax 都含“最高点”或“顶端”的意思。

summit 指“顶点”、“最高处”、“成就的顶峰”，如：talks at the summit 最高级会谈。

peak 指“山中的最高峰”、“山顶”，还可指“程度、数量、物体等的尖端”，如：the peak output 最高产量。

climax 指“兴趣、情绪或重要性的最高点”或“戏剧、小说等情节的高潮”，如：

♥ His quarrel with his father brought matters to a climax.
他与他父亲的争吵使得事态发展到了顶点。

attain　[əˈtein] *v.* **to succeed in achieving something after trying for a long time** 到达；获得

♥ He finally attained the position of the president of the company.
他终于当上了这家公司的总裁。

♥ Mary attained her ideal weight after hard exercise.
通过艰苦锻炼，玛丽达到了她理想的体重。

记忆点拨 at＋tain (to reach)

相关表达 attainable *adj.* 可到达的；可得到的

perilous [ˈperiləs] ***adj.* very dangerous 危险的**

♥ The aircraft caught fire, a perilous situation.

飞机起火，情况十分危险。

词组拓展 a perilous journey to the west 去西方的危险旅程

相关表达 hazardous; risky; dangerous 危险的

记忆点拨 peril (危险) ＋ ous (……的)

shudder [ˈʃʌdə] ***v.* to shake for a short time because you are afraid or cold, or because you think something is very unpleasant 不寒而栗**

♥ Jane shuddered as she walked in the dark forest.

简颤抖地走在黑暗的森林里。

♥ He shuddered at the thought that his mother could have been killed.

他一想到母亲差点被杀害就不寒而栗。

其他词性 *n.* 震动，颤抖

court [kɔːt] ***v.* to try hard to please someone, especially because you want something from them 追求**

♥ He has been courting wealth and fame.

他一向追求名利。

♥ A man courts a woman because he hopes to marry her.

一个男人追求一个女人是因为他希望可以和她结婚。

相关表达 chase; pursue; woo

其他词性 *n.* 法院，庭院，朝廷，奉承

solitary [ˈsɔlitəri] ***adj.*** **used to emphasize that there is only one of something** 唯一的

♥ There was a solitary horse in the field.
地里仅有一匹马。

♥ He spent twenty-five years in prison in solitary confinement.
他在监狱里被单独监禁了 25 年。

相关表达 **single** 单一的；个别的

记忆点拨 sol（alone）＋itary（*adj.*）

impoverish [imˈpɔvəriʃ] ***v.*** **to make someone very poor; to make something worse in quality** 使贫困

♥ The soil was impoverished by overuse.
过度耕作使土壤变得贫瘠。

♥ There are many families impoverished by debt.
许多家庭被债务弄得穷困潦倒。

记忆点拨 im＋pover（poor）＋ish（v.）

相关表达 **an impoverished man** 一个贫穷的人
spiritual impoverishment 精神贫乏

Alpine [ˈælpain] ***adj.*** **relating to the Alps（＝a mountain range in central Europe）or to mountains in general** 阿尔卑斯山的

♥ Tom loves the Alpine skiing.
汤姆喜欢在阿尔卑斯山滑雪。

♥ They are enjoying the breathtaking Alpine scenery.
他们正在欣赏那非凡的阿尔卑斯山景色。

相关表达 **alpine** ***adj.*** 高山的；**alpine plants** 高山植物

记忆点拨 Alp（s）（阿尔卑斯山）＋ ine（阴性词的形容词后缀）

flea-ridden [fliːridən] ***adj.*** 布满跳蚤的

♥ There has been nobody living in that flea-ridden room for five years.
那间满是跳蚤的房间已经 5 年没有人住了。

记忆点拨 flea（跳蚤）＋ ridden（全是……的）

coarse [kɔːs] *adj.* **having a rough surface that feels slightly hard 粗劣的**

♥ He is wearing a jacket of coarse tweed.
他穿着一件粗花呢的夹克。

♥ The President just told a coarse joke.
总统刚刚讲了一个粗俗的笑话。

词义辨析 **coarse, gross, indelicate, vulgar, obscene, ribald**

coarse 意指粗陋的和粗鲁的

♥ A clown performed a coarse imitation of the President.
滑稽演员粗劣地模仿总统。

gross 暗示缺乏文雅，近于野蛮

♥ "It is futile to expect a hungry and squalid population to be anything but violent and gross." (Thomas H. Huxley)
"期望饥饿和贫穷的居民不狂暴和粗野是无用的。"（托马斯 H. 赫克斯利）。

indelicate 意指缺乏雅致、得体或大方

♥ She was angered by the indelicate suggestion.
她对不得体的暗示发怒了。

vulgar 强调不合适的举止、粗鲁和缺乏教养的暗示

♥ The novel is full of language so vulgar it should have been edited.
小说充满着粗俗的语言，应予剪辑。

obscene 强调讨厌的淫荡和下流

♥ The movie is racy rather than obscene.
这部电影与其说是猥亵的，倒不如说是活泼的。

ribald 意指粗俗的、粗鲁的、缺乏生动的语言或举止令人可笑的

♥ "Peals of laughter were mingled with loud ribald jokes." (Washington Irving).
"一连串的大笑声掺杂着大声的下流笑话。"（华盛顿·欧文）

boast [bəust] *v.* **to talk too proudly about your abilities, achievements, or possessions** 自恃有

♥ Mike boasted that his daughter was a genius.
麦克吹嘘他的女儿是天才。

♥ He boasted of the new car he had just bought.
他夸耀他刚买的车。

parishioner [pə'riʃənə] *n.* **someone who lives in a parish, especially someone who regularly goes to a Christian church there** 教区居民

♥ The parishioners here go to the Christian church every week.
这里的教区居民每周去一次教堂。

♥ Mary has always been very faithful and very active parishioner.
玛丽一直是一个虔诚并且非常活跃的教区居民。

相关表达 parish *n.* 教区

记忆点拨 parish（教区）＋ ion（行为）＋ er（人）

shepherd ['ʃepəd] *n.* 牧羊人

♥ A shepherd's job is to take care of sheep in the fields.
牧羊人的工作就是看管地里的羊群。

♥ The poor boy became a shepherd at his age of ten.
那个可怜的男孩十岁就成了一个牧羊人。

其他词性 *v.* 引导；引领

♥ The teachers shepherded the students into the bus.
老师带领学生们上了公共汽车。

记忆点拨 she(e)p（羊）+ herd（兽群）（看管羊群的人）

linen [ˈlinin] ***n.*** **sheets, tablecloths etc.** 亚麻布床单

♥ The tablecloths are made of linen.
这些桌布是亚麻质地。

♥ He likes wearing his linen jacket.
他喜欢穿他那件亚麻外套。

相关表达 **bed linen** 床上用品
table linen 餐布（包括餐巾及桌布等）

the Alps ***n.*** 阿尔卑斯山脉

♥ Every year, many people from different countries visit the Alps to ski.
每年有很多来自不同国家的人们到阿尔卑斯山滑雪。

♥ The Alps are well-known that go through France, Switzerland, Italy, Germany, and Austria.
著名的阿尔卑斯山脉贯穿法国、瑞士、意大利、德国及奥地利等国家。

Lesson 4

solid [ˈsɔlid] ***adj.*** **strong and well made** 坚实的

♥ The 100-year old house is a very solid construction.
那座有 100 年历史的老房子是一座非常坚固的建筑。

♥ His company had a solid foundation.
他的公司有着坚实的基础。

相关表达 solidly *adv.* 坚固地；坚硬地
solidity *n.* 团结，一致，关联

其他词性 *n.* 固体，立体

记忆点拨 sol（溶胶）＋ id

safe [seif] ***n.*** **a strong metal box or cupboard with special locks where you keep money and valuable things** 保险柜

♥ Please keep your valuable things in the safe.
请将贵重物品放入保险柜。

♥ There is a huge safe in Tom's house.
汤姆家里有一个巨大的保险柜。

其他词性 *n.* 冷藏柜 a meat safe 肉类冷柜
adj. 安全的，可靠的，有把握的

Ulyanovsk [uːˈljɑːnɔfsk] ***n.*** 乌里扬诺夫斯克 苏联伏尔加河中游城市（旧称辛比尔斯克）

♥ Most people know Ulyanovsk as Lenin's birthplace.
大多数人知道乌里扬诺乌斯克是因为这里是列宁的出生地。

♥ Ulyanovsk was founded in 1648 on the site of a Tatar village as a strong-point to defend Russia's southern frontier.
乌里扬诺夫斯克于 1648 年建立在鞑靼人村庄遗址上，作为防卫俄罗斯南部边境的战略要点。

commission [kə'miʃən] *n.* 委员会

♥ His brother is working in the Federal Trade Commission.
他哥哥在联邦贸易委员会工作。

♥ The government established a commission to investigate false advertising.
政府建立委员会调查不实广告。

记忆点拨 com（加强意义）＋ mission（使命，任务）

opaque [əu'peik] *adj.* **opaque glass or liquid is difficult to see through and often thick** 不透明的

♥ There is a shower with an opaque glass door in the apartment.
公寓里有个装有不透明玻璃门的淋浴间。

♥ There is some opaque liquid in the glass.
玻璃杯里有一些不透明液体。

相关表达 **opaquely** *adv.* 不透明地；**opaqueness** *n.* 不透明
反义词 transparent *adj.* 透明的

记忆点拨 op（反）＋ aque(ous)（水的）

Lotto ['lɔtəu] *n.* **a game used to make money, in which people buy tickets with a series of numbers on them. If their number is picked by chance, they win money or a prize** 一种有编号的纸牌

♥ Those gamesters addict themselves to the Lotto.
那些赌徒沉溺于纸牌赌博游戏。

♥ Her father was staring at the TV and waiting for the Lotto result.
她的父亲目不转睛地盯着电视等待乐透的结果。

相关表达 the Lotto *n.* 乐透（国家彩票）

slipper [ˈslipə] *n.* **a light soft shoe that you wear at home** 拖鞋

♥ He bought a new pair of slippers for his daughter.
他给他的女儿买了一双新拖鞋。

♥ There are no slippers supplied in this hotel.
这家旅馆不提供拖鞋。

相关表达 slippery *adj.* 滑的，光滑的

记忆点拨 slip（滑动）＋（p)er（物品）

blindfold [ˈblaindfəuld] ***adj.* & *adv.*** **with your eyes covered by a piece of cloth** 被蒙上眼睛的（地）

♥ He said he could drive blindfold.
他说他可以蒙着眼睛开车。

♥ The blindfold acrobat is walking on the high wire.
那个蒙着眼睛的杂技演员正在走高空钢丝。

相关表达 blindfold *vt.* 将……眼睛蒙起，蒙骗；*n.* 眼罩，障眼物

记忆点拨 blind(盲）＋fold(包，蒙罩）

Lesson 5

leave [liːv] ***n.*** ***formal*** **permission to do something 允许**

♥ All that was done entirely without the leave of the boss.
没有得到老板的允许，那件事情就做完了。

♥ Have you been given leave to fish here?
你在这里钓鱼得到许可了吗？

其他词性 *n.*休假，假期

词组拓展 take leave (of): to say goodbye (to)（向……）告别；go away (from)（从……）离去

fundamentals [ˌfʌndəˈmentl] ***n.*** **the most important ideas, rules etc. that something is based on 基本原则**

♥ One of the fundamentals of good behavior is consideration for others.
良好行为的一个根本是体谅他人。

♥ If the children are going to camp for ten days by themselves, they will need to know the fundamentals of cooking.
孩子们如果要自己出去野营十天，就需懂得做饭的基本方法。

其他词性 *adj.* 基础的，基本的

相关表达 the fundamental laws of the nature 自然的基本规律

记忆点拨 fundament（基础）＋ al（关于，属于）＋ s（复数）

glorious [ˈglɔːriəs] ***adj.*** **having or deserving great fame, praise, and honour** 光辉灿烂的

♥ Our country has glorious traditions.
我们的国家有着光荣的传统。

♥ His army attained a glorious victory in the battle.
他的部队在战争中取得了辉煌的胜利。

相关表达 **gloriously** *adv.* 光辉灿烂地
gloriousness *n.* 光辉，光荣
近义词 magnificent
反义词 inglorious 不名誉的，可耻的

记忆点拨 glori（y）（荣誉）＋ous（……的）

splendid [ˈsplendid] ***adj.*** **beautiful and impressive** 灿烂的

♥ The emperor wears a splendid golden crown.
皇帝带着一顶金光灿烂的皇冠。

♥ The splendid images of the national heroes will forever live in the hearts of the people.
民族英雄们的光辉形象永远留在人民的心里。

相关表达 **splendidly** *adv.* 灿烂地；**splendidness** *n.* 灿烂
近义词 brilliant, glorious
反义词 ordinary 普通的，平凡的

rub [rʌb] ***n.*** **a particular problem is the reason why a situation is so difficult** 难题

♥ We'd like to travel, but the rub is that we have no time.
我们喜欢旅行，问题是我们没有时间。

♥ Everyone has to face the rubs and worries of life.
每个人都必须面对人生的磨难和烦恼。

相关表达 **rub** *v.* 摩擦；按摩；磨损；惹人恼怒
rubber *n.* 橡皮擦

identity [ai'dentiti] *n.* **someone's identity is their names or who they are** 身份

♥ The police have already been certain of the murderer's identity.
警察已经证实杀人犯的身份。

♥ Mark lost his identity card and is applying for a new one.
马克丢了身份证，正在申办一张新的。

相关表达 identify *v.* 认出，识别

♥ I identified the wallet at once; it was my mother's.
我立即认出了那个钱包，它是我母亲的。

记忆点拨 id (遗传素质) ＋ enti ＋ ty (……的条件)

dreary ['driəri] ***adj.*** **dull and making you feel sad or bored** 沉郁的

♥ Lucy complained about the dreary tasks that her boss had given to her.
露茜抱怨老板给她的枯燥任务。

♥ It is a dreary winter's day.
这是沉闷的冬日一天。

相关表达 近义词 boring, dull

记忆点拨 drear (阴沉的) ＋ y (充满……的)

commitment [kə'mitmənt] *n.* **a promise to do something or to behave in a particular way** 信奉

♥ The audience were deeply impressed by the energy and commitment shown by the players.
观众被选手的精神与信念深深地打动。

♥ We must honor our commitments to other countries.
我们必须遵守我们对其他国家的诺言。

相关表达　commit *v.* 交托；承担；致力于

记忆点拨　commit(交托；承担）＋ ment（……的状态）

mean　[miːn] ***adj.*** **not wanting to spend money, or not wanting to use much of something** 吝啬，小气

♥ He's too mean to buy toys for his kids.
他小气到不舍得给他的孩子买玩具。

♥ It was supposed to be curry soup, but they'd been a bit mean with the curry.
这应该是份咖喱汤，但是他们有些吝啬他们的咖喱。

相关表达　abject; ignoble

其他词性　*vt.* 意味，想要，预定；*vi.* 用意，有意义；*n.* 平均数，中间，中庸

social climber **追求更高社会地位的，向上爬的人**

♥ Social climbers are always striving for acceptance in fashionable society.
攀龙附凤之人总是不断争取被上流社会接受。

♥ The social climber will cleverly try to infiltrate this group of his liking.
向上爬的人会聪明地努力渗透到他所喜欢的人群中。

devotion　[di'vəuʃən] ***n.*** **the strong love that you show when you pay a lot of attention to someone or something** 热爱

♥ The devotion of too much time to music leaves too little time for working.
把过多的时间用于音乐就把太少的时间留给工作。

♥ Tim's mother has always shown intense devotion to him.
提姆的母亲总是对他表现出强烈的爱。

相关表达　近义词 affection

记忆点拨 devot[e]（奉献，投入于）+ ion（……的行为）

cosmic [ˈkɔzmik] *adj.* **relating to space or the universe** 宇宙的

One cosmic year is approximately equal to two hundred and twenty million years.

词组拓展 cosmic time and space 宇宙时空

相关表达 近义词 universal 宇宙的；世界的

suburban [səˈbəːbən] *adj.* **boring and typical of people who live in the suburbs** 见识不广的，偏狭的

♥ Jerry does not like his present suburban life style.
杰瑞不喜欢他目前的郊区生活方式。

♥ Tina doesn't like those narrow-minded and suburban attitudes of her mother-in-law.
蒂娜不喜欢她婆婆那些小心眼和见识浅的意见。

相关表达 **suburbanite** *n.* 郊区居民

记忆点拨 suburb（郊区）+ an（人）

conceited [kənˈsiːtid] *adj.* **someone who is conceited thinks they are very clever, skilful, beautiful etc. — used to show disapproval** 自高自大的

♥ Mary shouted at me that I was the most conceited, selfish person she had ever known.
玛丽对我喊道我是她认识的最自以为是而且自私的人。

♥ You're coarse, and you're conceited.
你很卑鄙，而且很自负。

相关表达 **conceitedly** *adv.* 自高自大地；**conceitedness** *n.* 自负
近义词 proud(中性词：骄傲的)
arrogant(贬义词：自大的)，vain(贬义词：虚荣的，自负的)

记忆点拨 conceit（狂妄）+ ed（……的）

presumptuous [priˈzʌmptjuəs] ***adj.*** **doing something that you have no right to do and that seems rude** 自以为是的，放肆的

♥ It is too presumptuous of your friend to do so.
你朋友这样做太放肆了。

♥ Would it be presumptuous of me to ask whether you are married or not?
如果我问你是否已经结婚，是否太冒昧？

相关表达 **presumptuously** *adv.* 自以为是地，放肆地
presumption *n.* 冒昧，放肆，自以为是

记忆点拨 pre（前）＋ sumptuous（奢侈的）

fatuous [ˈfætjuəs] ***adj.*** **very silly or stupid** 愚蠢的

♥ What a fatuous question!
多么愚蠢的问题！

♥ You'd better drop those fatuous thoughts.
你最好放弃你那些愚蠢的想法。

相关表达 **fatuously** *adv.*（愚蠢地），**fatuousness** *n.*（愚蠢）

记忆点拨 fat（丰满的，肥的）＋ u ＋ ous（有某种本质的）

cliché [kliːˈʃei] ***n.*** **an idea or phrase that has been used so much that it is not effective or does not have any meaning any longer** 陈词滥调

♥ From my point of view, it is a short story weakened by clichés.
从我的观点来看，这是一篇因内容常见而削弱其可读性的短篇小说。

♥ There is plenty of truth in the cliché that a stitch in time save nine.
老话里有很多真理比如“一针及时省九针”。

相关表达 **clichéd** *adj.* 陈词滥调的

Lesson 6

goodwill [gudˈwil] ***n.*** **kind feelings towards or between people and a willingness to be helpful** 友好

♥ A fund was set up as a goodwill gesture to refugees.
一个针对难民的慈善基金成立了。

♥ The exchange of goodwill missions greatly contributes to a better relationship and understanding between the two nations.
互派友好代表团大大有助于两国的相互关系及了解。

记忆点拨 good (好的) + will (意向)

cricket [ˈkrikit] ***n.*** **a game between two teams of 11 players in which players try to get points by hitting a ball and running between two sets of three sticks** 板球

♥ The university in this town is famous by their cricket team.
这座城市里的大学以他们的板球队闻名。

♥ Tom loves playing the game of cricket.
汤姆喜欢打板球。

相关表达 cricket *n.* 蟋蟀；cricketer 板球队员

inclination [ˌinkliˈneiʃən] ***n.*** **a feeling that makes you want to do something** 意愿

♥ My natural inclination was to be a doctor.
我本来打算当一名医生。

♥ He always follows his own inclinations instead of thinking of the feelings of his friends.
他总是随心所欲，而不考虑朋友们的感情。

相关表达 inclination *n.* 倾斜
incline *v.* 倾向于使（某人）感到……；倾斜

记忆点拨 inclin[e] 倾斜 + ation (行为)

contest ['kɔntest] ***n.*** **a competition or a situation in which two or more people or groups are competing with each other** 比赛

♥ There is a contest of skill being held in that hall.
礼堂里正在举行一场技术比赛。

♥ The teacher decided to hold a contest to see who could write the best essay.
老师决定举行一场竞赛看谁的文章写得最好。

词组拓展 beauty contest 选美；close contest 势均力敌的比赛

其他词性 **contest *v.*** 争论，争辩，竞赛，争夺

记忆点拨 con (共同) + test (测试)

orgy ['ɔːdʒi] ***n.*** **a wild party with a lot of eating, drinking, and sexual activity** 无节制，放荡

♥ The guys always got into the drunken orgies of their youth.
这帮家伙年轻时总是纵酒狂欢。

♥ Mary has an orgy of spending in recent days.
最近玛丽开始无节制地消费。

相关表达 orgiastic *adj.* 无节制的；放荡的

deduce [di'djuːs] ***v.*** **to use the knowledge and information you have in order to understand something or form an opinion about it** 推断

♥ From her age, I deduced that her father must be at least 60.

从她的年纪我推断她的父亲至少有 60 岁了。

♥ He deduced that it would be a very cold night because there was no cloud.

因为没有云，所以他推断那将是一个非常寒冷的夜晚。

相关表达 **deducible** *adj*. 能推论的；可推断的

deduction *n*. 推断，推论

induce *v*. 引诱；诱导

记忆点拨 de (使成……) ＋ duce (首领)

competitive [kəm'petitiv] ***adj*. determined or trying very hard to be more successful than other people or businesses** 竞争性的

♥ My boss was once a highly competitive sales representative.

我的老板曾经是一个有强烈竞争意识的销售代表。

♥ Some western industries are not as competitive as they have been in the past.

一些西方工业已经不如以前具有竞争力了。

相关表达 **competitively** *adv*. 竞争性地

compete *v*. 比赛；竞争

competition *n*. 竞争；竞赛

记忆点拨 compet(e) 竞争＋ it ＋ ive (……性质的)

patriotism ['pætriətizəm] ***n*. love of and devotion to one's country** 地方观念，爱国主义

♥ Patriotism means to stand by the country.

爱国主义意味着支持自己的国家。

♥ Some young persons are thought to be lacking of patriotism.

一些年轻人缺乏爱国主义精神。

相关表达 patriot *n.* 爱国者

patriotic *adj.* 爱国的；有爱国心的

记忆点拨 patriot(爱国者) ＋ ism(主义)

disgrace [disˈgreis] ***v.*** **to do something so bad that you make other people feel ashamed** 使丢脸

♥ The scandal of the son disgraced his whole family.

儿子的丑闻让整个家庭蒙羞。

♥ How could you disgrace your friends like that?

你怎么能让你的朋友那样丢脸？

其他词性 **disgrace *n.*** 耻辱，丢脸的人（或事）

记忆点拨 dis（相反）＋ grace（优雅）

savage [ˈsævidʒ] ***adj.*** **very violent or cruel** 野性的

♥ The inhabitants are still in the savage state.

那些居民仍处于未开化状态。

♥ There were lots of savage beasts in the jungle.

丛林里有很多野生动物。

相关表达 savagely *adv.* 野性地；savageness *n.* 野蛮

combative [ˈkɔmbətiv] ***adj.*** **ready and willing to fight or argue** 好斗的

♥ Tom had combative impulses of his youth.

汤姆年轻时有好斗的冲动。

♥ The Opposition is in a combative mood.

反对党处于一种斗争的情绪中。

相关表达 combatively *adv.* 好斗地；combativeness *n.* 好斗

记忆点拨 combat（战斗）＋ ive（……倾向的）

mimic warfare [ˈmimik] 模拟战争

♥ A mimic warfare between China and Russia was held last year.

中俄两国去年举行了一场模拟战争。

♥ In peacetime, mimic warfare is held for training soldiery.
和平时期用举行模拟战争来训练军人。

相关表达 mimic *adj.* 模拟的；warfare *n.* 战争；冲突

记忆点拨 war(战争) ＋fare(走，进行)

behaviour [bi'heivjə] ***n.*** **the things that a person or animal does** 行动，举止

♥ The scientists have been studying the behaviour of lions in their natural habitat.
科学家一直在研究天然环境中狮子的行为。

♥ The boy was punished by his father due to his bad behaviour at school.
男孩因为在学校恶劣的行为受到父亲的惩罚。

相关表达 behavioural *adj.* 行为的；行为方面的
behaviourally *adv.* 行为地，行为方面地

记忆点拨 behav[e]（举动）＋ iour

absurd [əb'səːd] ***adj.*** **completely stupid or unreasonable** 荒唐的

♥ His brother was wearing an absurd kind of hat.
他哥哥戴着一顶样式古怪的帽子。

♥ The idea that seeing black cat at night will bring bad luck is absurd.
认为夜晚看见黑猫就不吉利的想法是愚蠢可笑的。

相关表达 近义词 foolish *adj.* 愚蠢的；ridiculous *adj.* 荒谬的

记忆点拨 ab（自……）＋ surd（无道理的）

Lesson 7

bat [bæt] ***n.*** **a small animal like a mouse with wings that flies around at night** 蝙蝠

♥ Bat is not a bird but a flying mammal.
蝙蝠不是鸟类而是会飞的哺乳动物。

♥ The drunken man was driving like a bat out of the hell.
那个醉汉横冲直撞地开飞车。

strictly ['striktli] ***adv.*** **exactly and completely** 明确地

♥ Alcohol is strictly forbidden on driving.
酒后驾驶被明令禁止。

♥ That is strictly true.
那是完全正确的。

相关表达 strict *adj.* 严格的；严密的；完全的；精心的

记忆点拨 strict（完全的）＋ ly（……地）

utilitarian [ju:tili'tεəriən] ***adj. formal*** **intended to be useful and practical rather than attractive or comfortable** 实用的

♥ My sister invented some plain and utilitarian kitchenware.
我姐姐发明了一些简单实用的厨具。

♥ A good cloth jacket is more utilitarian than a fur one.
一件优质的布外套要比一件毛皮的更有用。

相关表达 utility *n.* 功用；效用

记忆点拨 utilit[y]（效用）+ arian

appreciation [əpriːʃi'eiʃən] ***n.*** **an understanding of the importance or meaning of something** 理解

♥ She has an appreciation of literature.
她对文学有鉴赏能力。

♥ My uncle has a keen appreciation of a joke.
我叔叔能深刻领会一个笑话的妙处。

相关表达 **appreciate** *v.* 意识到，领会，估计

记忆点拨 appreciat(e) + ion（动作，过程）

elapse [i'læps] ***v. formal*** **if a particular period of time elapses, it passes** 消逝，流逝

♥ Five years elapsed before her son returned.
过了 5 年她儿子才回来。

♥ Weeks elapsed before we could go back to school.
几周过去后我们才回到学校。

其他词性 ***n.*** 消逝

hull [hʌl] ***n.*** **the main part of a ship that goes in the water** 船体

♥ The hull of the oil tanker was made by the best material.
这艘油轮的船体是用最好的材料制成的。

♥ I have a wooden-hulled boat.
我有一艘木制的小船。

相关表达 **ship** *n.* 船

interval ['intəvəl] ***n.*** **the period of time between two events, activities etc.** 间隔

♥ It was a long interval between the last lightning flash and the following thunder.
上一次闪电与随后雷鸣之间的间歇时间较长。

♥ There is an interval of 50 meters between posts.
柱间距离是 50 米。

相关表达 **break; interim; interlude; intermission**

记忆点拨 inter(在……之间) ＋ val

receipt [riˈsiːt] ***n.*** ***formal*** **when someone receives something** 收到

♥ We are waiting for the receipt of further information.
我们正在等待接获进一步的消息。

♥ He denied the receipt of the package I sent to him.
他否认收到了我寄给他的包裹。

词义辨析 **receipt, reception** 这两个名词都是 receive 的同根名词，它们的一般含义是“收到”或“接收”。

receipt 的逻辑宾语通常是别人给与或邮寄来的钱钞、货物、信件或其他东西，其含义为“收到”或“接收”。

reception 的逻辑宾语可以是“人”，这时其含义为“接待”或“招待会”；当其逻辑宾语是“物”时，reception 有两层含义：其一，表示“接受”后的“容纳”；其二，指收音机或电视机的接受性能。

♥ I was honoured by reception of the Academy.
我被光荣地接纳入学会。

记忆点拨 recei(ve)（收到）＋ pt

apparatus [ˌæpəˈreitəs] ***n.*** **the set of tools and machines that you use for a particular scientific, medical, or technical purpose** 仪器

♥ A new electric scoring apparatus was used in the campus basketball games.
校园篮球赛使用了一台新的电子记分器。

♥ An automobile is a complicated apparatus.
汽车是台复杂的机器。

相关表达 equipment *n.* 设备；装置

shoal [ʃəul] ***n.*** **a large group of fish swimming together** 鱼群

♥ There is a shoal of goldfish in the pool.
池塘里有一大群金鱼。

相关表达 shoal *n.* 浅滩；沙洲

herring [ˈheriŋ] ***n.*** **a long thin silver sea fish that can be eaten** 青鱼；鲱

♥ The prickled herring is a very popular Scandinavian food item.
青鱼酱是非常受斯堪的纳维亚人欢迎的一种食物材料。

♥ Herring have supported some of the Alaska's oldest commercial fisheries.
青鱼曾是阿拉斯加部分最早渔业贸易的支柱。

词组拓展 red herring 提出不相干的事实或论点，以分散对主题的注意力

cod [kɔd] ***n.*** **a large sea fish that lives in the North Atlantic** 鳕鱼

♥ Cod is an important food fish of northern Atlantic waters.
鳕鱼是大西洋北部水域的一种重要食品鱼。

♥ One cod fillet, please.
一片鳕鱼肉，谢谢。

相关表达 cod *n.* 玩笑，骗局

squeak [skwiːk] ***n.*** **a very short high noise or cry** 尖叫声

♥ I was awaked by the squeak of the mouse.
我被老鼠吱吱的叫声吵醒。

♥ She was scared of the harsh squeak of the gate hinges.
她被大门铰链刺耳的嘎吱声吓到了。

相关表达 **squeal** *n.* 长而尖的声音
a squeal of brakes 刹车的嘎吱声

Lesson 8

slaughter ['slɔːtə] ***v.*** **to kill an animal, especially for its meat; to kill a lot of people in a cruel or violent way** 屠宰

♥ Thousands of people were needlessly slaughtered in the war.
成千上万的人在战争中被无辜杀戮。

♥ "I could not give my name to aid the slaughter in this war, fought on both sides for grossly material ends."（Sylvia Pankhurst）
"我不能用自己的名义去帮助这场双方为谋取巨额物质利益的战争中的大屠杀。"（西尔维亚·潘克赫斯特）

其他词性 **slaughter** ***n.*** 屠杀；残杀
massacre ***v.*** **&*n.*** 残杀，集体屠杀

fit [fit] ***adj.*** **suitable or good enough for something** 适合

♥ It is not a fit time for flippancy.
现在不是放肆的时候。

♥ She is not fit to take care of young kids.
她不适合照顾幼儿。

相关表达 近义词 suitable *adj.* 适当的

♥ The toy is not suitable for small children.
这个玩具不适合小孩玩。

反义词 unfit *adj.* 不适当的
an unfit parent 不合格的家长

grace [greis] *v.* 给……增光

♥ They were graced with the presence of their chairman.
主席光临，他们感到不胜荣幸。

♥ His painting graces the wall of the sitting room.
他的画给客厅的墙壁增色。

其他词性 *n.* 优美，优雅

tariff ['tærif] *n.* **a tax on goods coming into a country or going out of a country** 关税

♥ The government may impose tariffs on exports.
政府可能要征收出口关税。

♥ The government decided to cut import tariffs on cars and computers.
政府决定削减汽车和计算机的进口税。

相关表达 近义词 tax *n.* 税；税金；duty *n.* 税

standard ['stændəd] *n.* **the level that is considered to be acceptable, or the level that someone or something has achieved** 标准

♥ He was a teacher who set high standards for his students.
他曾经是一位对学生高标准要求的老师。

♥ The government has an official standard for the purity of gold.
政府对于黄金的纯度定有官方的标准。

相关表达 近义词 benchmark *n.* 基准；criterion *n.* 标准，规范

记忆点拨 stand（立场）＋ ard

dialysis [dai'ælisis] *n.* **the process of taking harmful substances out of someone's blood using a special machine, because**

their KIDNEYS do not work properly 分离，分解；透析，渗析

实际应用　a dialysis machine 透析机

♥ His grandfather has been on dialysis for the past two years.

他父亲两年来一直在做透析。

相关表达　**dialytic** *adj.* 透析的

记忆点拨　dialys[e]（分离，透析）＋ is

electrocute　[ɪlektrəkjuːt] ***v.*** **if someone is electrocuted, they are injured or killed by electricity passing through their body** 使触电身亡

♥ A worker hired by Tom was electrocuted by a high-tension wire.

汤姆雇用的一名工人被高压电线电死。

♥ Last month a housewife was electrocuted by her microwave oven.

上个月一个家庭主妇被微波炉电死。

相关表达　**electrocute** *v.* 处电刑

记忆点拨　electro（电版）＋ cute

eliminate　[i'limineit] ***v.*** **to completely get rid of something that is unnecessary or unwanted** 消灭

♥ We have been making the effort to eliminate capital punishment.

我们一直在为取消死刑努力。

♥ Greasy foods should be eliminated from the diet.

日常食物中应该消除油腻的食品。

词义辨析　**eliminate, eradicate, liquidate, purge**

这些动词共有的中心意思是“消除不期望的某人或某物，尤指通过极端的手段，例如放逐或处死”：

eliminate political opposition 消除政治对手
eradicate guerrilla 消灭游击战
liquidating traitors 肃清叛徒
purge all the dissidents 清除所有持不同意见者

accord [ə'kɔ:d] *n.* **a formal agreement between countries or groups** 协议

♥ the Helsinki accord on human rights
赫尔辛基人权协议

♥ the American accords with Turkey and Greece
美国同土耳其和希腊的防卫协定

相关表达 agreement *n.* 协议

记忆点拨 ac（加强意义）＋cord（束缚）

device [di'vais] *n.* **a machine or tool that does a special job** 仪器，器械

♥ The clever boy invented a device for opening bottles at his age of ten.
那个聪明的男孩十岁时就发明了一个开瓶子的装置。

♥ The newly-designed device for sharpening pencils will appear on the exhibition next week.
这件新设计的削铅笔装置将在下周的展览会上展出。

相关表达 apparatus *n.* 器械，设备；machine *n.* 机器，机械

记忆点拨 de（去除）＋vice（缺陷）

hammer out 推敲

♥ The boss tried to hammer out an agreement with his workers on overtime pay.
老板煞费苦心设法和工人达成了一项加班工资的协议。

♥ He tried to hammer out a plan on the renovation of his company.
他经过仔细研究制定出公司改革的计划。

pact [pækt] ***n.*** **a formal agreement between two groups, countries, or people, especially to help each other or to stop fighting** 合同，条约，公约

实际应用 the Warsaw pact 华沙公约

♥ The two governments have signed a non-aggression pact.
两国政府签订了互不侵犯条约。

相关表达 **agreement** ***n.*** 协议
alliance ***n.*** 联盟；联合

Unit 2

Lesson 9

espionage ['espiənidʒ] ***n.*** **the activity of secretly finding out secret information and giving it to a country's enemies or a company's competitors** 间谍活动

实际应用 counter-espionage 反间谍

♥ He was planning a campaign of industrial espionage against his main rival.
他在计划一个针对主要竞争对手的商业间谍战。

♥ Two persons have been arrested on espionage charge.
两个人被指控犯间谍活动罪而被捕。

相关表达 **espier** *n.* 窥见者；**espial** *v.* 窥探，侦察

记忆点拨 espi[al] 侦察 ＋ on ＋ age 行为，活动

Alfred ['ælfrid] **871～899** 年间任英国国王
阿尔弗烈德：英格兰韦塞克斯王国国王（871～899年）、学者及立法者，曾击败了丹麦人的侵略并使英格兰成为统一的王国。

Danish ['deiniʃ] ***adj.*** 丹麦的，丹麦人的，丹麦语的

实际应用 Danish blue 丹麦青纹干酪
Danish pastry 丹麦酥皮饼

♥ Many young couples love Danish modern furniture.
许多年轻夫妇喜欢丹麦式样的家具。

相关表达 **Denmark** *n.* 丹麦

记忆点拨 Dan[mark] ＋ ish（……的）

minstrel [ˈminstrəl] ***n.*** **a singer or musician in the Middle Ages** 中世纪的吟游歌手

♥ A minstrel was a traveling entertainer to sing and recite poetry.
吟游诗人是个游历各地的表演者，歌唱或朗诵诗歌。

♥ He is a wandering minstrel, a link to a bygone era.
他是一个流浪的吟游歌手，连接了过去的时代与现在。

相关表达 bard *n.* 吟游诗人，troubadour *n.* 行吟诗人

wandering [ˈwɔndəriŋ] ***adj.*** 漫游的

♥ There are still some wandering tribes in the west of China.
中国西部仍然有一些游牧部落。

♥ His brother is a wandering Jew who has traveled half of the world.
他哥哥是个旅游各国的人，已经走遍了半个地球。

相关表达 wander *v.* 漫步；徘徊

记忆点拨 wander（漫步，徘徊）＋ ing（……的）

harp [hɑːp] ***n.*** 竖琴

♥ The girl began to play harp when she was only 8 years old.
那个女孩 8 岁就开始弹竖琴。

♥ Harp playing is quite difficult for me.
弹奏竖琴对我来说太难了。

其他词性 *v.* 用竖琴弹奏

ballad [ˈbæləd] ***n.*** **a slow love song** 民歌

♥ He was a famous ballad singer in his country.
他曾是他们国家有名的民歌歌手。

♥ Her father created a lot of excellent ballad compositions.
她父亲创作了大量优秀的民歌作品。

相关表达 ditty *n.* 小调；poem *n.* 诗歌；song *n.* 歌曲

acrobatic [ˌəkrəuˈbætik] ***adj.*** **acrobatic movements involve moving your body in a very skilful way** 杂技的

♥ The artists performed some amazing acrobatic feats.
艺术家表演了一些令人惊叹的杂技技艺。

♥ With a sudden acrobatic action, he picked the pear off the tree.
它像杂技演员般地做了个动作，从树上摘下了梨。

相关表达 acrobatics *n.* 杂技
acrobat *n.* 杂技演员

conjuring [ˈkʌndʒərɪŋ] ***n.*** **the skill of performing clever tricks in which you seem to make things appear, disappear, or change by magic** 魔术

♥ The magician did some conjuring tricks for the children.
魔术师给孩子们表演了几个戏法。

♥ He made a conjuring gesture.
他做了个变戏法的手势。

相关表达 magic *n.* 魔法；戏法

记忆点拨 conjur［e］（变戏法，施魔法）＋ ing（……的）

Athelney [ˈæθəlni] ***n.*** 阿塞尔纳（英国一个小岛）

♥ Athelney once stood as a lone hill among miles of marshes.
阿塞尔纳曾经是一座立于大片沼泽地中的孤独小山。

Chippenham *n.* 切本哈姆（英国一个城市）

- Chippenham Rugby Football Club unveiled their new sponsors before Saturday's home game.
切本哈姆橄榄球俱乐部在周六主场比赛前宣布了他们的新赞助商。

thither [ˈðiðə] *adv.* in that direction 向那里

- The kids were running hither and thither in the field.
孩子们在地里到处跑。
- How the footprint came thither I knew not, nor could in the least imagine.
那脚印是怎么留在那儿的，我既不知道也丝毫猜不出。

相关表达 hither *adj.* 这里

Dane [dein] *n.* 丹麦人

- The husband of his sister is Dane.
他的姐夫是个丹麦人。
- The famous Dane, Hans Christian Andersen created 168 fairy tales in his life.
著名的丹麦人，汉斯·克里斯蒂安·安徒生一生创作了 168 篇童话作品。

slack [slæk] *adj.* not taking enough care or making enough effort to do things correctly 涣散的

- You have been slack in your work in recent days.
你最近的工作一直很懈怠。
- Slack defending by AC Milan allowed Rome to score.
AC 米兰队的松懈防守使得罗马队得分。

相关表达　tight *adj*. 紧的；严厉的

conqueror　[ˈkɔŋkərə] ***n.*** 征服者

♥ He was a conqueror of the South Pole.
他成功地登上了南极。

相关表达　conquer *v.* 征服；战胜

记忆点拨　conquer（征服）＋ or(……者)

casual　[ˈkæʒjuəl] ***adj.*** **without any serious interest or attention**马虎的，随便的

♥ He was so angry with the casual attitude of his son toward drugs.
他非常生气儿子对毒品的听任态度。

♥ He was wearing casual clothes, not his work ones.
他穿着他的便服，不是他的工作服。

其他词性　**casual *n.*** 临时雇员，短工
casuals *n.* 便服；便鞋

precaution　[priˈkɔːʃən] ***n.*** **something you do in order to prevent something dangerous or unpleasant from happening** 预防，警惕

♥ We took every precaution against SARS.
我们对非典采取了所有的预防措施。

♥ It was impossible to take precaution in those dire circumstances.
在紧迫的环境下无暇再去周密慎重。

相关表达　forewarning *adj*. 预先警告的

记忆点拨　pre（预先）＋ caution（小心，谨慎）

proceeds　[ˈprəusiːdz] ***n.*** **the money that is obtained from doing something or selling something** 所得

♥ We sold the business and bought a villa by the sea with the proceeds.
我们结束了买卖，用所得的钱买了一栋海边的别墅。

♥ The proceeds of the basketball game will go to charity.
这场篮球赛的收入都将捐给慈善机构。

相关表达 **earnings** *n.* 所得；**income** *n.* 收入；收益

记忆点拨 proceed（*v.* 发生，进行）＋ s（复数后缀）

assemble [əˈsembl] ***v.*** **if you assemble a large number of people or things, or if they assemble, they are gathered together in one place, often for a particular purpose** 集合

♥ All the people assembled at the square.
所有的人都聚集在广场上。

♥ If we can assemble everybody quickly then we can leave.
如果我们能把大家都很快地集中起来，我们就可以走了。

相关表达 **collect** *v.* 聚集；集中；**congregate** *v.* 聚集

记忆点拨 as（促进）＋ semble

trivial [ˈtriviəl] ***adj.*** **not serious, important, or valuable** 微不足道的

♥ You don't need to get angry over such trivial matters.
你不必为这些琐事生气。

♥ I was punished for the most trivial offences.
我因为一次极为微不足道的过错而受到惩罚。

词义辨析 **trifling, paltry, petty**

trifling *adj.* 指的是某物太小或太不重要以至于几乎不值得注意

♥ "I regret the trifling narrow contracted education of the females of my own country." (Abigail Adams)
"我对于自己国家给予女性的微不足道的、狭隘的、有限的教育表示遗憾。"(阿比盖尔·亚当斯)

paltry *adj.* 尤其用来形容那些完全没有达到要求的或希望的标准而引起鄙视情绪的

♥ "He…considered the prize too paltry for the lives it must cost." (John Lothrop Motley)
"他……认为奖金与它所夺去的生命相比太微不足道了。"(约翰·洛斯罗浦·莫特莱)

petty *adj.* 可以指那些重要性或大小是较小或第二位的东西；这个词也会令人想起精神上的偏狭或小气

♥ "Our knights are limited to petty enterprises." (Sir Walter Scott)
"我们的骑士被局限于琐碎的事情上。"(华尔特·司各特爵士)

记忆点拨 trivia (琐事) + (a) l (……的)

prolonged [prəˈlɔŋd] ***adj.*** **continuing for a long time** 持久的

♥ The prolonged exposure to the sun will hurt skin.
持续在太阳下曝晒会伤害皮肤。

♥ The audience gave the young pianist prolonged applause.
观众给了那个年轻的钢琴家长时间的掌声。

相关表达 prolong *v.* 延长；拖延

记忆点拨 pro (前进) + long (长) + ed (已发生的……)

commissariat [ˌkɔmiˈsɛəriət] ***n.*** **a military department that is responsible for supplying food** 军粮供应

♥ My brother is working in a commissariat.
我哥哥在一个军需处工作。

♥ A commissariat is an important department of an army in charge of providing food and other supplies for the troops.
军粮部门是军队的一个重要部门，为军队提供食品和其他供应品。

相关表达 commissary *n.* 军营超级市场，军需官

episode [ˈepisəud] ***n.* an event or a short period of time during which something happens** 一个事件，片断

♥ "South Africa may remain one of history's most tragic episodes."(Bayard Rustin)
"南非可能仍是保留历史上最悲惨的事件之一的地方。"（贝亚德·拉斯廷）

♥ It was one of the funniest episodes in my life.
那是我一生中最好笑的一件事。

相关表达 event *n.* 事件
experience *n.* 经历

记忆点拨 epi（在……上）＋ sode

epic [ˈepik] ***n.* a book, poem, or film that tells a long story about brave actions and exciting events** 史诗

♥ The Iliad is an epic of ancient Greece.
《伊里亚特》是古希腊的一首史诗。

相关表达 lyric *n.* 抒情诗

harry [ˈhæri] ***v.* to keep attacking an enemy; to keep asking someone for something in a way that is upsetting or annoying** 骚扰

♥ The pirates harried the towns along the coast.
海盗抢劫了沿海城市。

♥ We have to harry Tim for money.
我们不得不常常缠着蒂姆要钱。

相关表达 besiege *v.* 围攻；invade *v.* 侵略，侵袭

assail [əˈseil] ***v.* to attack someone or something violently** 袭击

♥ The Opposition assailed the Prime Minister on the question of tax increase.
反对党就增加赋税问题向首相提出质疑。

♥ He was assailed by conflicting arguments.
他为互相矛盾的论点所困扰。

相关表达 同义词 attack *v.* 攻击
反义词 defend *v.* 防卫

skirmish [ˈskəːmiʃ] ***n.* a fight between small groups of soldiers, ships etc., especially one that happens away from the main part of a battle** 小规模战斗

♥ Her brother was killed in a skirmish with government troops.
她的兄弟死在一场与政府军队的冲突当中。

♥ There were always skirmishes between those two countries.
那两国间总是有小规模战争。

相关表达 近义词 conflict *n.* 斗争；冲突

Lesson 10

integrated ['intigreitid] *adj.* **an integrated system, institution etc. combines many different groups, ideas, or parts in a way that works well** 综合的

♥ There is an integrated public transport system in that town.
那座城市里有完整的公共交通系统。

实际应用 Integrated Production Systems 综合生产制度

记忆点拨 integrate(使成整体) + (e)d

circuit ['sə:kit] *n.* **A closed path followed or capable of being followed by an electric current** 线路，电路

♥ His grandfather used to run three circuits of the track every morning.
他的爷爷以前每天早晨沿跑道跑三圈。

♥ The workers are rebuilding the television circuit of the old building.
工人们正在改造那幢老房子的电视线路。

记忆点拨 cir(围绕) +cuit(走)

California [kæli'fɔ:njə] *n.* 加利福尼亚（美国州名）

♥ California is often called the Golden State because of its sunny climate and the discovery of gold during its pioneering days.
由于其阳光明媚的气候，并在拓荒年代发现了金矿，加利福尼亚常被称为金色之州。

♥ The city Los Angeles in California is well-know for the Hollywood.
位于加利福尼亚的洛杉矶市以好莱坞而著名。

workstation [ˈwɜːksteɪʃən] *n.* **An area, as in an office, outfitted with equipment and furnishings for one worker, often including a computer or computer terminal**
工作站

♥ A computer workstation will improve the efficiency.
电脑工作组可以提高工作效率。

记忆点拨 work(工作) ＋ station(站)

chip [tʃip] *n.* **a small piece of SILICON that has a set of complicated electrical connections on it and is used to store and PROCESS information in computers** 芯片，集成电路片，集成块

♥ The entire content of a book will be located on a single silicon chip.
整本书的内容只用一片硅芯片就可以装下。

♥ This mug has a chip in it.
这个缸子上有个缺口。

newsletter [ˈnjuːzˌletər] *n.* **a printed report giving news or information of interest to a special group** 时事通信

♥ The society publishes a newsletter once a year.
社团每年发行一份时事通信。

♥ The newsletter just published by my university aims to raise awareness of new sources of information on the Internet.
我的大学刚刚发表的时事通信旨在提高互联网作为新的信息来源的认知度。

记忆点拨 news(新闻) ＋letter(文字)

Macintosh [ˈmækintɔʃ] ***n.*** **a type of personal computer** 麦金托什机，一种个人电脑

♥ Macintosh is a trademark licensed to Apple Computer, Inc..
麦金托什机是苹果公司注册的商标。

♥ The Macintosh was the first personal computer to use a graphical user interface.
麦金托什机是最早使用了图形用户界面的个人计算机。

penalize [ˈpiːnəlaiz] ***v.*** **to subject to a penalty, especially for infringement of a law or an official regulation** 处罚，惩罚

♥ The German football team was penalized for intentionally wasting time.
德国足球队因故意拖延时间而受罚。

♥ Tom and his sister were penalized very differently for the same offence.
汤姆和他妹妹犯了同样的错误却得到了很不一样的惩罚。

相关表达 同义词 punish *vt.* 惩罚；处罚

记忆点拨 penal[刑事的] +ize[使……]

customize [ˈkʌstəməraiz] ***v.*** **to make or alter to individual or personal specifications** 按顾客具体需要制造

♥ The factory produces customized cars.
这家工厂生产客户订制的汽车。

♥ He customized a pair of NIKE sneakers for his son.
他为他的儿子订制了一双耐克运动鞋。

记忆点拨 custom(er)(顾客) +ize (……化)

spawn [spɔːn] ***v.*** **to make a series of things happen or start to exist** 引起，酿成

♥ Tyranny spawned revolt.

残暴统治激起了叛乱。

♥ New business opportunities have been spawned new technology.

新技术产生了新的商机。

相关表达 近义词 engender *v.* 造成；spawn *n.* 卵

thrive [θraiv] ***v.*** **to become very successful or very strong and healthy** 兴旺，繁荣

♥ Plants can thrive in tropical rainforests.

植物可以在热带雨林茁壮成长。

♥ Mike thrived on the adulation of his henchmen.

麦克是靠下属的奉承而发迹的。

相关表达 近义词 prosper *v.* 昌盛；兴隆

anarchy [ˈænəki] ***n.*** **a situation in which there is no effective government in a country or no order in an organization or situation** 无政府状态，混乱

♥ The jail is close to anarchy.

监狱近乎混乱状态。

♥ The county is in danger of falling into anarchy.

国家面临无政府状态的危险。

记忆点拨 an(无) ＋arch(统治者) ＋y

oriental [ˌɔːriˈentl] ***n.*** **a word for someone from the eastern part of the world, especially China or Japan, now considered offensive** 东方人

♥ This oriental legend is fascinating.

这个东方传说很吸引人。

He specializes in oriental history.
他专门研究东方史。

相关表达 occidental *n.* 欧美人；西方人

记忆点拨 orient(东方) ＋al

constitute [ˈkɔnstitjuːt] ***v.*** **to be the elements or parts of 构成**

Correct grammar and sentence structure do not in themselves constitute good writing.
正确的语法和句子结构本身并不能构成一篇好文章。

England, Wales, Scotland, and Northern Ireland constitute the United kingdom.
英格兰、威尔士、苏格兰和北爱尔兰组成联合王国。

相关表达 近义词 compose *v.* 组成

记忆点拨 con(加强意义) ＋stitue(设立)

drove [drəuv] ***n.*** **crowds of people; a group of animals that are being moved together 群**

Tourists come in droves to see the Palace Museum.
游客成群结队地来参观故宫博物院。

There is a drove of cattle on the grassland.
草原上有一群牛。

记忆点拨 drove—drive 的过去式

innovator [ɪnəuveɪtər] ***n.*** **someone who introduces changes and new ideas 发明者**

One of the workers who followed in his steps as an innovator was his sister.
还有一个跟他闹革新的工人，那就是他妹妹。

The new principal is going to be the innovator in school customs.
新校长打算改进学校的风气。

记忆点拨 innovat(e)(创新) ＋or(者)

forge [fɔːdʒ] *v.* **to develop something new, especially a strong relationship with other people, groups, or countries 发展**

♥ In the 1980s, they were attempting to forge a new kind of rock music.

20 世纪 80 年代，他们尝试创作一种新的摇滚乐。

♥ The two women had forged a close relationship.

两位女士发展成一种亲密的关系。

相关表达 同义词 form *v.* 形成

memory-chip ***n.*** 内存条

♥ My computer did not work due to the broken of its memory-chip.

由于内存条损坏，我的电脑不能用了。

实际应用 semiconductor memory chip 半导体存储器芯片

记忆点拨 memory(记忆) ＋chip(芯片)

Kansas [ˈkænzəs] ***n.*** 堪萨斯（美国州名）

♥ Kansas was admitted as the 34th state in 1861.

堪萨斯于 1961 年被批准为第 34 个州。

♥ Kansas is in the central US, which produces large amounts of wheat.

堪萨斯位于美国中部，盛产小麦。

Missouri [miˈzuəri] ***n.*** 密苏里（美国州名）

♥ Jefferson City is the capital and St. Louis the largest city of Missouri.

杰斐逊城是密苏里州首府，圣路易斯为最大城市。

♥ Missouri is an industrial and farming area.

密苏里是工业和农业区。

Lesson 11

oppress [əˈpres] ***v.* to treat a group of people unfairly or cruelly, and prevent them from having the same rights that other people in society have 忧郁，压抑**

♥ Before the independent war, Americans were highly oppressed by the British colonist.
在独立战争以前，美国人民受到英国殖民者的高度压迫。

♥ The gloomy atmosphere of house oppressed him since the first day he moved in.
从他搬进这座房子的第一天开始，黑暗阴沉的气氛就让他觉得很压抑。

相关表达 **oppressor** *n.* 暴君

记忆点拨 op(强意) ＋press(压)

justification [dʒʌstɪfɪˈkeɪʃən] ***n.* a good and acceptable reason for doing something 正当理由**

♥ There is no doubt that poverty cannot be justification for shoplifting.
毫无疑问，贫困不能成为偷窃商品的正当理由。

♥ The defendant's attorney raised the issue of self-defense as a justification for the assault accusation.
被告律师提出自卫作为攻击罪行的正当理由。

相关表达 **just** *adj.* 正确的，正义的

记忆点拨 justifi[y]（证明……是正当的）＋ cation(行为)

justifiably [ˈdʒʌstifaiəbli] ***adv.* 无可非议地**

♥ All pregnant women are justifiably in unstable mood before their delivery.
所有的怀孕妇女在临产前都无可非议地处于不稳定的情绪中。

♥ After the death of the president, the vice-president justifiably resumed his official role temporarily.
在总统去世以后，副总统无可非议地暂时担当起了总统的职务。

相关表达 **justifiable** *adj.* 有理由的

记忆点拨 justify[y]（证明……是正当的）＋ able（……倾向）＋ly（……地）

cheat [tʃiːt] ***v.*** **to behave in a dishonest way in order to win or to get an advantage, especially in a competition, game, or examination** 欺骗

♥ The teacher warned the students not to cheat in the exam.
老师警告学生不要在考试中作弊。

♥ Mrs. White was cheated by the salesperson and paid much higher than a reasonable price.
怀特太太被推销员欺骗了，她支付的价钱远远高于合理的价格。

相关表达 **cheating** *adj.* 欺骗的

abject [ˈæbdʒekt] ***adj.*** **the state of being extremely poor, unhappy, unsuccessful etc.** 可怜的

♥ He is despised by his teammates as an abject coward because he withdrew right before the game began.
因为他在比赛开始前就退出了，所以他的队友们都鄙视他是个可怜的懦夫。

♥ A lot of African people lived in abject poverty because of the drought in continuous years.
由于连续几年的干旱，很多非洲人民都生活在可怜的贫困中。

ignoble [ig'nəubl] ***adj.*** **ignoble thoughts, feelings, or actions are ones that you should feel ashamed or embarrassed about** 不体面的，可耻的

♥ In the early twentieth century's American upper class society, it is still ignoble to get divorced.
在20世纪早期的美国上流社会，离婚仍然是一件不体面的事。

♥ It is such an ignoble act for the swimming athletes to take analeptic before the game.
对一个游泳运动员来说，在比赛前服用兴奋剂是一种可耻的行为。

记忆点拨 ig(不，相反）+noble(高尚的)

impersonal [im'pəːsənl] ***adj.*** **not showing any feelings of sympathy, friendliness etc.** 超脱个人感情影响的

♥ To be a good umpire, you need to make impersonal judgment in the competition.
要成为一个好裁判，你需要在比赛中作出客观的判断。

♥ An impersonal corporation is not attractive to the employers.
对雇员们来说，缺少人情味的公司没有吸引力。

记忆点拨 im(不，非）+personal(个人的)

ego ['iːgəu] ***n.*** **the opinion that you have about yourself** 自我

♥ People with a big ego are usually not easy to make friends with.

比较自我的人都不容易交朋友。

♥ Ego is a concept first invented by Freud in psychology.
自我是由弗洛伊德在心理学里首先提出的。

recede [ri'si:d] ***v.*** **if something you can see or hear recedes, it gets further and further away until it disappears** 退去

♥ The flood receded finally after two months' sweep.
在两个月的泛滥后，洪水终于退去了。

♥ By the passage of time, my childhood memories gradually receded.
随着时间的流逝，我童年的记忆慢慢消退。

相关表达 **ebb** *v.*（潮水）退去；**retreat** *v.*（军队）撤退

记忆点拨 re(回，向后) ＋ cede(放弃)

increasingly [ɪn'kri:sɪŋlɪ] ***adv.*** **more and more all the time** 日益，不断

♥ Education has been an increasingly important factor in one's career success.
对于一个人事业上成功与否，教育已经成为一个越来越重要的因素。

♥ The size of the factory's output has been increasingly expanded since last year.
从去年以来，这个工厂的生产规模就在不断扩大。

记忆点拨 increase[e]（增加，增长）＋ing(状态) ＋ ly(……地)

passionately ['pæʃənitli] ***adv.*** 激昂地

♥ The audience gave the speaker a big applause after he passionately finished the speech.
在演讲者激昂地结束演讲后，听众热烈鼓掌。

♥ The tenorist passionately gave a tenor solo at the end of the drama.
在歌剧结束时，这位男高音歌手情绪激昂地表演了一段男高音独唱。

相关表达 passionate *adj.* 充满热情的

painlessly ['peinlisli] ***adv.*** 毫无痛苦地

♥ His grandfather passed away painlessly during a deep sleep.
他的祖父在沉睡中毫无痛苦地去世了。

♥ With the aid of anesthetic, he took the surgery painlessly.
使用了麻醉剂后，他的手术毫无痛苦。

相关表达 painless *adj.* 无痛的

记忆点拨 pain 痛苦 ＋ less(没有，不) ＋ly(……地)

vitality [vai'tæliti] ***n.*** **great energy and eagerness to do things** 精力

♥ Since the beginning of opening and reform, China's economy has been full of vitality for the last decade.
自从改革开放以来，近十几年来中国经济始终充满活力。

♥ The plants lost the vitality after the removal from the seed to the pot.
这棵植物自从土壤里移植到花盆里后就失去了活力。

记忆点拨 vit(生命) al ＋ ity

weariness ['wiərinis] ***n.*** 疲惫

♥ You can feel his weariness through his facial expression.
通过他脸上的表情你能感觉到他的疲惫。

♥ After one full day's labor, he was stricken down by the weariness.
劳动了一整天后，他疲惫不堪。

词组拓展　wear and tear 磨损

记忆点拨　weari[y]（疲倦的）＋ ness

Lesson 12

current [ˈkʌrənt] ***adj.*** **happening or existing now** 通用的，流行的

♥ Ren Ming Bi is the current money in the People's Republic of China.
人民币是中华人民共和国的通用货币。

♥ College students are very concerned about the world current events.
大学生们很关注当前国际形势。

相关表达 prevalent *adj.* 普遍的；流行的

account [əˈkaunt] ***n.*** **an arrangement in which a bank keeps your money safe so that you can pay more in or take money out** 账户

词组拓展 saving account 储蓄账户 checking account 支票账户

♥ Usually a couple will open a joint account after marriage.
一般来说，在婚后夫妻会开一个联名账户。

♥ The account number is printed at the bottom of your cheques.
你的账户号码印在支票的底部。

相关表达 accountant *n.* 会计

记忆点拨 ac（关于……）+count（计算，计数）

cash [kæʃ] ***n.*** **money in the form of coins or notes rather than cheques, credit cards etc.** 现金

♥ The supermarket has a cash flow of ＄30,000 a month.
这家超市的流动现金为每月 3 万美元。

♥ You can't pay by Credit Card in McDonald's, because they only accept cash.
在麦当劳你不能用信用卡付账，他们只收现金。

cheque [tʃek] ***n.*** **a printed piece of paper that you write an amount of money on, sign, and use instead of money to pay for things** 支票

♥ You can deposit this cheque into your bank account.
你可以把这张支票存到你的银行账户里。

♥ Please write this cheque payable to "Beijing University".
请将支票的收款人写为北京大学。

debtor [ˈdetə] ***n.*** **a person, group, or organization that owes money** 借方

♥ Being a responsible debtor, you need to pay back the debt in installment in time.
作为一个负责任的债务人，你应该按时分期还债。

♥ If he lacks the capacity to pay the debt off, then he becomes an insolvent debtor.
如果他失去还钱能力，那他就是无力偿付的债务人。

记忆点拨 debt（债务）＋or(……人)

creditor [ˈkreditə] ***n.*** **a person, bank, or company that you owe money to** 贷方

♥ It is wise for the creditor to investigate the debtor's credit history before loaning the money.
对贷款方来说，在贷款以前调查一下借款方的信用背景是明智的。

♥ Bank is usually the largest creditor in modern society.
在现代社会里，银行通常是最大的贷款方。

相关表达 credit *n.* 信用

记忆点拨 credit（信用）＋or(人)

obligation [ˌɔbliˈgeiʃən] ***n.* a moral or legal duty to do something** 义务

♥ The policemen have the obligation to provide a safe environment to the citizens.
警察有义务为市民提供一个安全的环境。

♥ The safeguards have the obligation to maintain the safety inside the garden.
门卫有义务维持公园的安全。

记忆点拨 obligat[e]（使付义务）＋ation(行为)

complication [ˌkɔmpliˈkeiʃən] ***n.* a problem or situation that makes something more difficult to understand or deal with** 纠纷

♥ The lack of a clearly drafted contract may lead to complications in the future.
缺少一份条文清楚的合同会导致将来的纠纷。

♥ A mediator tried to solve the complication through mediation rather than litigation.
一个调解员试图通过调解而不是诉讼来解决纠纷。

相关表达 complicated *adj.* 复杂的

记忆点拨 complicat[e]（变复杂）＋ ation(过程，行为)

debit [ˈdebit] ***v.* to record in financial accounts the money that has been spent or that is owed** 把……记入借方

♥ When you use a debit card, the transaction amount will immediately be debited to your bank account.
当你使用借记卡时，交易金额就会马上从你的银行账户中划走。

♥ The bank debited my online transaction from the account immediately.

银行马上把我网上购物的金额从账户中扣除了。

记忆点拨 de（使……成为）＋bit(辅币)

specimen ['spesimin] ***n.*** **a small amount or piece that is taken from something, so that it can be tested or examined; a single example of something, often an animal or plant** 样本

♥ The researcher is carefully examining the specimen of the plants.

那位研究员正在认真检验植物的样本。

♥ He collects specimens of butterfly.

他收集各种蝴蝶的标本。

forge [fɔːdʒ] ***v.*** **to illegally copy something, especially something printed or written, to make people think that it is real** 伪造

♥ That smuggler forged his passport and was caught by the custom officer.

那个走私犯因为伪造护照被海关官员抓住了。

♥ It is hard to tell a forged signature from an authentic one by naked eyes.

只用肉眼很难鉴别真假签名。

相关表达 **falsify** *v.* 伪造

forgery ['fɔːdʒəri] ***n.*** **a document, painting, or piece of paper money that has been copied illegally; the crime of copying official documents, money etc.** 伪造（文件、签名等）

- At first he believed the painting was an original by Monroe, but by careful observation he found out that it was a forgery.
  起初他认为那幅油画是莫纳的真迹，可是仔细一看他发现那是一件赝品。
- He was sentenced to 10 years for forgery.
  他因伪造证件被判刑 10 年。

相关表达 **forger** *n.* 伪造者

记忆点拨 forge（伪造）＋ ry

adopt [ə'dɔpt] ***v.*** **to start to deal with or think about something in a particular way 采用**

- The bank begin to adopt the newly computerized banking system.
  这个银行开始采用新型的银行电脑系统。
- Their business education has adopted the case analysis method from Harvard.
  他们的商业培训已经采用了哈佛的案例分析方法。

相关表达 **adoption** *n.* 收养

adapt *vt.* 使适应；改编

facilitate [fə'siliteit] ***v.*** **to make it easier for a process or activity to happen 使便利**

- In order to facilitate the Sino-US business relationship, the Presidents of these two countries have signed a trade memo.
  为了促进中美两国商贸关系，两国领导人签署了一份贸易备忘录。
- The establishment of this community center has facilitated the communication of the residents.
  社区中心的建立便利居民们交流。

记忆点拨 facilit[y]（便利）＋ate

Lesson 13

mineral [ˈminərəl] ***adj.*** **of or relating to minerals 矿物的**

♥ China owns rich sources of mineral deposits.
中国拥有丰富的矿产资源。

♥ People began to focus on the mineral deposits deep under the sea.
人们开始关注埋藏在海底的矿产资源。

记忆点拨 mine（矿）＋r＋al(有关的)

boring [ˈbɔːriŋ] ***n.*** **making a deep round hole in a hard surface 钻孔**

♥ Once a boring sample is obtained, we can be sure of whether there is mineral deposits underneath.
当获得岩心取样后，我们就能确定到底地底下有没有矿产。

♥ A qualified oilman knows how to conduct a boring machine.
一个合格的石油工人知道如何操作钻孔机器。

其他词性 *adj.* 无聊的

记忆点拨 bor[e]（钻，凿）＋ing(状态)

derrick [ˈderik] ***n.*** **a tall tower built over an oil well, used to raise and lower the drill 井架**

♥ There are several derricks standing on the ground.
工地上耸立着好几座井架。

♥ Derrick is an essential instrument for an oil company.
对于石油公司来说，钻井架是很重要的工具。

block and tackle **a piece of equipment with wheels and ropes, used for lifting heavy things 滑轮组**

♥ Block and tackle is used to haul heavy goods.
滑轮组可以用来提升重物。

♥ Small block and tackle is often used in Physics experiment.
小型滑轮组经常被用于物理实验中。

haul [hɔːl] ***v.*** **to pull something heavy with a continuous steady movement 拖，拉**

♥ You can use a trolly to haul these piles of books into the library.
你可以用手推车把这么一大堆书运到图书馆里去。

♥ It is much easier to haul these pieces of furniture by truck than by your hand.
用卡车来拖这些家具比徒手容易得多。

rotate [rəu'teit] ***v.*** **to turn with a circular movement around a central point, or to make something do this 使转动**

♥ The earth rotates round the sun once every year.
地球一年绕太阳转一圈。

♥ The biology department rotates the first year graduate students among several labs.
生物系让一年级的研究生在不同的实验室轮换。

cutting bit 钻头

♥ This sharp cutting bit can be used to shape a diamond.
这个锋利的钻头可以用来切割钻石。

geologist [dʒi'ɔlədʒist] ***n.*** **地质学家**

♥ Geologists usually spend a lot of time working outdoors.
地质学家需要长时间在户外工作。

♥ Li, Siguang is the most famous geologist in China after 1949.
1949 年以后李四光是中国最著名的地质学家。

相关表达 geologic *adj.* 地质的

记忆点拨 geolog[y]（地质学）+ist(专家)

coring [ˈkɔːriŋ] ***n.*** **removing the centre from 取芯**

♥ Coring is a process to sample the central part of the rock.
岩石取芯就是截取岩石中心的一截做标本。

记忆点拨 cor[e]（中心）+ing(行为)

cylinder [ˈsilində] ***n.*** **a shape, object, or container with circular ends and long straight sides 圆柱体**

♥ The gate of the building is hold by several pillar of cylinder.
大门是由几个圆柱形的柱子支撑起来的。

♥ This is a bucket of cylinder.
这是一个圆柱形的桶。

词组拓展 function on all cylinders 工作效率很好，竭尽全力地干，运转正常

circulate [ˈsəːkjuleit] ***v.*** **to move around within a system, or to make something do this 注入，环流**

♥ The water in this swimming pool was circulated every three hours.
这个游泳池里的水每隔 3 个小时就循环一次。

♥ A human being's blood circulates through his body.
一个人的血液在身体内不停循环。

相关表达 circulation *n.* 循环；流通；发行额

记忆点拨 circu（四周，到处）+late

gusher [ˈɡʌʃər] ***n.*** **a place in the ground where oil or water comes out very forcefully, so that a pump is not needed 喷油井**

♥ When Iraqi troops withdrew from Kuwait, they set those gushers on fire.

当伊拉克军队从科威特撤军时，他们点燃了很多喷油井。

♥ The oil spewed some 20 to 30 feet into the air from the gusher.

喷油井中喷出差不多 20～30 英尺高的油柱。

相关表达 gush *v.* 喷涌

记忆点拨 gush（涌出）＋er(……物)

Lesson 14

forecast [ˈfɔːkɑːst] ***n.*** **a description of what is likely to happen in the future, based on the information that you have now 预报**

♥ The financial expert gave the forecast that the stock market will be in rising trend soon.
金融专家预测：股市将马上进入上升状态。

♥ The farmers were very concerned about the weather forecast during the harvest season.
农民在农忙季节都很关注天气预报。

记忆点拨 fore（在前面）＋cast(计算)

speculative [ˈspekjulətiv] ***adj.*** **based on guessing, not on information or facts 推测的**

♥ These numbers are not supported by reliable sources, and they are, at best, speculative.
这些数字都没有可靠信息支持，最多也就是推测的。

♥ The speculative news of the resignation of the principal was never confirmed by the authority.
关于校长辞职的推测消息根本没有得到官方的证实。

记忆点拨 speculat[e]（推测）＋ive（……的）

blizzard [ˈblizəd] ***n.*** **a severe snow storm 暴风雪**

♥ The heavy blizzard blocked the traffic of the city.
猛烈的暴风雪堵塞了城市交通。

♥ The TV was broadcasting a blizzard attack warning.
电视里正播放暴风雪袭击的警报。

deteriorate [di'tiəriəreit] ***v.*** **to become worse** 变坏

♥ His health condition has been deteriorated since last health examination.

自从上次体检以来他的健康状况越来越坏。

♥ The city's environment deteriorated since the founding of the chemical factory.

自从化工厂建立以来，城市的环境越来越差了。

multiply ['mʌltipli] ***v.*** **to do a calculation in which you add a number to itself a particular number of; to increase by a large amount or number, or to make something do this** 乘，增加

♥ 8 multiplied by 5 is 40.

8 乘以 5 等于 40。

♥ To multiply one's chances of success, persistence is very important.

要增加个人成功的机会，坚持不懈是很重要的。

相关表达 divide *v.* 相除

记忆点拨 multipl[e]（倍数）＋y

cascade [kæs'keid] ***v.*** **to flow, fall, or hang down in large quantities** 瀑布似地落下

♥ The snowball cascaded into small pieces from the top of the snow mountain.

雪球从雪山顶上碎成小块瀑布般落下来。

♥ The explosion broke the windows into pieces of glass cascading to the floor.

爆炸把窗户都震碎成小片玻璃，瀑布一样落到地上。

turbulent ['təːbjulənt] ***adj.*** **a turbulent situation or period of time is one in which there are a lot of sudden changes; turbulent air or water moves around a lot** 狂暴的

- The first half of 20th century was a turbulent period in Chinese history.
  20 世纪上半期是中国历史上动荡的时期。
- The turbulent rapids overthrew the small boat.
  湍急的水流把小船掀翻了。

dust devil 小尘暴，尘旋风

- Spring is the season that Beijing often suffers from the dust devil.
  春天是北京经常遭受沙尘暴袭击的季节。
- Experts agree the root cause of the dust devil is unsustainable land use — namely overgrazing.
  专家承认导致沙尘暴的根本原因是不持续性的土地使用，也就是过度放牧。

squall [skwɔːl] ***n.*** **a sudden strong wind, especially one that brings rain or snow** 暴风雪

- The weather forecaster pointed out at the weather map that the front squall line is approaching the city.
  气象预报员在气象地图上指出暴风雪的前锋带正在接近城市。
- There is snow accompanying the strong wind in a squall.
  暴风雪通常是大雪夹着劲风。

eddy [ˈedi] ***n.*** **a circular movement of water, wind, dust etc.** 旋涡

- The racing boat caused swirling eddies in the river.
  赛艇在河水里激起了阵阵旋涡流。
- The racing cars disappeared in eddy of dust.
  赛车在一片扬尘的涡流中不见了。

grid [grid] ***n.*** **a pattern of straight lines that cross each other and form squares** 坐标方格

♥ New York City's streets form a grid.
纽约城市的街道形成了一个网。

♥ The output of the blueprint needs to be grid paper.
这幅设计图需要打印在方格图纸上。

sensor [ˈsensə] ***n.*** **a piece of equipment used for discovering the presence of light, heat, movement etc.** 传感器

♥ China leads an advanced position in the world about the research technology of satellite sensors.
中国在卫星传感器的研究方面处于世界领先地位。

♥ The NASA satellite sensor and field experiment shows aerosols cool the surface but warm the atmosphere of the earth.
美国国家航空和宇宙航行局的卫星传感器和实地考察表明空气中的浮尘颗粒能使地球表面降温但却让大气升温。

记忆点拨 sens[e]（官能，感觉）＋or（……物）

humidity [hjuːˈmiditi] ***n.*** **the amount of water contained in the air** 湿度

♥ Humidity is usually highest in summer season.
通常夏季湿度最高。

♥ The weather forecast announced that today's humidity is 80％.
气象预报播报说今天的湿度是百分之八十。

相关表达 **humid** *adj.* 潮湿的

记忆点拨 humid（潮湿的）＋i＋ty(条件)

meteorologist [ˌmiːtjəˈrɔlədʒist] ***n.*** 气象学家

- Meteorologist cannot do research on the weather forecasting without the data obtained by those satellite sensors.
  没有来源于卫星遥感器的数据，气象学家无法从事气象预测的研究。
- Meteorologists need to carry out field experiment in outdoor fields even desert.
  气象学家需要去野外甚至沙漠里从事实地考察。

相关表达 **meteorological** *adj.* 气象学的

记忆点拨 meteor（大气现象）＋olog[y]（学科）＋ist（专家）

fuctuation [ˌflʌktjuˈeiʃən] ***n.*** **a change in a price, amount, level etc. 起伏，波动**

- The price fluctuation of rice caused the chaotic people.
  米价的起浮导致人群的混乱。
- The fluctuation of the gas price is dependent on the oil output of those Mideast countries.
  油价的起伏取决于中东国家的出油量。

记忆点拨 fluctuat[e]（波动）＋ation(状态)

deviation [ˌdiːviˈeiʃən] ***n.*** **a noticeable difference from what is expected or acceptable 偏差**

- His dress style is a deviation from the normal type.
  他的衣服款式和普通款截然不同。
- Parents of teenagers cannot tolerate their deviations from norms.
  十几岁年轻人的父母们都不能容忍他们离经叛道的行为。

相关表达 **deviationism** *n.* 异端

记忆点拨 deviat[e]（背离，偏离）＋ation(状态)

Lesson 15

secrecy ['siːkrisi] ***n.* the process of keeping something secret, or when something is kept a secret** 秘密

♥ The secrecy of the Coca-Cola receipt is estimated to worth about billions of dollars.
可口可乐配方的秘密估计价值数十亿美元。

♥ People have never stopped to find out the secrecy of mummies in the Egypt pyramid.
人们从来没有停止过探寻埃及金字塔中木乃伊的秘密。

记忆点拨 secre[t]（秘密）+cy

effectiveness [i'fektivnis] ***n.*** 成效，效力

♥ The effectiveness of the new working arrangement is quite significant.
这种新的工作方法的有效性非常显著。

♥ Scientists are very conservative about the effectiveness of this new anti-cancer medicine.
科学家们对于这种抗癌新药的成效都持保留态度。

相关表达 effective *adj.* 有效的

记忆点拨 effect（效果）+ive(性质的）+ ness(名词后缀）

inquiry [in'kwaiəri] ***n.* the act or process of asking questions in order to get information** 调查研究

词组拓展 make inquires 查询，探听，调查
on inquiry 经询问；经调查

♥ The marketing company began the inquiry about the popularity of the new trademark.
这个市场调查公司开始进行关于这个新商标普遍性的调查研究。

♥ The inquiry about the company's financial report has been carried out for months.
这个关于公司财务报告的调查已经进行了好几个月。

词义辨析 **inquiry, inquest, investigation** 都是关于知识、数据或者真相的调查。

♥ filed an inquiry about the lost shipment
把有关丢失货物的调查归档

♥ Holding an inquest to determine whether the dead man had been murdered.
通过验尸从而确定这位死者是否被谋杀。

♥ a criminal investigation
犯罪调查

记忆点拨 inquir[e]（询问，查究）＋y

positive [ˈpɔzətiv] ***adj.*** **if you are positive about things, you are hopeful and confident, and think about what is good in a situation rather than what is bad** 确实的

♥ I am positive that he is going to win.
我很确定他会赢。

♥ He is persuaded finally by this positive proof.
他最终被这份确实的证据说服了。

process [ˈprəses] ***n.*** **a series of actions that are done in order to achieve a particular result** 过程

♥ The whole process of the manufacture has been videotaped and analyzed.
整个生产过程都被录像而且分析了。

♥ The identity of the suspect was established by the process of elimination.
嫌疑犯的身份是通过排除的过程确定的。

记忆点拨 pro(向前) +cess(进行)

patent [ˈpeitənt]

***n*. a special document that gives you the right to make or sell a new INVENTION or product that no one else is allowed to copy** 专利

***v*. to obtain a special document giving you the right to make or sell a new INVENTION or product** 得到专利权

♥ Patent attorney need to pass the patent bar before practice.
专利律师需要在执业前通过专利律师资格考试。

♥ The inventor succeeded in patenting his product after 5 years.
发明人终于在五年后成功地取得了他的产品的专利权。

agent [ˈeidʒənt] ***n*. someone who works for a government or police department, especially in order to get secret information about another country or organization** 情报人员

♥ All the agents employed by CIA have received strict training in tracing information.
所有美国中央情报局的情报人员都接受过严格的情报探测训练。

♥ Though he was employed by company A, he acted secretly as the agent for company B.
虽然他受雇于 A 公司，可却是 B 公司的秘密情报人员。

Lesson 16

physiological [ˌfiziəˈlɔdʒikəl] ***adj.*** **being in accord with or characteristic of the normal functioning of a living organism** 生理的

♥ Mental health will have influence on people's physiological status.

精神健康影响人的生理状态。

♥ There are specialists who are focused on research about athletics physiological status.

有专门从事运动员生理研究的专家。

记忆点拨 physiologi[y]（生理学）+cal（……的）

maximum [ˈmæksiməm] ***adj.*** **the maximum amount, quantity, speed etc. is the largest that is possible or allowed**最大限度的

♥ The city's electricity demand in the summer has exceeded the maximum supply of the power plant.

城市夏季的电力需求已经超过了电厂的最大供电量。

♥ The maximum class load a student can take for each semester is 16 credits.

一个学期每个学生最多能拿 16 个学分。

相关表达 **minimum** *adj.* 最少的

记忆点拨 max（至多）+imum

consideration [kənsidəreiʃən] ***n.*** **careful thought and attention, especially before making an official or important decision** 考虑

♥ It is emphasized that during the admission process, equal considerations shall be given to students of different races.

需要强调的是在录取过程中，不同种族的学生应该给予平等的考虑。

♥ During the construction of the building, the designers have given enough considerations to the safety against earthquake.

在建房子的过程中，设计师充分考虑到了防震的安全性。

相关表达 considerate *adj.* 体贴的

记忆点拨 consider（考虑）＋ation(行为)

descendant [dɪˈsendənt] ***n.* someone who is related to a person who lived a long time ago, or to a family, group of people etc. that existed in the past** 子孙，后代

♥ It is important to have descendant to carry the family tree in traditional Chinese notions.

在传统的中国观念里，后继有人是很重要的。

♥ We need to protect the environment for the benefit of our descendants.

为了我们的子孙后代，我们应该保护环境。

记忆点拨 descend（遗传）＋ant

artificial [ˌɑːtiˈfiʃəl] ***n.* not real or not made of natural things but made to be like something that is real or natural** 人工的

♥ Most of the seafood sold in the supermarket grew up in artificial environment rather than in the sea.

超市里出售的海鲜食品大多数都不是海里自然生长的，而是人工环境里养殖的。

♥ Artificial intelligence has been a hot topic since the end of last century.

从上世纪末以来，人工智能就成为了一个热门话题。

记忆点拨 arti[y]（艺术家气派的）＋ficial

impose [im'pəuz] ***v.*** **if someone in authority imposes a rule, punishment, tax etc., they force people to accept it** 强加

♥ The government imposed heavy duties on the entertainment business.

政府对娱乐经营场所强行征重税。

♥ The safety regulations are imposed on those fireworks factories.

烟花生产厂家被强制执行安全条例。

记忆点拨 im（强调意义）＋pose(放置)

dimension [di'menʃən] ***n.*** **the length, height, width, depth, or diameter of something** 尺寸

♥ You need to measure the dimension of the garden before decide how to landscape it.

在决定如何对花园景观设计以前，你需要丈量一下它的面积。

♥ The dimension of the bookcase is larger than that of the trunk. Therefore it cannot fit into.

这个书柜的尺寸大于车后箱的尺寸，所以无法放进去。

相关表达 **dimensional** *adj.* 尺寸的

skyscraper ['skaɪskreɪpə(r)] ***n.*** **a very tall modern city building** 摩天大楼

♥ Sears is the highest skyscraper in Chicago.

Sears 是芝加哥最高的摩天大楼。

♥ People first believe that skyscraper can solve the problem of scarcity of land in the city.
人们最初以为摩天大楼能解决城市里土地紧张的问题。

记忆点拨 sky(天) ＋scraper(刮的人)

tenant [ˈtenənt] ***n.*** **someone who lives in a house, room etc. and pays rent to the person who owns it** 租户

♥ The tenant moved out of the apartment without noticing the landlord.
租户没有通知房主就搬出了公寓。

♥ Tenants are responsible to keep the house clean.
租户们有责任保持房子的洁净。

civilized [ˈsɪvɪlaɪzd] ***adj.*** **a civilized society is well organized and developed, and has fair laws and customs** 文明的

♥ Monogamy is common nowadays in civilized society.
一夫一妻制在现代文明社会很普遍。

♥ The NAZI slaughter shocked the whole civilized society.
纳粹的大屠杀震惊了整个文明社会。

相关表达 barbarous *adj.* 野蛮的；uncivilized *adj.* 不文明的

记忆点拨 civil (有礼貌的) ＋ize(形成) ＋ (e)d (……的)

banal [bəˈnɑːl] ***adj.*** **ordinary and not interesting, because of a lack of new or different ideas** 平庸的

♥ I am so bored by my banal life.
我厌烦了这种平庸的生活。

♥ This newly published banal book was not sold well in the market at all.
这本新出版的平庸的书在市场上卖得一点也不好。

相关表达 banality *n.* 陈词滥调

luxury [ˈlʌkʃəri] ***n.*** **very great comfort and pleasure, such as you get from expensive food, beautiful houses, cars etc.** 豪华

♥ More than 200 guests attended their luxury wedding in Hawaii.

有两百多宾客参加了他们在夏威夷举办的豪华婚礼。

♥ They live in luxury in a very big house near the beach.

他们在海边一所很大的房子里过着奢侈的生活。

deprive [diˈpraiv] ***v.*** **to prevent someone from having something, especially something that they need or should have** 剥夺

♥ The parents deprive the girl of her childhood happiness by forcing her to learn playing piano.

父母强迫小女孩去学钢琴，剥夺了她的童年乐趣。

♥ The wild animals were deprived of their freedom by locked in the cage of zoo.

野生动物们被关在动物园的笼子里，被剥夺了自由。

词组拓展 deprive sb. of… 剥夺某人的……，使某人丧失……；免去某人（职务）

记忆点拨 de（除去，取消）＋ prive

monstrous [ˈmɔnstrəs] ***adj.*** **shockingly hideous or frightful.** 畸形的

♥ They complained that monstrous buildings destroyed the city's landscape.

他们抱怨说那些畸形的建筑物破坏了城市的景观。

♥ Without proper designing, the school gate building turned out to be a monstrous giant.
由于缺乏合适的设计，学校大门变成了一个畸形的巨人。

相关表达 monster *n.* 怪物

记忆点拨 monst［e］r（怪物）＋ous（……性质的）

edifice ['edifis] ***n.* a building, especially a large one** 大厦

♥ The Citibank has its headquarter in an imposing edifice.
花旗银行的总部在一栋宏伟的大厦里。

♥ There are two emergency exists at the two ends of the edifice.
大厦的两头分别有两个紧急出口。

相关表达 近义词 building *n.* 建筑物；construction *n.* 建筑物

toxic ['tɔksik] ***adj.* containing poison, or caused by poisonous substances** 有毒的

♥ The villagers got sick by drinking the toxic water in the well.
村民们由于饮用了有毒的井水生病了。

♥ You need to be careful of this toxic gas when doing experiment.
做实验的时候你要注意这些有毒气体。

相关表达 poisonous *adj.* 有毒的

记忆点拨 tox（总氧化剂）＋ic（……的）

ceaselessly ['siːslisli] *adv.* 不停地

♥ The train station is crowded ceaselessly by passengers passing by.
火车站里挤满了来来往往的旅客。

♥ He kept ceaselessly looking at the entrance.
他不停地朝入口处看。

记忆点拨 cease（停止）＋less（不，相反的）＋ly（……地）

throng [θrɔŋ] *v.* **if people throng a place, they go there in large numbers** 挤满，拥塞

♥ The tunnel is thronged with vehicles in rush hour.
在高峰期，隧道里挤满了汽车。

♥ The time square is thronged with celebrating people at New Year's Eve.
新年前夜，时代广场挤满了庆祝的人群。

相关表达 近义词 crowd *v.* 群集；拥挤

Unit 3

Lesson 17

settlement ['setlmənt] *n.* **when a lot of people move to a place in order to live there, especially in a place where not many people have lived before** 新居地

♥ California is the settlement for those west explorers.

加州是那些西部开拓者的新居地。

♥ The settlement of Africa by white colonists started 500 years ago.

由白人殖民者进行的向非洲移民开始于 500 年前。

词组拓展 marriage settlement 结婚财产契约

记忆点拨 settle (定居)＋ment(地方)

enterprising ['entəpraiziŋ] *adj.* **having the ability to think of new activities or ideas and make them work** 有事业心的

♥ The enterprising owner expanded the shop by twice as large as before.

有事业心的店主把商店面积扩充了一倍。

♥ The wife complained that her enterprising husband cared too little about the family.

妻子抱怨说她有事业心的丈夫太不关心家庭。

相关表达 enterprise *n.* 企业；enterpriser *n.* 企业家

记忆点拨 enterprise[e] (事业心)＋ ing(状态)

settler ['setlə] *n.* **someone who goes to live in a country or area where not many people like them have lived before, and that is a long way from any towns or cities** 移居者

♥ There have been more and more new Chinese settlers in Vancouver since the late 1990s.
从20世纪90年代末开始，温哥华出现越来越多的中国新移居者。

♥ The US is a country built by new settlers to the North American continent.
美国是移居北美大陆的移居者建立起来的国家。

记忆点拨 settl[e]（定居）+er(者)

promiscuous [prəˈmiskjuəs] ***adj.*** **having many sexual partners; involving a wide range of different things** 混乱的

♥ The room was messed by a promiscuous heap of clothes on the floor.
房间被地上堆的一堆杂乱无章的衣服搞得很乱。

abandon [əˈbændən] ***n.*** **if someone does something with abandon, they behave in a careless or uncontrolled way, without thinking or caring about what they are doing** 放任，纵情

♥ The fans shouted in abandon in the rock n' roll concert.
在摇滚音乐会上，爱好者们放肆地大叫。

♥ People hurled pieces of wood into the bonfire with abandon.
人们纵情地往篝火里扔一块块的木柴。

overrun [əuvərʌn] ***v.*** **if unwanted things or people overrun a place, they spread over it in great numbers** 蔓延，泛滥

♥ Locus overran the whole farmland.
蝗虫在整片田里肆虐。

♥ The gutter was overrun by mice.
贫民区老鼠猖獗。

记忆点拨　over(越过) ＋ run(趋向)

devastation　[ˌdevəsˈteiʃən] ***n.*** **to damage something very badly or completely** 破坏，劫掠

♥ The earthquake brought immense devastation to the city.
地震给城市带来了巨大的破坏。

♥ Forest devastation is a big problem China has to face in this century.
森林的破坏是中国在21世纪必须面对的一个巨大问题。

相关表达　**devastating** *adj.* 破坏性的，极坏的

记忆点拨　devastate[e]（毁坏）＋ation(行为)

burrow　[ˈbʌrəu] ***v.*** **to make a hole or passage in the ground** 挖，掘

♥ Rabbits like to burrow into grounds for residence and food.
兔子喜欢往地里打洞做窝和觅食。

♥ The construction workers burrowed through the mountain for the train tunnel.
建筑工人挖山来修建火车隧道。

susceptible　[səˈseptəbl] ***adj.*** **likely to suffer from a particular illness or be affected by a particular problem** 易受感染的

词组拓展　be susceptible to 对……敏感的；容易受到

♥ Infants are susceptible to all kinds of virus.
婴儿对各种病毒都易受感染。

♥ People are susceptible to flu in spring.
春季人们易感染流行感冒。

记忆点拨　suscept（感病体）＋ible(倾向的)

virus ['vaiərəs] ***n.* a very small living thing that causes infectious illnesses 病毒**

♥ My computer is down because of the computer virus.
我的电脑因为感染病毒死机了。

♥ Nowadays we still cannot effectively control the HIV virus.
今天我们还是不能有效地控制艾滋病病毒。

infect [in'fekt] ***v.* to give someone a disease 传染**

词组拓展 be infected with 感染，沾染上

♥ One of the children in the class had a fever and he soon infected other children.
班上的一个孩子发烧了，不久他就传染上了其他孩子。

♥ You need to clean the wounds every day, otherwise it will be infected.
你需要每天清洗伤口，否则就会被感染。

相关表达 近义词 contaminate *v.* 污染

记忆点拨 in（入）＋fect

epidemic [ˌepi'demik] ***n.* a large number of cases of a disease that happen at the same time 流行病**

♥ Chicken pox was an epidemic easily infected by children.
水痘是很容易传染给小孩的一种流行病。

♥ The University health center is giving free flu shot for curbing the epidemic outbreak of the influenza.
大学的校医院免费提供流感疫苗以控制流行性感冒的爆发性蔓延。

相关表达 近义词 prevalent *adj.* 普遍的；流行的；widespread *adj.* 分布广泛的；普通的

mosquito [məsˈkiːtəu] *n.* **a small flying insect that sucks the blood of people and animals, sometimes spreading the disease MALARIA** 蚊虫

♥ I have been bitten by mosquitoes for several bites this afternoon.
这个下午我已经被蚊子叮了好几口了。

♥ You need to spray some insecticide in the room to kill the mosquitoes.
你应该在屋里喷点杀虫剂来杀死蚊子。

carrier [ˈkæriə] *n.* **someone who passes a disease or GENE to other people, especially without being affected by it themselves** 带菌者，运送者

♥ Flies can be carriers for numerous diseases.
苍蝇可以成为多种疾病的带菌者。

♥ The carrier can deliver the package from the company to their clients overnight.
运送者只需要隔夜就可以把包裹从公司送到客户处。

记忆点拨 carri[y]（运送）+er(者)

exterminate [iksˈtəːmineit] *v.* **to kill large numbers of people or animals of a particular type so that they no longer exist** 消灭

♥ Human beings do not have right to exterminate any spices living on the earth.
人类没有权利消灭任何生存在地球上的物种。

♥ It is impossible to exterminate the grass by fire.
用火烧是无法斩草除根的。

相关表达 destroy *v.* 破坏；毁坏；消灭，eliminate *v.* 排除；消除

记忆点拨 ex（使）+terminate（终止）

ironically [aiə'rɔnikəli] *adv.* **used when talking about a situation in which the opposite of what you expected happens or is true** 具有讽刺意味地

♥ Ironically he had to team up with the girl he dislikes most.

具有讽刺意味的是，他不得不和他最讨厌的女孩合作。

♥ Ironically she lost the game to the adversary she despised most.

具有讽刺意味的是，她输给了她最看不见的对手。

相关表达 **irony** *n.* 反话；讽刺；讽刺之事

记忆点拨 iron[y]（讽刺）＋ical(涉及）＋ly（……地）

bequeath [bi'kwiːð] *v.* **to officially arrange for someone to have something that you own after your death; to pass knowledge, customs etc. to people who come after you or live after you** 把……传给

♥ The Queen will bequeath the regime to the princess.

女王将把政权传给王子。

♥ Our ancestor bequeathed us the spirit of braver and hardworking.

我们的祖先把勤劳勇敢的精神传给了我们。

相关表达 **bequeathal** *n.* 遗产

pest [pest] *n.* **a small animal or insect that destroys crops or food supplies** 害虫，有害动物

♥ From our human being's point of view, insects that eat crops are pests.

从人类的角度来讲，吃庄稼的昆虫是害虫。

♥ Pest can spread disease quickly.

害虫能迅速传染疾病。

相关表达　pesthole *n.* 传染病地区，瘟疫区

pestilence　[ˈpestiləns] ***n.* a disease that spreads quickly and kills a lot of people** 瘟疫

An effective means to control pestilence is quarantine.

有效控制瘟疫的方法是隔离。

With the development of modern sanitation, human beings are more capable to control pestilence than before.

随着现代公共卫生事业的发展，人类比原先更有能力控制瘟疫的发生。

相关表达　pestilent *adj.* 致命的

记忆点拨　pest（有害物）＋ilence

confine　[ˈkɔnfain] ***n.* limits or borders** 范围

词组拓展　beyond the confine of 超出……的范围

within the confines of 在……（范围）之内

A country can exercise its sovereignty independently within the confine of its land.

一个国家能在自己领土之内独立行使主权。

This question is beyond the confine of the stud－ents'curriculum.

这个问题超出了学生的课程范围。

相关表达　近义词 scope *n.* 范围；机会；余地；border *n.* 边界；国界；

记忆点拨　con(共同) ＋ fine(好)

domesticate　[dəˈmestikeit] ***v.* to make an animal able to work for people or live with them as a pet** 驯养

Cattle are very help domesticated animals to farmers.

牛对农民们来说是非常有用的驯养动物。

♥ Domesticated horses can be an effective means of transportation in older days.
以前驯养的马匹是非常有效的交通工具。

相关表达 domestic *adj.* 家庭的，驯服的

记忆点拨 domestic（驯服的）＋ate

Lesson 18

porpoise [ˈpɔːpəs] ***n.*** **a sea animal that looks similar to a dolphin and breathes air** 海豚

♥ Porpoise are very smart animals and have their own language to communicate.
海豚是很聪明的动物，有自己的交流语言。

♥ Porpoise can be trained to perform water show before audience.
海豚经过训练可以在观众面前表演水中节目。

mariner [ˈmærinə] ***n.*** **a sailor** 水手

♥ To be a qualified mariner, you need to be a good swimmer and have a strong body.
要想成为一名合格的水手，需要是游泳好手，并有强健的体魄。

♥ Mariners are required to learn some marine knowledge.
水手们都被要求学习海事知识。

相关表达 近义词 seaman; sailor

记忆点拨 marin[e] 海运业 ＋ er 人

shark [ʃɑːk] ***n.*** **a large sea fish with several rows of very sharp teeth that is considered to be dangerous to humans** 鲨鱼

♥ Sharks usually find food from the bottom of the sea by smell.
鲨鱼通常靠嗅觉从海底寻找食物。

♥ The net is placed along the beach to protect the attack of sharks.
防鲨网放在海边是为了防止鲨鱼的进攻。

formation [fɔːˈmeiʃən] ***n.*** **the way in which a group of things are arranged to form a pattern or shape 队形**

♥ The coach carefully designed the formation of the soccer team before the game.
教练员在比赛前精心设计足球队的队形。

♥ The emphasis of the formation is put on defense.
队形的重点放在了防守上。

记忆点拨 form（排列）＋ation(行为)

dolphin [ˈdɔlfin] ***n.*** **a very intelligent sea animal like a fish with a long grey pointed nose 海豚科动物**

♥ The tourists are happily feeding the dolphins in the pool.
游客们正在高兴地给池里的海豚喂食。

♥ The dolphins are jumping up and down in the water.
海豚们在水中跳上跃下。

unconscious [ʌnˈkɔnʃəs] ***adj.*** **unable to see, move, feel etc. in the normal way because you are not conscious 不省人事的**

♥ The patient's brain was hurt during the car accident, and he has been unconscious since then.
这个病人在车祸中脑部受伤，一直不省人事。

♥ After stood under the sun for too long, she passed out and become unconscious.
在太阳下站立太久后，她昏迷了过去，不省人事。

相关表达 近义词 senseless *adj.* 无意识的；无感觉的；unaware *adj.* 不知道的；没觉察到的

记忆点拨 un(不）＋conscious（有意识的，有知觉的）

beaver [ˈbiːvə] ***n.*** **a North American animal that has thick fur and a wide flat tail, and cuts down trees with its teeth 海狸**

♥ People use the fur of beaver to manufacture high-quality clothes.
人们利用海狸皮来生产高质量的衣服。

♥ Beavers are pests for forest, because they can cut down young trees by their teeth.
海狸对森林有害，因为他们会用牙齿咬断幼树。

ashore [əˈʃɔː] ***adv.*** **on or towards the shore of a lake, river, sea etc. 向岸地**

♥ The mariners tried to pull the boat ashore.
船员们努力把船拉上岸。

♥ Army troops wade ashore on "Omaha" Beach during the "D-Day" landings.
在诺曼底登陆日，军队在名叫奥马哈的海滩上岸了。

词组拓展 go ashore 上岸，登陆

相关表达 反义词 adrift *adv.* 随波逐流地

记忆点拨 a(向……) ＋shore(岸)

waterlogged [ˈwɔːtəlɔgd] ***adj.*** **a waterlogged area of land is flooded with water and cannot be used 浸满水的**

♥ Policemen finally found the waterlogged dead body from the surface of the sea.
警察最终在海面上找到了这具浸满水的尸体。

♥ It will cost thousands of dollars to salvage this waterlogged ship from the bottom of the sea.
要从海底打捞起这艘灌满水的船需要花费数千美金。

记忆点拨 water(水) ＋logged

scent [sent] ***n.*** **a pleasant smell that something has 香味**

♥ This perfume adds a pleasant scent to my clothes.
这种香水使我的衣服发出一种令人愉快的香味。

♥ Dogs have an amazing memory about all kinds of scent.
狗对各种气味有惊人的记忆力。

相关表达 近义词 fragrance *n.* 芬芳，香味；odor *n.* 气味，名声

ensue [in'sjuː] ***v.*** **to happen after or as a result of something 接着发生**

♥ What will ensue from this incident?
这样的事件会产生什么结果呢？

♥ The host gave an exciting speech, and then a heated debate ensued.
主持人发表了一番激动人心的演讲，然后紧接着是一场激烈的辩论。

词组拓展 ensue (from, on) 结果是

相关表达 近义词 follow *v.* 跟随；result *v.* 导致

intrigue [in'triːg] ***v.*** **if something intrigues you, it interests you a lot because it seems strange or mysterious 引起兴趣**

♥ The sci-fi novel intrigued the children to learn more about robotics.
这本科幻小说激起孩子们去更多地了解机器人的兴趣。

♥ The clone technology intrigued the biologists.
克隆技术激发了生物学家的兴趣。

indignity [in'digniti] ***n.*** **a situation that makes you feel very ashamed and not respected 侮辱**

♥ He will never submit to indignity.
他从来不屈服于侮辱。

♥ She suffered many such indignities in school.
在学校里她经受了很多这样的侮辱。

词组拓展 put an indignity upon sb. 贬损某人的尊严，侮辱某人

记忆点拨 in(不) +dignity (尊贵，高贵，庄严)

snout [snaut] ***n.* the long nose of some kinds of animals, such as pigs** 口鼻部

♥ The dolphin can play balls with his snout.
这只海豚能用鼻子玩球。

♥ The two dolphins kissed each other by snouts.
两只海豚用鼻尖互相亲吻。

shove [ʃʌv] ***v.* to push someone or something in a rough or careless way, using your hands or shoulders** 硬推

♥ We need two persons to move this machine. One is going to pull, and the other will shove.
我们需要两个人来挪动这个机器。一个人拉，另一个人推。

♥ People frequently shove one another in the crowds.
人们在人群中互相推来推去。

词组拓展 shove along 推着走

aquaplane [ˈækwəplein] ***n.* a thin board that you stand on while you are pulled over the water by a fast boat** 驾浪滑水板

♥ The main difference between aquaplane and sailboard is the aquaplane is pulled over the water by a motorboat.
滑水板和帆板的主要区别在于滑水板是由摩托艇在水上牵引的。

♥ The tip to play aquaplane is keeping balance.
玩滑水板的窍门在于保持平衡。

相关表达　aquaplaner *n.* 滑水运动员

记忆点拨　aqua（水）＋plane(平面)

oceanarium　[ˌəuʃəˈnɛəriəm] ***n.*** **a large aquarium for the study or display of marine life** 水族馆

♥ Children can learn all kinds of ocean animals in the oceanarium.

孩子们可以在海洋水族馆里认识各种海洋动物。

♥ The biggest oceanarium in Texas is located in San Antonio.

德克萨斯州最大的水族馆在圣安东尼奥。

相关表达　复数 oceanariums 或者 oceanaria

近义词 aquarium

记忆点拨　ocean（海洋）＋arium(场所，地点)

swoop　[swuːp] ***v.*** **if a bird or aircraft swoops, it moves suddenly down through the air, especially in order to attack something** 猛扑

♥ The eagle swooped down on a chicken.

老鹰猛扑小鸡。

♥ The bird swooped down to the lake.

这只鸟猛扑到湖上。

词组拓展　swoop (down; on; upon)

相关表达　近义词 dive; plunge

belly　[ˈbeli] ***n.*** **the front part of your body between your chest and your legs** 腹部

♥ Belly dance is a traditional Turkish dancing.

肚皮舞是一种传统的土耳其舞蹈。

♥ The pregnant woman has a round belly.

那个怀孕的妇女大腹便便。

相关表达　近义词 abdomen *n.* 腹部；stomach *n.* 胃部

equilibrium [ˌiːkwiˈlibriəm] ***n.*** **a balance between different people, groups, or forces that compete with each other, so that none is stronger than the others and a situation is not likely to change suddenly 平衡**

♥ One way to protect the environment is to maintain the equilibrium of the nature.

保护环境的一种方法是保持自然生态的平衡。

♥ Even if you want to lose weight, you still need to maintain nutritious equilibrium of your body.

即使你要减肥，你仍然需要保持身体的营养均衡。

相关表达 近义词 balance

记忆点拨 equilibr[ate]（使平衡）＋ium（名词后缀）

butt [bʌt] ***v.*** **to hit or push against something or someone with your head 碰撞**

♥ He felt a little dizzy and butted his head against the wall.

他感到有点头晕于是一头撞到了墙上。

♥ The bull butted toward the matador.

公牛一头撞向斗牛士。

crack [kræk] ***n.*** **a sudden loud sound like the sound of a stick being broken 重击**

♥ I got a crack on the head as I went through the low doorway.

当我经过那个低矮的门口时，头被撞了一下。

♥ The hijacker raised the baseball bat and gave him another crack on the head.

那个强盗举起棒球棒，又重重地击打了他脑袋一下。

Lesson 19

speculation [ˌspekjuˈleiʃən] ***n.*** **when you guess about the possible causes or effects of something without knowing all the facts, or the guesses that you make 推测**

♥ Speculations cannot be court evidence.
推测不能作为法庭证据。

♥ Their speculations were all quite close to the truth.
他们的揣测都很接近于事实。

词组拓展 lead to the speculation 引起猜测

相关表达 speculative *adj.* 投机的

记忆点拨 speculat[e]（推测）＋ion(行为)

literally [ˈlitərəli] ***adv.*** **to believe exactly what someone or something says rather than trying to understand their general meaning 确实**

♥ Don't take her words literally.
别把她的话当真。

♥ The final of Europe Cup was watched by literally millions of people.
欧洲杯的决赛确实有数百万人观看。

相关表达 近义词 actually; really

记忆点拨 literal（无夸张的）＋ly(……地)

odd [ɔd] ***adj.*** **different from what is normal or expected, especially in a way that you disapprove of or cannot understand 奇特的，奇怪的**

♥ An odd phenomenon is that almost all the villagers have a life span around 90 years.
一个奇特的现象是几乎所有的村民都有 90 岁左右的寿命。

♥ Our neighbor is so odd that he never go out at daytime.
我们的邻居很奇怪，从来不在白天出门。

相关表达 近义词 peculiar; strange

tissue [ˈtisjuː] *n.* **the material forming animal or plant cells** 组织

♥ Human body has four basic types of tissue: muscle, nerve, epidermal, and connective.
人体拥有四种基本的组织：肌肉、神经、表皮和连接。

♥ The doctor told her that there is something wrong with her brain tissue.
医生说她的脑组织出了一些问题。

plausible [ˈplɔːzəbl] *adj.* **reasonable and likely to be true or successful** 似乎有理的

♥ Although her excuse sounds plausible, I know she is lying.
虽然她的借口听起来可信，但我知道她在撒谎。

♥ Only after the plausible theories have been proved by reality, can we rely on them.
只有用事实检验过这些似乎有理的理论后，我们才能依赖它们。

hypothesis [haiˈpɔθisis] *n.* **an idea that is suggested as an explanation for something, but that has not yet been proved to be true** 假说

♥ This is only a sort of scientific hypothesis that has not been proved by experiments.
这仅仅是一个尚未被实验证明的科学假说。

♥ The paper elaborates the scholar's hypothesis clearly and vividly.
这篇论文很清晰生动地阐述了这个学者的假设。

相关表达 复数 hypotheses

记忆点拨 hypo（低，次）+thesis(论题，论文)

electrode [ɪ'lektrəʊd] ***n.*** **a small piece of metal or a wire that is used to send electricity through a system or through a person's body** 电极

♥ We need to recharge the cells by the two electrodes.
我们需要通过两电极来给电池充电。

♥ Look closely at the signs of the electrodes before you put these cells in.
在放电池前，仔细看清楚两极的符号。

记忆点拨 electro（电版）+de

scalp [skælp] ***n.*** **the skin on the top of your head** 头皮

♥ Native American warriors used to take the scalps of the opponents as a battle trophy.
印第安武士曾经将敌人头皮剥下作为战利品。

♥ One of the functions of scalp is to protect the brain.
头皮的一个作用是保护大脑。

词组拓展 have the scalp of …剥取某人的头皮；打败（某人）

psychiatrist [saɪ'kaɪətrɪst] ***n.*** **a doctor trained in the treatment of mental illness** 精神病学家

♥ Psychiatrists can give professional consulting to people in mental disorder.

精神病学家可以给精神混乱的人提供专业咨询。

♥ Psychiatrist can provide testimony as an expert witness in court.

精神病学家可以作为专家证人在法庭上作证。

记忆点拨 psychiatr[y]（精神病学）＋ist(专家)

punctuate [ˈpʌŋktjueit] *v.* **to be interrupted by something, especially when this is repeated** 不时介入

♥ The movie was occasionally punctuated by the audiences'laughter.

电影中不时介入观众的笑声。

♥ Feel free to punctuate my presentation by any questions you have.

如果对我的演示有任何问题，随时可以打断。

相关表达 **punctuation** *n.* 标点符号

jerky [ˈdʒəːki] *adj.* **jerky movements are rough, with many starts and stops** 急动的

♥ It is so dangerous to have a jerky break on highway.

在高速公路上急刹车是很危险的。

♥ The jerky train ride made her begin to vomit.

颠簸不平的火车让她呕吐。

记忆点拨 jerk（急拉，颠簸地行进）＋y(……的)

disorder [disˈɔːdə] *n.* **a mental or physical illness which prevents part of your body from working properly** 失调

♥ Eating disorder can lead to death.

厌食症可以导致死亡。

♥ The power cut made the life of the residents into a disorder state.
停电使居民的生活陷入无序的状态。

相关表达 反义词 order *n.* 秩序

记忆点拨 dis（相反）+order（秩序）

implication [ˌimpliˈkeiʃən] ***n.*** **a suggestion that is not made directly but that people are expected to understand or accept** 含意，暗示

♥ Did you get the implication of this novel?
你能明白这篇小说的言外之意吗？

♥ The implication of his words is not friendly.
他的话外之音并不友好。

词组拓展 by implication 含蓄地，用寓意

相关表达 imply *v.* 暗示

记忆点拨 implicat［e］（暗示）+ion（行为，状态）

Lesson 20

saliva [səˈlaivə] ***n.*** **the liquid that is produced naturally in your mouth** 唾液

♥ Saliva is imperative to people since it helps digest food.
唾液对于人们来说至关重要因为它可以帮助消化。

♥ Infants like to spit saliva when feeding them milk.
给婴儿喂奶时他们喜欢吐唾液。

digestive [diˈdʒestiv] ***adj.*** **connected with the process of digestion** 助消化的

♥ You'd better have something digestive since you ate too much tonight.
你最好吃点助消化的东西，你今晚吃太多了。

♥ He has an amazing digestive power.
他有惊人的消化力。

相关表达 digest *v.* 消化

记忆点拨 digest（消化）＋ive(……性质的)

defy [diˈfai] ***v.*** **to refuse to obey a law or rule, or refuse to do what someone in authority tells you to do** 藐视，使……难于

♥ As a statesman, Bush should not defy public opinion of Islamic world to continue the war in Iraq.
作为一个政治家，布什不应该藐视伊斯兰国家的看法而发动对伊拉克的战争。

♥ The pain defies description.
那是无法形容的痛苦。

analysis [ə'nælisis] ***n.*** **a careful examination of something in order to understand it better 分析**

♥ Even the most accurate analysis cannot thoroughly predict the trend in stock market.

即使是最精确的分析也无法完全预测股市的走向。

♥ Although we seldom use calculus in daily life, learning it helps our ability of analysis.

虽然我们在日常生活中很少用到微积分，但学习它有助于我们的分析能力。

相关表达 近义词 synthesis *n.* 综合，合成

记忆点拨 analys[e]（分析）＋ is

prey [prei] ***n.*** **an animal, bird etc. that is hunted and eaten by another animal 被捕食的动物**

♥ Usually the world is ruthless. You can either be a prey or a preyer.

大自然很残酷，你或者是猎物或者是扑食者。

♥ The eagle played its prey in its claws.

这只鹰用爪子玩耍着捕获物。

词组拓展 be a prey to（动物）被捕食

easy prey 容易上钩者

相关表达 **preyer** *n.* 猛兽

fierce [fiəs] ***adj.*** **a fierce person or animal is angry or ready to attack, and looks very frightening 凶猛的**

♥ Most people regard tigers as fierce animals but actually they will not attack people unless they are threatened.

很多人都认为老虎是凶猛的动物，其实如果不是受到威胁，它们一般不会攻击人类。

♥ Sometimes people are more dangerous than fierce animals.

有时候人比凶猛的动物更危险。

tussle [ˈtʌsl] *n.* **a fight using a lot of energy, in which two people get hold of each other and struggle 扭打**

♥ Their quarrel became tussle since neither of them can keep sane.

因为他们都不够理智，所以争吵最终成了扭打。

♥ The policeman stopped their tussle and brought them into custody.

警察制止了他们的扭打，然后把他们都扣押了下来。

相关表达 近义词 battle; fight

carnivore [ˈkɑːnivɔː] *n.* **an animal that eats flesh 食肉动物**

♥ Carnivores are more dangerous to people since they probably will attack people when feeling hungry.

因为食肉动物饥饿时会攻击人类，所以也许对于人类它们更危险。

♥ He is like a carnivore. He can eat meat all day without vegetables or fruit.

他就像个食肉动物，可以整天只吃肉，不需要蔬菜和水果。

相关表达 反义词 Herbivore *n.* 食草动物

vertebrate [ˈvəːtibrit] *n.* **a living creature that has a backbone 脊椎动物**

♥ Vertebrates are the highest in the chain of evolvement.

在进化链中脊椎动物是最高级的。

♥ Fish is a vertebrate in water.

鱼是水中的脊椎动物。

记忆点拨 vertebra（脊椎骨）＋te

lizard [ˈlizəd] *n.* **a type of reptile that has four legs and a long tail 蜥蜴**

♥ Although lizards are ugly, sometimes they are raised as pets by people.
虽然蜥蜴很难看，可是还有人把它们当作宠物。

♥ In summer, lizard can help us get rid of mosquito.
夏季蜥蜴可以帮助我们消灭蚊子。

concoct [kən'kɔkt] ***v.*** **to make something, especially food or drink, by mixing different things, especially things that are not usually combined** 调制

♥ He concocted a splendid cocktail in the party.
他为聚会调制出了很棒的鸡尾酒。

♥ Remarkably, it took four writers to concoct this farce.
惊讶的是，需要四位作家来编造这出闹剧。

相关表达 近义词 create; devise

记忆点拨 con（共同，合起来）＋coct

potency ['pəutənsɪ] ***n.*** **the power that something has to influence people; the strength of something, especially a drug, on your mind or body** 效力

♥ In the new movie of *Harry Potter*, the young wizard lost much of his potency.
在《哈利·波特》的新电影中，年轻的巫师失去了他的魔力。

♥ At *Troy*, Achilles distinguished himself as an undefeatable warrior with super potency.
在《特洛伊》中，阿克硫斯是一个力大无穷，无法打败的战士。

相关表达 **potecary** ***n.*** 药剂师；药房

记忆点拨 potenc[e]（能力）＋y

conversion [kən'vəːʃən] ***n.*** **when you change something from one form, purpose, or system to a different one** 转变

♥ His conversion to Christianity in his late years is regarded as one of the most important events in his life by historians.

历史学家们认为他晚年成为基督徒是他一生中很重要的事件。

♥ You need special instrument to complete the conversion from digital code to video.

你需要特殊的仪器才能完成从数字代码到图像的转变。

记忆点拨 convers[e]（相反的事物，逆行）＋ion(行为)

arsenic [ˈɑːsənik] ***n.*** **a very poisonous chemical substance that is sometimes used to kill rats, insects, and weeds. It is a chemical element** 砒霜

♥ Arsenic is a deadly poison for people as well as animals.

砒霜对于人和动物来说都是致命的毒药。

♥ It is required that Arsenic can only be obtained by prescription.

根据要求砒霜只能通过处方获得。

venom [ˈvenəm] ***n.*** **a liquid poison that some snakes, insects etc. produce when they bite or sting you** 毒液

♥ Snake venom is highly modified saliva produced by modified saliva glands.

蛇毒是通过唾液腺分泌高度浓缩的唾液的。

♥ Venom can be transmitted by snake' bites.

蛇毒可以通过被蛇咬伤传播。

viperine [ˈvaipərin] ***adj.*** **of, resembling, or characteristic of a viper** 毒蛇的

♥ Scientists' results have a number of implications on the taxonomy of viperine snakes, which will be discussed in this symposium.
科学家的研究成果对毒蛇的分类有了很多改变，我们将在研讨会上讨论。

♥ This snake looks like viperine, but it turns out to be not.
这条蛇看上去好像有毒，但最后发现没有。

记忆点拨 viper（毒蛇）＋ine（……的）

Lesson 21

supreme [sju:'pri:m] ***adj.*** **having the highest position of power, importance, or influence** 首屈一指

♥ As the supreme student in the class, he went to Beijing University to pursue his study.
作为班上的尖子生，他考上了北大继续深造。

♥ He was awarded this prize for his supreme performing talents.
为了表彰他顶尖的表演才华，他被授予这个奖项。

相关表达 近义词 greatest; top

记忆点拨 super（特级的，极好的）＋ eme

protagonist [prəu'tægənist] ***n.*** **the most important character in a play, film, or story** 主角

♥ The protagonist in *Cast Away* made Tom Hanks, the actor who plays it, the nominee of the best actor of the Academic Award.
汤姆·汉克斯因为扮演电影《荒岛余生》的主角而获得了奥斯卡最佳男主角的提名。

♥ The competition of the protagonist selection is very fury.
主角的挑选竞争非常激烈。

outlaw ['autlɔ:] ***n.*** **someone who has done something illegal, and who is hiding in order to avoid punishment - used especially about criminals in the past** 逃犯，亡命之徒

♥ National Association for Outlaw and Lawman History is a non-profit, educational organization whose aim is to discover, share, and promote the true stories of outlaws and lawmen in the frontier West.
全美逃犯和警察历史协会是一个非赢利性的教育组织，目的是为了发现、分享和传播在西部开发中真实的逃犯和警察的故事。

♥ In those west movies, the outlaw is always depicted as a hero.
在西部片电影中，逃犯常被塑造成英雄。

相关表达 近义词 convict; exile

记忆点拨 out(外) +law(法律)

framed [freimd] *adj.* 遭到陷害的

♥ *Who Framed Roger Rabbit* is a very famous movie.
《谁陷害了兔子罗杰》是一部很有名的电影。
He was framed by the real criminals, but finally proved innocent.
他被真正的罪犯所诬陷，最终洗脱罪名。

记忆点拨 fram[e]（陷害）+ed(被……的)

vicious [ˈviʃəs] *adj.* **violent and cruel in a way that hurts someone physically** 恶毒的

♥ The stepmother of Princess Snow White is a vicious woman that she try to kill the Princess with poisonous apple.
白雪公主的继母是个恶毒的女人，企图用毒苹果毒害白雪公主。

♥ The vicious witch put a curse on all the villagers.
恶毒的巫婆诅咒全村老少。

相关表达 近义词 bad; evil

mythology [mi'θɔlədʒi] *n.* **a set of ancient myths 神话**

♥ In Greek Mythology different gods and goddesses have different status, just like what it is in human society.

希腊神话里不同的神仙地位不同，就像人类社会一样。

♥ Mythology of different nations is a set of cyclopedia.

各国不同的神话就像一部百科全书。

记忆点拨 myth（神话）＋ology(学科)

vanished ['væniʃd] *adj.* **disappeared suddenly, especially in a way that cannot be easily explained 消失了的**

♥ Amy is an American citizen who 'vanished' while aboard a foreign vessel in international waters.

爱米是一个美国公民，当她乘坐的外国轮船航行在国际公海时，她消失了。

♥ The vanished diamond ring mysteriously reappeared on the table.

消失了的钻戒又神秘地在桌上重现。

记忆点拨 vanish（消失）＋ed(被……的)

absurdly [əb'səːdli] *adv.* **surprisingly or unreasonably 荒诞地**

♥ Due to the large amount of food, the price of rice is absurdly cheap in this country.

由于大量的食物，这个国家的大米价格低得可笑。

♥ Don't act absurdly on the stage.

不要在台上出丑。

记忆点拨 absurd（荒谬的）＋ly（……地）

arena [ə'riːnə] *n.* **a building with a large flat central area surrounded by seats, where sports or entertainments take place 竞技场**

♥ The arena of Roma is one of the most famous historical sight scene in Italy.
罗马的竞技场是有名的历史遗迹。

♥ The stadium looks like an arena in Roman time.
这个体育馆看上去像罗马时代的竞技场。

encroaching [in'krəutʃiŋ] *adj.* **gradually taking more of someone's time, possessions, rights etc. than you should** 渐渐渗入的

♥ The residents protest against the encroaching factories to their community.
居民们对于慢慢入侵他们社区的工厂表示抗议。

♥ The Chinese elders despised the encroaching western pop music.
中国的老人们讨厌这些慢慢渗入的西方流行音乐。

相关表达 **encroachment** *n.* 侵蚀；侵犯

记忆点拨 encroach（侵占）＋ ing(……过程的)

Indian ['indjən] *n.* **a member of one of the races that lived in North, South, and Central America before the Europeans arrived** 印第安人

♥ The Indians are the real natives of the American continental.
印第安人是美国大陆的真正原住民。

♥ Indian people are good at horsing and hunting.
印第安人擅长骑马和打猎。

bewilder [bi'wildə] *v.* **to confuse someone** 使手足无措

♥ Whenever I have to give a presentation publicly, I will be bewildered and flush all the time.
每次我要做公共的演示，我都会手足无措并脸红。

♥ The general manager's compliment on her bewildered her.
总经理的称赞让她手足无措。

记忆点拨 be（使）＋wilder（迷失，困惑）

alien [ˈeiljən] ***adj.*** **belonging to another country or race** 外来的

♥ You need to file the tax form for alien resident.
你需要填写给外国居民的税表。

记忆点拨 a（无）＋lien（置留权）

taboo [təˈbuː] ***n.*** **a custom that says you must avoid a particular activity or subject, either because it is considered offensive or because your religion does not allow it** 戒律

♥ In Islamic world pork is a taboo for the believers.
伊斯兰国家里，猪肉是教民的戒律。

♥ It is taboo to have sex before marriage in ancient China.
古代中国婚前性行为是戒律。

disinherit [ˈdisinˈherit] ***v.*** **to take away from someone, especially your son or daughter, their legal right to receive your money or property after your death** 剥夺……的继承权

♥ Since the intensive relationship between the spouses, they decided to disinherit each other.
由于夫妇间紧张的关系，他们决定剥夺各自的继承权。

♥ According to the old man's will, the remarriage of his wife will automatically disinherit her from his estate.

根据这个老人的遗嘱，他妻子的再婚会自动剥夺她对他财产的继承权。

记忆点拨 dis（消除）+inherit（继承）

undeclared [ˈʌndiˈklɛəd] ***adj.*** **not officially announced or called something** 未经宣布的

♥ In a standard academic paper, an undeclared quotation is invalid.

对于正规的论文来说，未经宣布的引用是无效的。

♥ The undeclared attack on the Pearl Harbor shocked the US people.

偷袭珍珠港震惊了美国人民。

记忆点拨 un（未）+ declare [e]（宣布）+ed（被……的）

hypocrisy [hiˈpɔkrəsi] ***n.*** **when someone pretends to have certain beliefs or opinions that they do not really have-used to show disapproval** 伪善

♥ Some citizens claim that the biggest single problem the federal government has is its hypocrisy.

有人指出联邦政府的最大问题就是伪善。

♥ His hypocrisy made me sick, and I don't want to be friend with him any more.

他的伪善让我恶心，我再也不要和他做朋友了。

记忆点拨 hypo（下，次）+crisy

chicanery [ʃiˈkeinəri] ***n.*** **the use of clever plans or actions to deceive people** 诈骗

♥ Financial chicanery is the one of the most harmful problems to the economic development of a country.

金融诈骗是对国家经济发展最有害的问题之一。

♥ The general prosecutor's report revealed the chicanery and corruption of some high level officials.
总检察长的报告披露了高层官员的诈骗和贪污行为。

记忆点拨 chicane（诈骗）+ry（名词后缀）

impending [ɪm'pendɪŋ] ***adj.*** **an impending event or situation, especially an unpleasant one, is going to happen very soon** 迫近的，近在眉睫的

♥ The impending world oil shortage made the price of gasoline increase incredibly in US.
迫在眉睫的石油短缺使得美国国内的油价狂涨。

♥ The UN is trying to resolve the impending crisis of food supply worldwide.
联合国在尽力解决迫在眉睫的世界粮食短缺。

记忆点拨 impend（即将发生）+ing（进行的）

immolation [ˌɪməʊ'leɪʃən] ***n.*** **killing someone or destroy something by burning them** 杀戮

♥ The Afghan government is expressing concern over the growing number of women who have killed themselves through self-immolation.
阿富汗政府对日益增多的妇女参加到自杀攻击行为中表示关注。

♥ The immolation is anti-humane and need to be condemned by the world society.
杀戮行为是反人道的，应该受到国际社会的谴责。

记忆点拨 immolat [e]（牺牲）+ion（行为）

code [kəud] ***n.*** **a set of rules, laws, or principles that tell people how to behave** 准则

- As early as in the Tang dynasty, the criminal code of China has already been highly mature.
  早在唐朝，中国的刑法典就已经很规范了。
- Normally breaking the traffic code is not conviction unless it has really serious consequence.
  一般来说，违反交通法规不是严重罪行，除非造成很严重的后果。

词组拓展　civil code 民法

Lesson 22

loom [luːm] *v.* **to appear as a large unclear shape, especially in a threatening way 赫然耸起**

♥ If something looms large in our life, it becomes important and cost concern.
如果生活中某件事很突出，它就会变得很重要而且值得关注。

♥ Nuclear war is looming large in world today.
核战争是对全世界都很严重的问题。

词组拓展 loom large 显得严重（突出）

manifest [ˈmænifest] *adj.* **plain and easy to see 明显的**

♥ His advantage in the election was so manifest that nobody would doubt his success.
他在竞选中的优势很明显，没人怀疑他会获胜。

♥ His manifest superiority displeased his friends.
他如此明显的优越感让朋友们很不高兴。

相关表达 近义词 apparent

morality [məˈrælɪtɪ] *n.* **beliefs or ideas about what is right and wrong and about how people should behave 道德**

♥ The complementary instincts of morality and tribalism are easily manipulated.
道德与部落文化的互补特点很容易被利用。

♥ The society holds a higher standard for people's behavior in morality than in law.
社会对于人的行为要求而言，道德的标准是高于法律的。

相关表达 moral *adj.* 道德的

记忆点拨 moral（道德的）+ity(形成)

communicate [kəˈmjuːnikeit] ***v.* to exchange information or conversation with other people, using words, signs, writing etc.** 交流，交际

♥ With the trend of globalization, it is more and more important to communicate among countries.

随着全球化的趋势，各个国家之间的交流越来越重要。

♥ The non-stop flight between Beijing and Taipei will facilitate the communication between the two sides of the strait.

北京和台北的直航飞机可以促进两岸的交流。

记忆点拨 com（共同，在一起）+muni+cate

compound [ˈkɔmpaund] ***adj.* consisting of two or more substances, ingredients, elements, or parts** 复合的

♥ A compound word is made when two words are joined to form a new word.

复合词是由两个单词组成的一个新单词。

♥ Many insects have compound eyes.

很多昆虫有复合眼。

记忆点拨 com（共同）+pound

enhance [inˈhɑːns] ***v.* to improve something** 增进

♥ I believe the first priority is to have all students develop digital imaging skills.

我相信最重要的是让所有的学生掌握电子图像技术。

♥ The government is trying to enhance the living of the residents.

政府在努力增进居民的生活水平。

相关表达　近义词 improve; better

记忆点拨　en(使上) ＋hance(拱腰)

tempo ['tempəu] ***n.*** **the speed at which something happens** 速率

♥ In physics, the term, tempo, only means the low or high of speed without any indication of direction.
在物理中，速率是指速度的高低，跟方向无关。

♥ The song has a quick tempo which is good for disco dancing.
这首歌的节奏很快，适合跳迪斯科。

trickle ['trikl] ***n.*** **a thin slow flow of liquid** 涓涓细流

♥ This mountain area is famous for its numerous peaceful trickles.
这座山以众多平静的涓涓细流闻名。

♥ There was a trickle of blood from the wound.
血从伤口汩汩流出。

torrent ['tɔrənt] ***n.*** **a large amount of water moving very quickly and strongly in a particular direction** 滔滔洪流

♥ Heavy rainfall turns the river into a torrent.
暴雨使河水变成了激流。

♥ The torrent destroyed the raft bridge.
洪流冲毁了浮桥。

相关表达　近义词 burst; flood

humanity [hju(:)'mæniti] ***n.*** **people in general** 人类

♥ Humanity has dominated the earth for millions of years by its well-developed brain.
由于其高级的大脑，人类已经统治地球数百万年了。

♥ The discovery of the new medicine will benefit all humanity.
新药的研制会造福全人类。

记忆点拨 human（人）＋ity(性)

indifferently [in'difərəntli] *adv.* 不在乎地

♥ Stop taking the assignment indifferently. It is actually quite important to your grades.
别对这份作业满不在乎，它对你的成绩很重要。

♥ It is so rude to act indifferently to people's death.
听到别人去世的消息表现得无动于衷是非常没礼貌的。

记忆点拨 in(无）＋different(不同的）＋ly(……地）

grimly [grimli] *adv.* 可怕地

♥ Later Mr. Ashby left the court, grimly straightened his face and kept silent.
艾司比先生随后离开了法庭，阴沉着脸，一言不发。

♥ The gangster smiled at him grimly.
那个黑帮分子恐怖地朝他笑了。

记忆点拨 grim（严酷的）＋ly(……地）

whimsical ['hwimzikəl] *adj.* **unusual or strange and often amusing 怪诞的**

♥ Usually the more modern, the more whimsical an art is.
通常来说越现代的艺术就越怪诞。

♥ People felt lost after watching the whimsical drama.
看了这出荒诞剧后，人们觉得很迷惑。

记忆点拨 whims[y]（怪念头，奇想）＋ical(涉及……的）

shatter [ˈʃætə] ***v.*** **to break suddenly into very small pieces, or to make something break in this way 毁坏**

♥ His health was shattered by the cancer.
他的健康因癌症而恶化。

♥ The house was shattered by the earthquake.
房子被地震毁坏了。

相关表达 近义词 destroy

twofold [ˈtuːfəʊld] ***adj.*** **two times as much or as many of something 双重的**

♥ Psychological research shows that most people have twofold or even multi-fold characters.
心理学家研究表明大多数人都有双重甚至多重性格。

♥ He is busy with his twofold duty-both as teacher and mentor.
他的双重职务让他很忙，既是老师又当指导者。

记忆点拨 two(二) ＋fold(折)

Lesson 23

albatross ['ælbətrɔs] ***n.*** **a very large white sea bird** 信天翁

♥ To be a successful albatross means having some amazing skills, including the ability to make tremendous long-distance flights.
一只出色的信天翁拥有惊人的技能，包括艰巨的长途飞行能力。

♥ A group of albatross were flying accompany the ship.
一队信天翁在伴随船只飞行。

sustenance ['sʌstinəns] ***n.*** **the supporting of life or health; maintenance** 支撑力

♥ In reality, the person is going around in order to find the sustenance that is prescribed for him to pick up.
在现实生活中，人们总是在生活中不断寻找适合自己的支持力。

♥ When she was laid off, she found support in her religious belief.
当她失业的时候，她在宗教信仰里找到了支持力。

相关表达 近义词 support

glider ['glaidə] ***n.*** **a light plane that flies without an engine** 滑翔机

♥ To fly, a glider must reach flying speed, which is the speed at which the wings generate enough lift to overcome the force of gravity.
要想飞起来，滑翔机必须达到一定的飞行速度，也就是说翅膀要产生足够的上升力量来克服重力。

♥ A glider is an aircraft without engines.
滑翔机是没有引擎的飞机。

记忆点拨 glid[e]（滑翔）＋er(者)

harness [ˈhɑːnis] ***v.*** **to control and use the natural force or power of something** 利用

♥ It is a sustainable resource to harness the wind and waves as power.
利用风和海浪做能源是可持续的资源。

♥ If you can harness your intelligence, you will accomplish.
如果你能控制你的才智，你将获得成功。

相关表达 近义词 use

endow [inˈdau] ***v.*** **to make someone or something have a particular quality, or to believe that they have it** 赋有

♥ Endowed with gift, Mozart showed his talent in music in his boyhood.
天生聪慧，莫扎特幼年就展现出了音乐上的才能。

♥ Nature endowed her with a beautiful face.
大自然赋予她美丽的容颜。

记忆点拨 en(致使) ＋ dow(得以，能够)

ply [plai] ***v.*** **to continue supplying or offering to** 不断地供给

♥ Failing to ply food to the frontier in frozen winter, the German Army lost the war to the USSR.
未能在严冬给前线提供充足的食物，德国军队最终输给了苏联军队。

♥ Dealers are opening ply drugs on street at midnight.
半夜里毒贩们在街上公开供给毒品。

相关表达　近义词 supply

gale　[geil] ***n.*** **a very strong wind 大风**

♥ My hair was blown wild by the gales.
我的头发被风吹乱了。

♥ The gale drove the boat out of the harbor.
大风把小船吹出了港口。

相关表达　近义词 shout;tempest

partridge　[ˈpɑːtridʒ] ***n.*** **a fat brown bird with a short tail which is shot for sport and food 鹧鸪**

♥ Partridge has strong wings which is good at long distance flying.
鹧鸪有适合长途飞行的强劲的翅膀。

♥ She is as plump as a partridge.
她肥得像一只鹧鸪（胖乎乎的）。

suchlike　[ˈsʌtʃlaik] ***adj.*** **of the same kind;similar 类似的**

词组拓展　and suchlike 等等；诸如此类

♥ I am fond of apples, pears and suchlike.
我喜欢苹果、香蕉以及诸如此类的水果。

♥ I have no time for concerts, cinemas and suchlike.
我没有时间去欣赏音乐会、看电影以及诸如此类的消遣。

记忆点拨 such(这种，某一) + like (……般的)

propulsion [prəˈpʌlʃən] ***n.*** **the force that drives a vehicle forward** 推进力

♥ The Special Studies Program has examined alternative spacecraft propulsion concepts to meet performance objectives.
特别研究项目已经测试了其他的飞行推动力来达到表演的目标。

♥ The windmill propulsion cannot be ignored.
风的推进力不容忽视。

记忆点拨 prop [el] (推进) + ul+sion(性质)

utter [ˈʌtə] ***adj.*** **complete-used especially to emphasize that something was very bad, or that a feeling was very strong** 完全的

♥ It was an utter surprise when we heard that Bush won the presidential election in 2002.
当我们听到布什赢得了 2002 年总统大选时，都完全惊呆了。

♥ Reading this book was an utter waste of time.
读这本书完全是浪费时间。

相关表达 近义词 absolute; complete

slip [slip] ***v.*** **to slide a short distance accidentally, and fall or lose your balance slightly** 滑行

♥ Time slipped out quickly when we were enjoying the pleasant trip.
当我们尽情享受快乐的旅行时，时间飞快的过去了。

♥ An old lady slipped on the wet floor of the market.
一位老太太在市场的湿地上滑倒了。

相关表达 近义词 slide

adverse [ˈædvəːs] ***adj.*** **not good or favourable** 逆的，相反的

♥ Since 1966, this bimonthly publication has provided comprehensive coverage of the field of adverse drug reactions.

从 1996 年开始，这份双月刊已经在药物逆反反应领域进行了全面的报道。

♥ The school's discipline on the students may have adverse effect on their behaviors.

学校对学生的约束可能会让他们的行为产生相反的结果。

相关表达 近义词 opposite

记忆点拨 ad(朝向) +verse(反面)

omen [ˈəumen] ***n.*** **a sign of what will happen in the future** 预兆

♥ A lot of natural phenomenon can be regarded as omens by superstitious people.

很多自然现象都被迷信的人们当作预兆。

♥ People believe that seeing magpie in the morning is a good omen for that day.

人们相信早上看见喜鹊是一天的好兆头。

词组拓展 be of good (bad, ill) omen 兆头好（不好）

相关表达 近义词 indication; sign

Lesson 24

intense [inˈtens] *adj.* **having a very strong effect or felt very strongly** 强烈的

♥ The explosion of an atomic bomb will generate an intense heat.

原子弹的爆炸会产生强烈的热量。

♥ He has an intense desire to win the Nobel Prize.

他有着强烈的愿望想获得诺贝尔奖。

相关表达 intensive *adj.* 强烈的

记忆点拨 in(加强意义）＋tense(拉紧的）

aesthetic [iːsˈθetik] *adj.* **connected with beauty and the study of beauty** 审美的

♥ He is pretty good on aesthetic taste.

他的审美品位不错。

♥ The professor explained from the aesthetic point of view that how successful this photo is.

教授从审美的角度来说明这幅图片的成功。

相关表达 artistic *adj.* 艺术的，有美感的，风雅的

记忆点拨 aesthet [e]（审美家）＋ic(涉及的）

realm [relm] *n.* **a country ruled by a king or queen** 世界

♥ Genetic technology creates a new realm for agriculture.

基因工程为农业创造了一个新世界。

♥ After the death of the King, the realm stood in great jeopardy.
国王去世后，国家陷入严重危机中。

相关表达 kingdom *n.* 王国

serenity [si'reniti] ***n.*** **the state or quality of being serene; tranquillity 静谧**

♥ The serenity only lapsed for a while.
宁静只短暂持续了一下。

♥ The son's return had restored serenity to his mother's face.
儿子的归来让母亲的面容恢复了平静。

相关表达 近义词 tranquility

记忆点拨 seren [e](平静的) +ity(状态)

undeniable ['ʌndi'naiəbl] ***adj.*** **definitely true or certain** 不可否认的

♥ It is undeniable that China had make great progress in economy during the last decade.
不可否认的是在上个十年，中国在经济上取得了卓越的成绩。

♥ Based on the undeniable proof, the murder was sentenced to death.
根据无可否认的证据，杀人犯被判处死刑。

记忆点拨 un(不) +deny(否认) + -able(能的)

indefinable [ˌindi'fainəbl] ***adj.*** **an indefinable feeling, quality etc is difficult to describe or explain** 模糊不清的

♥ Since 9.11, Americans have an indefinable feeling of terror.

自从"九一一"后，美国人就有了一种说不清的恐惧感。

♥ In many cases, human beings' feeling is indefinable.

在很多情况下，人类的感觉是很难说清楚的。

相关表达　近义词 unspeakable

记忆点拨　in(非) ＋ defin [e](详细说明) ＋able(能的)

vulgar　['vʌlgə] *adj*. **deficient in taste, delicacy, or refinement 平庸的，粗俗的**

♥ This middle-aged woman put herself in an vulgar dress.

这个中年妇女穿着平庸。

♥ It is vulgar and contemptible to envy others' success.

嫉妒别人的成功是粗俗且让人鄙视的。

相关表达　近义词 indecent

radiance　['reɪdiəns] *n*. **a soft gentle light 发光**

♥ I was struck by the joyful radiance on her face.

我看着她容光焕发的脸呆住了。

♥ From her immortal head the radiance is from heaven and it embraces the earth.

在她信仰神灵的头脑里，光芒是来自于天堂并且笼罩着地球。

记忆点拨　radian [t](发光的) ＋ce(名词后缀)

intimation　[ˌinti'meiʃən] *n*. **an indirect or unclear sign that something may happen 暗示**

♥ The boy gave her an intimation of love.

那个男孩给了她一点爱的暗示。

♥ In many cases, intimations are better than speaking out.
在很多情况下，暗示比明说要好。

记忆点拨 intimat [e]（私下的）＋ion（行为）

unutterable [ʌnˈʌtərəbl] ***adj.*** **an unutterable feeling is too extreme to be expressed in words 不可言传的**

♥ In unutterable distress, the student dropped out of the university.
在不可言传的压力下，这个学生从大学退学了。

♥ I waited in unutterable expectation for the news that was to be announced.
我在不可言状的压力下等待即将宣布的消息。

记忆点拨 un（不）＋utter（发表）＋able（能……的）

invest [inˈvest] ***v.*** **to commit (money or capital) in order to gain a financial return; to endow with authority or power 授予，投资**

♥ The government needs to invest more in the people, in their jobs and in their future.
政府应该给予它的人民更多东西，对于他们的工作或者未来。

♥ I have money to invest, and you need it.
我有钱投资，而你又需要钱。

记忆点拨 in（使）＋vest（授予，归属）

Unit 4

Lesson 25

auditory [ˈɔːditəri] *adj.* **relating to the ability to hear** 听觉的

Some creatures have no auditory apparatus.
有些动物没有听觉器官。

There are some problems with the child's auditory nerve.

相关表达 **visual** *adj.* 视觉的

记忆点拨 audi(听觉) ＋tory（……的）

inadequate [inˈædikwit] *adj.* **not good enough, big enough, skilled enough etc. for a particular purpose** 不适当的；不充分的

词组拓展 be inadequate to do sth. 不适于做某件事

His knowledge of computers is inadequate for this project.
他的电脑知识不足以完成这个项目。

Five hours' sleeping is inadequate for normal persons.
对于寻常人来说，五个小时的睡眠不够。

相关表达 近义词 insufficient

记忆点拨 in(不) ＋adequate(适当的)

plea [pliː] *n.* **a request that is urgent or full of emotion** 要求

They were about to proceed to put him to death when he begged them to hear his plea for mercy.

他们就要准备把他处决时，他突然要求宽恕。

♥ No one responded to his plea.

没有人理会他的请求。

词组拓展 make a plea for 主张，请求

相关表达 近义词 request; appeal

abatement [ə'beitmənt] *n.* **diminution in degree or intensity; moderation** 减少

♥ A law to enforce noise abatement has been passed in the State Congress.

一个强制减少噪音的法规终于在国会通过了。

♥ The storm showed no signs of abatement.

这场暴风雨看上去没有减弱的迹象。

相关表达 反义词 addition

记忆点拨 abate(使减少) ＋ment(状态)

discredit [dis'kredit] *v.* **lack or loss of trust or belief; doubt** 怀疑

♥ The committee began to discredit the professor's experimental data.

委员会开始怀疑这个教授的实验数据。

♥ The judge will discredit your testimony if you are hesitant.

如果你吞吞吐吐，法官会怀疑你的证词。

相关表达 近义词 disbelieve; doubt

记忆点拨 dis(否定) ＋credit(信用)

allegation [ˌæli'geiʃən] *n.* **something alleged; an assertion** 断言

♥ Prove your allegation if you can.

如果可以请证明你的断言。

♥ The allegation that the Earth is round has been proved wrong.
关于地球是圆的断言已经被证实了。

相关表达 近义词 assertion

记忆点拨 alleg [e]（断言） ＋ation(行为)

caption [ˈkæpʃən] ***n.*** **a title, short explanation, or description accompanying an illustration or a photograph** 插图说明

♥ This paper includes many captions.
这篇论文包括很多插图。

♥ The captions in this book are created by his secretary.
这本书里的插图都是他的秘书绘制的。

词组拓展 film caption 电影字幕

wreck [rek] ***n.*** **a person who is physically or mentally broken down or worn out; the remains of something that has been wrecked or ruined** 废人；残骸

♥ He saw the wreck of an ambitious man—ruined by the pursuit of wealth and power.
他看到这个原来雄心勃勃的人由于追逐金钱权力而成为了一个废人。

♥ People in this town wanted to find the wreck of the Spanish ship.
镇上的人都想一睹这艘西班牙船只的残骸。

snag [snæg] ***n.*** **a problem or disadvantage, especially one that is not very serious, which you had not expected** 障碍

♥ The explorer overcame many snags.
探险者克服了很多阻碍。

♥ There might be snags or weeds around the pool.
在池塘边有很多阻碍的树桩或野草。

词组拓展 hit [strike, come upon, run into] a snag 触礁；碰到意外的障碍，遇到意外困难

anecdote ['ænikdəut] *n.* **a short account of an interesting or humorous incident** 轶闻

♥ Princess Diana's anecdotes have been composed into a book.
黛安娜王妃的轶闻已被编辑成书。

♥ It is a pleasure to recall all those anecdotes in our university time.
回忆大学时代的轶闻是多么愉快啊。

相关表达 近义词 story; tale

slander ['slɑːndə] *v.* **to say false things about someone in order to damage other people's good opinion of them** 诽谤

♥ He couldn't tolerate his colleague's slandering of his wife.
他不能容忍同事对自己妻子的诽谤。

♥ He slandered the young lady in front of the public.
他在公众面前造谣诽谤这个年轻女子。

相关表达 近义词 libel; slur

persecute ['pəːsikjuːt] *v.* **to treat someone cruelly or unfairly over a period of time, especially because of their religious or political beliefs** 迫害

♥ The house owner prosecuted the boy for trespass.
房主迫害擅自闯入其领地的男孩。

♥ The political dissident is scared to be persecuted by the government.
这个持不同政见者害怕受到政府的迫害。

词组拓展 persecute sb. with questions 给某人出难题

相关表达 persecutor *n.* 施加迫害的人

记忆点拨 per(完全) ＋sequi(追踪，跟随)

squadron [ˈskwɔdrən] ***n.*** **a military force consisting of a group of aircraft or ships** 中队

♥ The first squadron has moved out of the forest.
第一中队已经出了森林。

♥ The little squadron of canoes set sail with a favorable breeze.
这队炮兵中队随风出海了。

记忆点拨 squad(班) ＋ron

psychiatric [saɪkɪˈætrɪk] ***adj.*** **relating to the study and treatment of mental illness** 精神病学的

♥ That man has been dipagnosed in psychiatric disorder.
这个人被诊断为精神混乱。

♥ This is a psychiatric hospital.
这是个精神病院。

记忆点拨 psychiatr [y](精神病学) ＋ic (……的)

diagnosis [ˌdaiəgˈnəusis] ***n.*** **the process of discovering exactly what is wrong with someone or something, by examining them closely** 诊断

♥ The doctor wants to see if his diagnosis is correct.
大夫想看看他的诊断是否正确。

♥ He submitted this diagnosis to the committee.
他把诊断上交给了委员会。

词组拓展 form a correct diagnosis on [upon] a disease 确诊

相关表达 复数 diagnoses

记忆点拨 diagnos [e](诊断) +is(名词后缀)

orphanage [ˈɔːfənɪdʒ] *n.* **a large house where children who are orphans live and are taken care of** 孤儿院

♥ The congressman proposed to build an orphanage in this district.
参议员建议在这个地区建一个孤儿院。

♥ The poor girl died in the first week of her orphanage.
这个可怜的小女孩在孤儿院的第一个星期就死了。

相关表达 **orphan** *n.* 孤儿

记忆点拨 orphan(孤儿) +age(地方)

Lesson 26

preservation [ˌprezə(:)ˈveiʃən] ***n.*** **when something is kept in its original state or in good condition** 保存

♥ Robert worked as a volunteer for an environmental preservation organization for almost twelve years.
罗伯特在一个环境保护协会做志愿者工作已经有十二年了。

♥ Her doctor thesis is about study of the preservation development of cultural heritage in Changsha, China.
她的博士论文是关于如何保护中国长沙的文化遗产的研究。

词组拓展 cold preservation 冷藏

记忆点拨 pre(预先) ＋serv [e](供应) ＋ation(行为)

silt [silt] ***n.*** **sand, mud, soil etc. that is carried in water and then settles at a bend in a river, an entrance to a port etc.** 淤泥

♥ Long-term sustainable flood control in the Yellow River basin will ultimately be achieved by a significant reduction in the amount of silt entering the river.
长期有效的控制洪水终于可以通过减轻入河的泥沙量来实现了。

♥ There are a lot of organic compound in the water environment of heavy silt content.

水里的淤泥里有大量的有机化合物。

scavenger [ˈskævindʒə] ***n.*** **an animal, such as a bird or an insect, that feeds on dead or decaying matter 食腐动物**

♥ Research shows that there is a direct link between discard availability and discard use by a generalist predator and scavenger.
研究表明废弃物可用数量与被肉食动物和食腐动物对废弃物的消耗量有直接关系。

♥ Hyena is as much a hunter in his own right as the more familiar tag of a scavenger.
土狼既可被称为猎人，同时也是清道夫。

记忆点拨 scaveng [e][以（腐肉）为食] ＋er(者)

vole [vəul] ***n.*** **a small animal like a mouse with a short tail that lives in fields and woods and near rivers 野鼠，䶄鼠**

♥ The adult vole is a small rodent with a stocky and stubby body, short tail, and four short legs.
成年的䶄鼠是有着粗短身材、短尾、四肢短小的小型啮齿动物。

♥ The dramatic decrease of voles has caused a great damage to the balance of the biological chain.
䶄鼠数量的急剧减少严重破坏了生物链的平衡。

decompose [ˌdiːkəmˈpəuz] ***v.*** **to decay or make something decay 腐烂**

♥ Fungi are important in the process of decay, which returns ingredients to the soil, enhances soil fertility, and decomposes animal debris.

霉菌对于腐烂过程很重要，它们能把成分回收到土壤里，提高土壤的肥沃和分解动物遗体。

♥ You can apply heat to decompose organic compounds.

你可以加热来分解有机化合物。

相关表达 近义词 decay

记忆点拨 de(失出）＋compose(组成）

inaccessible [ˌinækˈsesəbl] ***adj.*** **difficult or impossible to reach** 不能到达的

♥ Despite the beauty and subtly of Chinese poems, for most foreigners, they remain inaccessible.

虽然中国古诗很美而且抽象，对于大多数外国人来说，它们还是遥不可及。

♥ Generally, the wildest and most inaccessible parts of the world are the places where wildlife is abundant and largely protected.

总的来说，世界上最荒凉且不能到达的地方也是野生生物保护最好、最多的地方。

记忆点拨 in(不）＋accessible(可达到的）

crevasse [kriˈvæs] ***n.*** **a deep open crack in the thick ice on a mountain** 缝隙

♥ Although crevasses are extremely common in both continental ice sheets and glaciers, the understanding of the initiation and growth of these features is limited.

虽然在大陆冰层和冰山上的缝隙非常常见，可是对于这些特征的起因和发展的研究还很有限。

♥ Since there is a danger of falling into a crevasse, climbers should never travel without roped.

因为有掉入缝隙的危险，所以登山者都应系好绳索。

Siberian [saiˈbiəriən] ***adj.*** **a very large area in Russia, between the Ural Mountains and the Pacific Ocean, where there are many minerals but very few people** 西伯利亚的

♥ Few plants and animals can survive the Siberian weather.

很少有植物或者动物能在西伯利亚的气侯下生存下来。

♥ The Siberian weather is extremely freezing all year long.

西伯利亚的气候四季都很寒冷。

记忆点拨 Siberia(西伯利亚) ＋n (……的)

palaeontological [ˌpælionˈtɔlədʒi] ***adj.*** 古生物学的

♥ This library offers a public enquiries service for the purpose of specimen identification for the general public, and houses all of the palaeontological collections.

这个图书馆可以回答公众有关标本确认的咨讯，并收藏了所有古生物学的资料。

♥ Some historical palaeontological fossils were found in mid China this year, which drew a lot of interest in the academia.

今年在中国又发现了历史性的古生物学化石，引起了学术界的极大兴趣。

记忆点拨 palaeontolog [y](古生物学) ＋ical(涉及)

sabre-toothed [ˈseibətuːθd] ***adj.*** 长着锐利的长牙

♥ He was freaked out when he saw a sabre-toothed dog standing in front of him after he got out of his apartment.

他出门以后就看见一只长着利牙的大狗在他面前，把他吓坏了。

♥ Sabre-toothed vampires are typical heroes in Hollywood horror movies.

长着利牙的吸血鬼常常是好莱坞恐怖电影的主角。

记忆点拨 sabre(马刀) ＋tooth(牙) ＋ed（……的）

venture [ˈventʃə] ***v.*** **to go somewhere that could be dangerous** 冒险

♥ If you venture nothing, you will have nothing.

如果你不冒险，你就会一无所获。

♥ He shield away from venturing into hazard.

他放弃了去探险。

相关表达 近义词 adventure

记忆点拨 vent(出口) ＋ure(行为，动作)

bogged [bɔgd] ***adj.*** 陷入泥沼的，陷入困境的

♥ She is really bogged down on the exam since she did not spend much time on it this semester.

她真的被考试难住了，因为她这学期没花多少时间在上面。

♥ The talks between Canada and China have bogged down once again.

中加两国的对话又一次陷入了困境中。

记忆点拨 bog(陷于泥沼) ＋（g)ed(被……的)

Lesson 27

galleon [ˈgæliən] ***n.*** **a sailing ship used mainly by the Spanish from the 15th to the 17th century** 大型帆船

♥ Galleon is largely used from 15th to 17th century.
大型帆船大量使用于15～17世纪中。

♥ Galleon is original manufactured in Spain.
大型帆船最初是在西班牙建造的。

flagship [ˈflægʃɪp] ***n.*** **the most important ship in a group of ships belonging to the navy** 旗舰

♥ Flagship is a ship that carries a fleet or squadron commander and bears the commander's flag.
旗舰是装有舰队或海军中队指挥官并悬有指挥官旗帜的船只。

♥ The German car factory opened its flagship store in Beijing.
这家德国车厂把自己的旗舰店开在了北京。

记忆点拨 flag(旗) ＋ship(船)

imperial [imˈpiəriəl] ***adj.*** **relating to an empire or to the person who rules it** 帝国的

♥ The movie *The Last Emperor* depicts the life of China's last imperial household.
电影《末代皇帝》描述了中国最后一个帝王家庭的生活。

♥ Princess Diana confessed that she is not happy with the imperial life.

戴安娜王妃袒露心声说自己的皇家生活并不快乐。

相关表达　近义词 royal

记忆点拨　imperia(统帅权) + (a)l (……的)

hurricane　[ˈhʌrikən] ***n.*** **a storm that has very strong fast winds and that moves over water** 飓风

♥ The weather forecast informed the villagers of the hurricane in advance.

天气预报提前把飓风的预告通知了村民。

♥ The hurricane flung their houses upon into the air.

飓风把他们的房子抛到空中。

相关表达　近义词 cyclone; tornado

记忆点拨　hurri [y](加速) +cane(藤条)

armament　[ˈɑːməmənt] ***n.*** **the weapons and military equipment used by an army** 军械

♥ The congress is planning to cut the budget of armament.

国会准备削减军备预算。

♥ Russian and the US are having a mutual talk about armament reduction.

俄罗斯和美国正在进行削减军备的双边谈判。

词组拓展　missile armament 导弹武器

记忆点拨　arm(武装) +a(连接字母) +ment(名词后缀)

triple　[ˈtripl] ***adj.*** **three times more than a particular number** 三倍的

♥ There are triple decks on the ship.

船上有三层的甲板。

♥ He is the world trip jump champion.

他是世界三级跳远冠军。

相关表达　double *adj*. 两倍的

记忆点拨　tri(三) ＋ple（……的）

mount　[maunt] ***v.*** **to fix securely to a support** 架有

♥ The mechanic mounted a new engine into his car.
机修工给他的车装了个新的发动机。

♥ Can you help me to mount the staircase to the house?
你能帮我忙把屋子的楼梯架好吗？

相关表达　近义词 fix；place

bronze　[brɔnz] ***n.*** **a hard metal that is a mixture of copper and tin** 青铜

♥ The statute is made of bronze.
雕塑是青铜做的。

♥ His skin was tanned by sun and had the color of bronze.
他的皮肤被太阳晒黑了，像青铜的颜色。

词组拓展　bronze medal 铜牌

相关表达　gold *n.* 金；silver *n.* 银

cannon　[ˈkænən] ***n.*** **a large heavy powerful gun that was used in the past to fire heavy metal balls** 加农炮

♥ The Cannon fired at the city gate.
大炮向城门开火。

♥ All the warships were equipped with the best cannons.
所有的军舰上都装备了最好的大炮。

Lesson 28

skeptical [ˈskeptikəl] *adj.* **tending to disagree with what other people tell you** 怀疑的

♥ Being skeptical is an essential trait of a good scientist.

质疑的态度是成为优秀科学家的重要性格。

记忆点拨 skeptic(怀疑论者)＋al（……的）

forefather [ˈfɔːˌfɑːðə] *n.* **the people, especially men, who were part of your family a long time ago in the past** 祖先

♥ The forefathers of Anglo-Americans are from the European continent.

盎格鲁血统的美国人的祖先都来自于欧洲大陆。

♥ Most of the Chinese-Americans speak Cantonese.

很多美籍华人的祖先都是说粤语的。

相关表达 近义词 ancestor

记忆点拨 fore(以前的)＋father(父亲)

fervently [ˈfəːvəntli] *adv.* 热情地

♥ He prayed to the God fervently for his mercy.

他热情地向上帝祈祷请求宽恕。

♥ Her family and friends fervently kept her memory alive after her tragic death.

在她不幸去世以后，她的家人和朋友都强烈地保持对她的回忆。

记忆点拨 fervent(炽热的)＋ly（……地）

curative ['kjuərətiv] ***adj.*** **able to, or intended to cure illness 治病的**

♥ As a doctor, she is concerned with the prevention of illness rather than with curative medicine.
作为医生，她更关心疾病的预防而不是治病的药。

♥ The curative value of Yoga is that it can activate the energy your body has accumulated and stagnated.
瑜珈的治疗作用在于它能使身体里郁积的热量释放出来。

记忆点拨 cure(治疗) ＋ate＋ive

astronomical [æstrə'nɔmɪk(ə)l] ***adj.*** **relating to the scientific study of the stars 天文学的**

♥ In the planetarium, the kids have many opportunities to see special astronomical phenomenon.
在天文馆里，孩子们能有很多机会见到各种特别的天文现象。

♥ The government seemed willing to spend astronomical sums on weapons development.
政府看来想在军备发展上花费天文数字。

词组拓展 astronomical figures 天文数字

记忆点拨 astronom [y](天文学) ＋ical(相关的)

tangible ['tændʒəbl] ***adj.*** **clear enough or definite enough to be easily seen or noticed 实实在在的**

♥ The fast development of high technology has made the Internet more tangible.
高科技的发展使互联网成为现实。

♥ This movie uses visuals to create a tangible texture of skin.

这部电影应用图片来显示皮肤真实纹理。

相关表达　近义词 palpable; concrete

remedy [ˈremidi] *n.* **a medicine to cure an illness or pain that is not very serious 药物**

♥ It is said that laughter is the best remedy in the world.
人们都说笑是最好的良药。

♥ This medicine is an effective remedy for acid indigestion.
这药据说是治疗消化不良的有效药。

词组拓展　be past [beyond] remedy 无法补救的；治不好的

相关表达　近义词 cure; treat

ointment [ˈɔintmənt] *n.* **a soft cream that you rub into your skin, especially as a medical treatment 药膏**

♥ After the ointment was applied on the wound, he felt so much better now.
在伤口上涂上药膏后，他现在觉得好多了。

♥ He became a millionaire immediately after selling off the formulae for the ointment handed down from his forefather.
在出售了他祖父传给他的药膏秘方后，他立即成为了一个百万富翁。

prescribe [prisˈkraib] *v.* **to say what medicine or treatment a sick person should have 开药方**

♥ The doctor prescribed some drugs for treating my cold.
大夫给我开药治疗感冒。

♥ In the United States, the patient must have his or her doctor to prescribe the needed medicine before they can buy from the pharmacy.
在美国，病人需要有医生的处方才能从药房买到药。

记忆点拨 pre(预先) ＋scribe(写下)

indisposition [ˌindispəˈziʃən] ***n.*** **a slight illness 小病**

♥ Since it is only an indisposition, he resumed his work soon after he came back from the clinic.
因为只是小病，在去过诊所后他就马上继续上班了。

♥ People tend to suffer from disposition of all kinds when they are getting old.
当人慢慢衰老时，就会开始被各种各样的小病困扰。

记忆点拨 in(不) ＋disposition(生理特性)

inconvenience [ˌinkənˈviːnjəns] ***n.*** **problems caused by something which annoy or affect you 令人讨厌的**

♥ Slow food is not an inconvenience but a goal to free the people from the side effect of fast food.
精心烧制的食物并不令人讨厌，并且帮助人们摆脱了快餐的副作用。

♥ Despite all the inconvenience, he helped her with all his heart.
即使很麻烦，他还是全心全意地帮助她。

记忆点拨 in(非，不) ＋convenience(便利，方便)

Lesson 29

hovercraft [ˈhɔvəkrɑːft] ***n.*** **a vehicle that travels just above the surface of land or water, travelling on a strong current of air that the engines produce beneath it** 气垫船

♥ A hovercraft can support many hundreds of pounds and thus serve as a very convenient means of transportation over both land and water.

气垫船可以支撑起数百磅的重物，因此成为了水陆都很有效的交通工具。

♥ Commercial hovercraft is widely available for purchase or lease in some parts of the country.

商用气垫船到处都可以买到，或者有些地方也能租到。

记忆点拨 hover(翱翔) ＋craft(船)

cushion [ˈkuʃən] ***n.*** **a cloth bag filled with soft material that you put on a chair or the floor to make it more comfortable** 座垫

♥ A cushion is a very ancient article of furniture and is only furnished in palaces and great houses in the early middle ages.

座垫是很古老的家居用品，在中世纪时，只有宫殿或者豪宅才有。

♥ Cushion may be used for sitting or kneeling upon, or to soften the hardness of a chair or couch.

座垫可以坐也可以跪，或者用来减轻椅子或者沙发的硬度。

ring [riŋ] ***v.*** **to surround something** 围

- The students ringed the stage watched the clown performing on it.
  学生围坐在舞台周围，观看小丑表演。
- Police ringed the building after received the threatening phone.
  接到恐吓电话后，警察马上包围了大楼。

sensation [sen'seiʃən] ***n.*** **extreme excitement or interest, or someone or something that causes this** 轰动

- The news created a great sensation on campus.
  新闻在校园里引起了轰动。
- Many newspapers are fond of dealing in sensation so as to attract more readerships.
  报纸都喜欢轰动消息，以此来吸引更多读者。

相关表达 sensational *adj.* 使人感动的，非常好的

记忆点拨 sensate [e] (可感觉的) ＋ion(状态)

dune [djuːn] ***n.*** **a hill made of sand near the sea or in the desert** 沙丘

- Barren as it is, endless wavelike dunes can make a magnificent landscape photo.
  虽然很贫瘠，但无边的波浪似的沙丘能拍成很壮观的景观图片。
- The Great Sand Dunes National Park in southern Colorado is a geologic wonderland that contains 30 square miles of dunes.

在南科罗拉多的大沙丘自然公园是一个拥有 30 平方英里的大沙丘的地理奇观。

plantation [plæn'teiʃən] ***n.*** **a large area of land in a hot country, where crops such as tea, cotton, and sugar are grown** 种植园

♥ Historically, plantation is a place where enslaved African Americans raised crops and tended livestock.

历史上，种植园是被奴役的美国黑人种植庄稼和饲养家畜的地方。

♥ George Washington's childhood was spent in a beautiful plantation house.

乔治·华盛顿的童年生活在一个美丽的种植园里。

词组拓展 coffee plantation 咖啡种植园

相关表达 **plantationlike** *adj.* 种植园的

记忆点拨 plant(种植) +ation(行为)

hovertrain ['hɔvətreɪn] ***n.*** 气垫火车

♥ Early versions of the hovertrain rested on a cushion of air, like a hovercraft that travels on sea or land.

早期的气垫火车是悬浮在气体上的，就像气垫船在海上或陆地上漂浮一样。

♥ People hope that hovertrain can be a viable and clean alternative to the expensive air travel and congested highways.

人们希望气垫火车能够替代昂贵的飞机和拥挤的高速公路，成为一种既可行又环保的交通工具。

记忆点拨 hover(盘旋) +train(火车)

Lesson 30

navigation [ˌnæviˈgeiʃən] ***n*.** **when someone sails a ship along a river or other area of water 航海**

♥ Ancient people relied on compass to provide accurate navigation capability.

古代人依靠指南针提供精确的航海导向。

♥ The Global Positioning System may be the single most significant advance in equipment of sea navigation.

全球定位系统可能是航海设备中最重大的进步。

词组拓展 navigation coodinate 导航坐标

air navigation 航空学，空中导航

相关表达 **navigate** *v.* 导航

记忆点拨 navigat [e](航行，航海) ＋ion(行为)

sounding [ˈsaundiŋ] ***n*.** **a measured depth of water 水深度**

♥ Scientists used high speed computers to examine the thousands of sounding points obtained in the sea floor survey.

科学家使用高速计算机来检测从海底勘测得到的成千上万的水深点。

♥ New acoustic technology was used to obtain sounding lines of new harbor area.

最新的声测技术被用来探测新港口地区的水深线。

词组拓展 take soundings in 测……的水深；悄悄地调查事态的发展

记忆点拨 sound(声) + ing(名词后缀)

fathom [ˈfæðəm] *n.* **a unit for measuring the depth of water, equal to six feet or about 1.8 metres** 寻（1 寻等于 1.8 米）

♥ People use fathom almost exclusively to indicate the depth of water nowadays.
现在人们只把寻这种度量单位用于指明水深。

porcupine [ˈpɔːkjupain] *n.* **an animal with long, sharp parts growing all over its back and sides** 箭猪

♥ Porcupine is a rodent, which has black or brownish-yellow fur, and strong short legs.
箭猪是一种有黑色或黄褐色皮毛、有强壮的短腿的啮齿类动物。

♥ The most recognizable feature of a porcupine is its quills, which are used to defend attackers.
箭猪最显著的特征是它用来抵抗来犯之敌的钢毛。

dredge [dredʒ] *v.* **to remove mud or sand from the bottom of a river, harbour etc., or to search for something by doing this** 挖掘

♥ Archaeologists dredged up to forty meters to get artifacts left in the ancient city.
考古学家们挖掘至四十米深的地层来寻找古代城市遗留下来的器具。

♥ Geologists found rich gold deposits after dredging deeply into the ocean floor.
地质学家深入挖掘大洋底之后找到了丰富的金矿储藏。

相关表达 近义词 dig; excavate

expedition [ˌekspiˈdiʃən] *n.* **a long and carefully organized journey, especially to a dangerous or unfamiliar place, or the people that make this journey** 远征

♥ Darwin took an expedition to remote islands to find evidence of evolution.
达尔文远赴偏远的海岛去寻找生物进化的证据。

♥ NASA planned to sponsor a manned Mars expedition by 2012.
美国国家航天局计划在 2012 年之前资助一次到火星的远航。

词组拓展 go [start] on an expedition 去远征 [探险，考察]

相关表达 近义词 journey; voyage

记忆点拨 ex(外) ＋ped(脚) ＋ition(行为)

physicist [ˈfɪzɪsɪst] *n.* **a scientist who has special knowledge and training in physics** 物理学家

♥ The little boy dreamed that he would be a great physicist when he grew up.
那个小男孩梦想他长大后成为一名伟大的物理学家。

♥ It took physicists many years to figure out the structure of an atom.
物理学家们花了很多年才搞清楚原子的结构。

记忆点拨 physic [s](物理学) ＋ist(专家)

magnitude [ˈmægnitjuːd] *n.* **the great size or importance of something** 很多

♥ The new CEO underestimated the magnitude of the financial difficulties before he took over the position.

新总裁在上任之前低估了财务困境的规模。

♥ The magnitude of the policy changes made by the new state governor is unprecedented.
新州长作出了前所未有的政策变化。

词组拓展 of the first magnitude 头等重要的

相关表达 近义词 enormity; scale

记忆点拨 magni(量大的) ＋tude

topography [tə'pɔgrəfi] *n.* **the shape of an area of land, including its hills, valleys etc. 地形**

♥ The topography changes in this area are reflected accurately on the digital satellite images.
这片地区的地形变化精确地反映在数字卫星图像上。

♥ The topography of this coastal areas was studied carefully by the state government who would like to build a new port there.
州政府在决定修建港口之前仔细地研究了海岸地区的地形。

相关表达 近义词 landscape

记忆点拨 topic(地方的) ＋graphy

crust [krʌst] *n.* **the hard outer layer of the Earth 地壳**

♥ The thickness of earth's crust has baffled people for hundreds of years before modern science provided the answer.
在现代科学给出答案之前，地球地壳的厚度困惑了人们数百年。

♥ The crust is the outermost major layer of the earth, ranging from about 10 to 65 km in thickness worldwide.

地壳是地球最外面的一层，厚度从10公里到65公里不一。

相关表达　近义词 coating; shell

rugged　[ˈrʌgid] ***adj.*** **land that is rugged is rough and uneven** 崎岖不平

♥ The small start-up company faces a rugged road to survive in this tough economy.
在这个困难的经济环境下，这个小公司生存的道路坎坷不平。

♥ Many Indian tribes used to live in the rugged mountains of South Carolina.
过去很多印第安部落生活在南卡来罗纳州起伏的山脉里。

相关表达　近义词 rocky; uneven
反义词 even; flat

记忆点拨　rug(地毯) ＋ (g)ed(粗糙的)

tableland　[ˈteibllænd] ***n.*** **a large area of high flat land** 高地

♥ Aboriginals have been living on the tableland along west Australian coast for hundreds of years.
土著居民已经在西澳洲海岸的高地上生活了上百年。

♥ A venture was formed quickly to explore the gold deposits in the barren tableland after the new geology report came out.
当新的地理研究报告得出后一个新的风险投资公司很快成立起来到荒凉的高地上寻找金矿。

记忆点拨　table(平桌) ＋land(地)

sediment [ˈsedimənt] ***n.*** **solid substances that settle at the bottom of a liquid 沉淀物**

♥ Scientists found rich information about glacier activities from the samples of sediment.

从沉积物的取样中科学家们找到了很多关于冰川活动的信息。

♥ Fossils were found in the sediments on seabed which provided scientists evidence of evolution.

在海底沉积物里找到的化石为科学家提供了生物进化的证据。

相关表达　近义词 remains

terrace [ˈterəs] ***n.*** **one of a series of flat areas cut out of a hill like steps, and used to grow crops 阶地**

♥ The terrace at the top of the mountain was selected by ancient people to build a church.

古代人选择在山顶的平地上建造一座教堂。

♥ The Hanging Gardens of Babylon, one of the Seven Wonders of the World, were a serious of terraces filled with plants.

世界七大奇迹之一的巴比伦空中花园是一系列种满了花草的阶地。

erode [iˈrəud] ***v.*** **if the weather erodes rock or soil, or if rock or soil erodes, its surface is gradually destroyed 侵蚀**

♥ As waves hit the shoreline, rocks were eroded gradually and broken into pieces.

海浪拍打沙滩，海边的岩石被逐渐侵蚀并裂成碎片。

♥ The market share of this computer company was eroded rapidly as cheap products from Asia continued to be brought in.
由于亚洲的廉价货物持续涌入，这家计算机公司的市场份额被快速的侵蚀。

相关表达 近义词 corrode; wear away

记忆点拨 e(外，出) ＋ rode(驱使，推进)

Lesson 31

color-blind [ˈkʌləblind] *adj.* **unable to see the difference between all or some colours** 色盲的

♥ Those people are just too color-blind to appreciate the splendor of this gothic church.
那些人就像色盲一样不会欣赏这个哥特式教堂的辉煌。

♥ Most people who are color-blind just have a hard time telling the difference between several colors.
大多数色盲的人只是不能分辨几种颜色。

记忆点拨 color(颜色) ＋blind(瞎的)

perception [pəˈsepʃən] *n.* **the way that you notice things with your senses of sight, hearing etc.** 知觉

♥ The photos taken by him are so vivid that they give people a perception of rhythm.
他的照片十分生动，给人一种节奏感。

♥ The temple built by ancient Greek people struck people with strong visual perception of grandeur and magnificence.
古希腊人造的神庙给人一种视觉上强烈的庄严和宏大的感觉。

词组拓展 aesthetic perception 美感；审美观念

相关表达 **observation** *n.* 观察；注意
近义词 sensation

记忆点拨 percept(知觉的对象) ＋ion

comprehend [ˌkɔmpriˈhend] *v.* **to understand something that is complicated or difficult 理解**

♥ The little girl could not comprehend what the teacher was talking about and raised her hand.
那个小女孩不能理解老师的讲话，举起了手。

♥ Few people could comprehend the relativity theory when Einstein published his research.
当爱因斯坦提出相对论时很少有人能够理解。

相关表达 近义词 understand; figure out

spatial [ˈspeiʃəl] *adj.* **relating to the position, size, shape etc. of things 空间的**

♥ NASA spent billions of dollars every year on advanced spatial technology research.
美国国家航天局每年花上百亿美元在先进空间技术研究上。

♥ The spatial scheme of ancient church conveys people with some sacred feelings.
这个古代教堂的空间布局给人一种神圣的感觉。

记忆点拨 space ＋ial

visualize [ˈvɪzjʊəlaɪz] *v.* **to form a picture of someone or something in your mind 使具形象，设想**

♥ It is hard to visualize the beauty of the lake just from words.
很难仅从词语中想象那个湖的美丽。

♥ He could hardly visualize how he would pass the hard examination.
他很难想象能通过那么难的考试。

相关表达 近义词 envision; imagine

记忆点拨 visual(形象的) +ize(使成为)

reminiscence [ˌremiˈnisns] *n.* **a spoken or written story about events that you remember** 回忆，联想

♥ The old album gave him a reminiscence of his days in college.
那本老像册使他怀念大学的时光。

♥ Those songs left people with a reminiscence of days in eighties.
这些歌使人回忆起 80 年代。

相关表达 近义词 memory; nostalgia

记忆点拨 reminisc [e](回忆) +ence(名词后缀)

tadpole [ˈtædpəul] *n.* **a small creature that has a long tail, lives in water, and grows into a frog or toad** 蝌蚪

♥ The little girl had spent hours in watching the tadpoles swim.
小女孩花了好几个小时看蝌蚪游泳。

♥ It usually takes 8 weeks for a tadpole to develop into a frog.
蝌蚪要花八周时间长成青蛙。

mushroom [ˈmʌʃrum] *n.* **one of several kinds of fungus with stems and round tops, some of which can be eaten** 蘑菇

♥ It is sometimes hard to tell edible mushrooms from poison ones.
有时很难分辨哪些蘑菇能食用、哪些有毒。

♥ Beautiful wild mushrooms could be seen everywhere in the forest after the rains.
雨后森林里美丽的野蘑菇到处可见。

记忆点拨 mush(软块) +room(屋子)

carrot [ˈkærət] *n.* **a long pointed orange vegetable that grows under the ground 胡萝卜**

♥ The carrot and stick policy was often used by U.S. government to deal with tough international conflicts.
胡萝卜加大棒的政策经常被美国政府用来对付困难的国际冲突。

♥ Carrots are considered to be healthy food which provides rich vitamins to people's diet.
胡萝卜被认为是一种健康的食品，给人们的饮食带来丰富的维生素。

bud [bʌd] *n.* **a young tightly rolled up flower or leaf before it opens 花蕾**

♥ The green leaves protect flower buds from storms.
绿叶保护花蕾不受暴风雨侵扰。

♥ The little girl was eager to see the red rose bud turning into a flower.
小女孩焦急地等待花蕾开放。

词组拓展 in bud 发芽；含苞欲放

lark [lɑːk] *n.* **a small brown singing bird with long pointed wings 云雀**

♥ Her singing was compared to lark in the morning.
人们把她的歌声比作早晨的云雀。

♥ Every morning he was awoke by the singing of larks.
每天早上他被云雀的歌声叫醒。

词组拓展 as happy as a lark 兴高采烈，非常快乐

ladybird [ˈleɪdɪbɜːd] ***n.*** **a small round beetle(=a type of insect) that is usually red with black spots** 瓢虫

♥ The naughty boy put a ladybird into the pocket of the girl.
淘气的男孩把一只瓢虫放进女孩的口袋里。

♥ Lots of ladybirds were found in the vineyard after the rain.
雨后葡萄园里到处都是瓢虫。

bulrush [ˈbulrʌʃ] ***n.*** **a tall plant that looks like grass and grows by water** 芦苇

♥ There was bulrush all over the wetland.
湿地里到处都是芦苇。

♥ Bulrush, when dried, can be made into paper.
晒干后的芦苇可以用于造纸。

记忆点拨 bul + rush(灯芯草)

Lesson 32

controversy [ˈkɔntrəvəːsi] *n.* **a serious argument about something that involves many people and continues for a long time** 争议，争论

♥ Whether the methodology used by the company to avoid tax is legal or not has sparked intense controversy in public.

这个公司用来避税的方法在公众中引起很大争议。

♥ There was huge controversy over the economic growth rate among economists.

经济学家们对于经济增长速度有很大争议。

词组拓展 without controversy 无可争议

相关表达 近义词 argument; debate

反义词 agreement, consensus

记忆点拨 controver [t] (辩论) ＋sy(名词后缀)

dust [dʌst] *n.* **dry powder consisting of extremely small bits of dirt that is in buildings on furniture, floors etc. if they are not kept clean** 纠纷，骚动

♥ The savvy businessman postponed all his procurement until the dust around import policy was settled.

这个精明的生意人把所有的采购订单都推迟到进口政策明确之后。

♥ The new research result about the origin of the cosmos stirred up dust in academics.

有关宇宙起源的新研究成果引起了学术界很大争议。

相关表达　近义词 chaos; turmoil

clash [klæʃ] ***n.*** **a short fight between two armies or groups—used in news reports** 冲突

♥ Clash of civilizations has been a hot topic in global politics these days.

文明之间的冲突是当代全球政治的热门话题。

♥ The High price of AIDS drugs has caused intense clash between developing and developed countries.

艾滋病药物的高价导致了发展中国家和发达国家间的剧烈冲突。

相关表达　近义词 conflict; collide

inquisition [ˌinkwiˈziʃən] ***n.*** **a Roman Catholic organization in the past whose aim was to find and punish people who had unacceptable religious beliefs**（罗马天主教的）宗教法庭

♥ The Inquisition was a permanent institution in the Catholic Church charged with the eradication of heresies.

宗教法庭是天主教会用来消灭异教的机构。

♥ Conflicts between science and religion were full of the history of Roman Inquisition in the Middle Ages.

中世纪罗马宗教法庭的历史充满了科学和宗教的冲突。

记忆点拨　inquisit [e]（审讯）＋ion（行为）

perspective [pə'spektiv] ***n.*** **a way of thinking about something, especially one which is influenced by the type of person you are or by your experiences 观点，看法**

♥ The economist's perspective on global economic trend was popular among academics.
这个经济学家对于全球经济走势的观点在学术界很流行。

♥ Goldman Sachs published its perspective on stock market quarterly.
高盛银行每个季度都发布它对于股市的看法。

词组拓展 in the right perspective 正确地、客观地、全面地（观察事物）

相关表达 近义词 view; point

记忆点拨 per(贯穿，全）＋spect(看）＋ive

despise [dis'paiz] ***v.*** **to dislike and have a low opinion of someone or something 蔑视**

♥ Theft behavior was despised by people in all cultures.
偷窃行为在所有的文化中都受到鄙视。

♥ The slow economic growth offered yet another reason for people to despise the president incumbent.
缓慢的经济增长使人们又多了一个原因蔑视现任总统。

相关表达 近义词 scorn; deride
反义词 respect; admire

generalize ['dʒenərəlaiz] ***v.*** **to form a general principle or opinion after considering only a small number of facts or examples 归纳**

♥ It is not always appropriate to generalize the moral standard in one culture to another.
把一种文化标准推广到另一种文化上并不总是合适的。

♥ The teacher showed students how to generalize the use of mathematical rule to a series of problems.
老师教导学生们怎样把数学法则归纳应用到一系列问题上去。

记忆点拨 general(综合的，概括的) ＋ize(使成为)

undercurrent [ˈʌndəˌkʌrənt] *n.* **a hidden and often dangerous current of water that flowes under the surface of the sea or a river 潜流**

♥ New undercurrent of stock market fear was formed soon after the war news came out.
战争的消息传出后，新的股市恐慌的暗流很快形成了。

♥ Under the calm surface of the ocean exist dangerous undercurrents.
平静的海洋下面是危险的暗流。

记忆点拨 under(在……下面) ＋current(水流)

theoretical [θiəˈretikəl] *adj.* **relating to the study of ideas, especially scientific ideas, rather than with practical uses of the ideas or practical experience 理论上的**

♥ Scientists were amazed by the experiment result which was completely different from theoretical prediction.
科学家们对于和理论预言完全不同的实验结果感到吃惊。

♥ Sometimes theoretical economic rules can't apply to real world.
有时理论经济法则并不适用于现实世界。

相关表达 近义词 notational
反义词 practical

记忆点拨 theor [y](理论) +etical (……的)

potentiality [pəˌtenʃi'æliti] ***n.*** **an ability or quality that could develop in the future 潜能**

♥ The potentiality of information technology is yet to be fully exploited.
信息技术的潜能还没有被完全开发。

♥ People are optimistic at the potentiality of Asian economic growth.
人们对于亚洲经济发展的潜能感到乐观。

词组拓展 tap potentialities 挖掘潜力

记忆点拨 potential(潜在的，可能的) +ity(形成的条件)

intimate ['intimid] ***adj.*** **very detailed knowledge of something as a result of careful study or a lot of experience 详尽的**

♥ That biologist has intimate knowledge of the insects living in rain forest.
那个生物学家对于生活在热带雨林里的昆虫有很详尽的知识。

♥ The newspaper showed intimate plan of the city highway.
报纸上发表了城市高速公路的详尽计划。

相关表达 近义词 close; thorough
反义词 rough

记忆点拨 inti(之间）＋mate(同伴）（亲密的）

familiarity [fəˌmiliˈæriti] ***n.*** **a good knowledge of a particular subject or place** 熟悉的

♥ His familiarity of the area surprised people since he had not been back for twenty years.
人们对于他熟悉这片地区感到吃惊，因为他已经离开二十年了。

♥ Familiarity of computer programming made him a star in his research team.
他对于计算机编程的熟悉使他成为研究团队的明星。
近义词 acquaintance

记忆点拨 familiar(熟悉的）＋ity(形成的条件）

culpable [ˈkʌlpəbl] ***adj.*** **deserving blame** 应受遣责的

♥ People are not sure who is culpable of the series murder.
人们不知道谁应对系列谋杀负责。

♥ Some people think that the inappropriate interest changes might be culpable for the economic recession.
有些人认为经济衰退应归咎于不恰当的利率变化。

相关表达 近义词 guilty; blameworthy

记忆点拨 culp [a]（疏忽，罪）＋able（……倾向的）

Aristotelian [ærɪstəˈtiːlɪən] ***n.*** 亚里士多德学派的人

♥ That historian has spent many years in the study of Aristotelian.
那个历史学家花了很多年研究亚里士多德学派。

♥ Aristotelians did lots of valuable research in logic and psychology.

亚里士多德学派在逻辑和心理学上做了很多有价值的研究。

记忆点拨 Aristotle(亚里士多德)＋ian（……的人）

Aristotle ['æristɔtl] ***n.*** 亚里士多德（公元前 384～322 年，古希腊哲学家）

♥ Aristotle was a famous philosopher in ancient Greece.

亚里士多德是古希腊有名的哲学家。

♥ The works done by Aristotle two thousand years ago are still studies by many historians.

亚里士多德两千多年前写的书至今还被历史学家研究。

Ptolemy 托勒密（公元 90～168 年，古希腊天文学家）

♥ Very little is known about Ptolemy's personal life.

人们对于托勒密的私生活知之甚少。

♥ Few people know that Ptolemy wrote a famous book on astrology, which was a reputable field of study in his days.

很少有人知道托勒密写了一本著名的关于“占星术”的书，占星术在他的那个时代是受人尊重的学科。

Leaning Tower of Pisa 比萨斜塔

♥ Leaning Tower of Pisa attracted thousands of tourists every year.

比萨斜塔每年吸引成千上万的游客来访。

♥ Leaning Tower of Pisa is famous for leaning fourteen and a half feet.

比萨斜塔因为倾斜十四英尺半而出名。

spiral [ˈspaiərəl] *adj.* **circling around a center at a continuously increasing or decreasing distance 螺旋状的**

♥ Spiral stairways were typical design among Ancient European castles.
螺旋状楼梯是欧洲古堡的普遍设计。

♥ Scientists concluded that the molecule must have a spiral shape from experiment result.
科学家们从实验结果中推出分子是螺旋状的。

相关表达 近义词 coiled; twisted

记忆点拨 spir [e]（尖顶）＋al(形状的）

nebula [ˈnebjulə] *n.* **a mass of gas and dust among the stars, which often appears as a bright cloud in the sky at night 星云**

♥ A few nebulas are visible to the unaided eye.
有些星云能被肉眼观测到。

♥ An unknown nebula discovered via Hubble Space Telescope raised intense interests among scientists.
科学家们对于哈勃空间望远镜发现的星云产生了浓厚的兴趣。

scratch [skrætʃ] *n.* **a thin mark or cut on the surface of something 擦痕**

♥ He threw the CD away after he found a few scratch on it.
他看到光盘上的划痕后把它扔掉了。

♥ The boy showed the cat scratches on his hand to his mother.

小男孩给他的妈妈看他手上被猫抓的痕迹。

词组拓展　from scratch 最开始的

contrivance　[kən'traivəns] ***n.*** **a machine or piece of equipment that has been made for a special purpose** 器械

♥ The R&D department came out with a contrivance which is effective at stopping bleeding.

研发部门做出了新的器械，在止血方面很有效。

♥ Any electrical contrivance sold to consumers must comply with federal standards.

出售给消费者的电器必须符合联邦标准。

词组拓展　an automatic contrivance 自动装置

相关表达　近义词 device; appliance

记忆点拨　contriv [e]（发明，设计）＋ance(物品)

distort　[dis'tɔːt] ***v.*** **to change the appearance, sound, or shape of something so that it is strange or unclear** 歪曲

♥ The inaccurate market data distorted the real picture of economy.

经济的真实情况被不准确的市场数据扭曲了。

♥ The judge suspected that the attorney distorted the truth in his defense.

法官认为律师在辩护中歪曲了事实。

词组拓展　distort sb.'s motives 曲解某人的动机

相关表达　近义词 deform

反义词 straighten

记忆点拨　dis(使) ＋tort(侵权行为)

Unit 5

Lesson 33

adverse [ˈædvəːs] *adj.* **not good or favourable** 不利的

♥ The small company has made a successful IPO despite of the adverse stock market sentiment.
尽管股市气氛不利，这家小公司的上市非常成功。

♥ The government provided additional agricultural aids to help farmers fight adverse climate changes.
政府为农民提供了附加农业贷款帮助他们与不利的气候做斗争。

词组拓展 be adverse to 跟……相反，不利于，反对

相关表达 reverse *adj.* 相反的
近义词 unfavorable, opposing
反义词 favorable, constructive

记忆点拨 ad(向……) ＋verse(反面)

purchasable [ˈpəːtʃəsəbl] *adj.* **that can be bought** 可买到的

♥ Some people believe that anything is purchasable for a price.
有些人认为用钱能买任何东西。

♥ Nowadays many things are purchasable on internet.
现在很多东西都能在互联网上买到。

相关表达 近义词 available

记忆点拨 purchase(买) ＋able（……可能的）

preacher ['priːtʃə(r)] ***n.*** **someone who talks about a religious subject in a public place, especially at a church** 传教士

♥ That preacher has been to Africa several times when he was in college.

那个传教士在大学时就去过非洲好几次。

♥ The famine of the small African village would be unknown to outside world without the help of a preacher come from Europe.

没有那个欧洲传教士的帮助，这个非洲小村庄的饥荒一定不为人所知。

相关表达 近义词 priest; cleric

记忆点拨 preach(鼓吹) ＋er(者)

defendant [di'fendənt] ***n.*** **the person in a court of law who has been accused of doing something illegal** 被告

♥ This would be a hard case to the defendant as all evidence pointed against him.

这案子被告很难赢，因为所有的证据都对他不利。

♥ The Fifth Amendment to the U. S. Constitution provides that a defendant has the right to remain silent.

美国宪法第五修正案规定被告有权保持沉默。

相关表达 反义词 plaintiff 原告

记忆点拨 defend(辩护) ＋ant (……的人)

outlook ['autluk] ***n.*** **a view from a particular place; your general attitude to life and the world** 视野

♥ The hotel has some rooms with perfect outlook to the sea.

这旅馆有些房间有很好的看海视野。

The relationship of the two countries has never been closer from historical outlook.

历史上来看现在这两个国家的关系最好。

词组拓展　be on the outlook for sth. 监视着，提防着；留心，注意

相关表达　近义词 view

记忆点拨　out(向外）＋look(看）

capacity　[kəˈpæsiti] ***n.*** **someone's ability to do something** 能力

The production capacity of this company could not meet the rapid growth of market demand.

这家公司的生产能力不能满足快速增长的市场需求。

I can hardly believe that this small restaurant has the capacity to host more than a hundred people at the same time.

我几乎不能相信这家小餐馆能同时容纳上百人。

词组拓展　at full capacity 满功率，满负载

相关表达　近义词 ability; aptitude

记忆点拨　capa [ble](有能力的）＋city(名词后缀）

democratic　[ˌdeməˈkrætik] ***adj.*** **organized according to the principle that everyone in a society is equally important, no matter how much money they have or what social class they come from** 民主的

People believed that ancient Greece was a democratic society in which government was elected by all its citizens.

人们认为古希腊是民主社会，政府由所有公民选举产生。

♥ Donkey is widely accepted as Democratic party's symbol in United States.
驴在美国是民主党的象征。

相关表达　反义词 autocratic; dictatorial

记忆点拨　democra [cy](民主主义) +tic (……的)

tribal　['traibəl] *n.* **relating to with a tribe or tribes** 部落的

♥ There will an exhibition of Indian tribal arts in the city museum.
城市博物馆要有一个印第安部落的艺术展览。

♥ Tribal affairs were usually determined by the eldest man according to the Indian traditions.
按印第安人的传统，部落事务有最老的人决定。

相关表达　**tribalism** *n.* 部落制度

记忆点拨　trib [e](部落) +al (……的)

tribe　[traib] *n.* **a social group consisting of people of the same race who have the same beliefs, customs, language etc., and usually live in one particular area ruled by their leader** 部落

♥ Some tribes in East Africa still live the same way as they did several hundred years ago.
东非的一些部落现在的生活和几百年前没什么区别。

♥ Many historians in America are very interested in the history of Indian tribes who used to live on the Great Plains.
很多美国历史学家对生活在大平原上的印第安部落史很感兴趣。

相关表达　近义词 clan

illiterate　[i'litərit] *n.* **someone who has not learned to read or write 文盲**

♥ The illiterates among young and middle-aged Chinese had decreased to less than 5% according to Ministry of Education.

教育部宣布文盲在中国中青年中的比例降到了百分之五以下。

♥ People who have difficulty using computers are considered illiterate in modern society.

在现代社会里不会使用计算机的人被认为是文盲。

记忆点拨　il＝in(不，没有）＋literate(有文化的）

相关表达　近义词 uninformed

反义词 educated

记忆点拨　il(否定）＋literate(学者）

compulsory　[kəm'pʌlsəri] *adj.* **something that is compulsory must be done because it is the law or because someone in authority orders 义务的**

♥ People need to take 9-year compulsory education accord to law in China.

按中国法律规定人们必须完成九年义务教育。

♥ Army service is compulsory in some countries.

在某些国家里必须义务服兵役。

词组拓展　compulsory execution 强迫执行

相关表达　近义词 obligatory

反义词 voluntary

记忆点拨　com(共同）＋ pulse(脉搏）＋（o)ry（……的）

deem [diːm] ***v.*** **to think of something in a particular way or as having a particular quality 认为**

♥ The climbing oil price was deemed to be the major threat to economy recovery.
上升的油价被认为是经济复苏的首要威胁。

♥ The old woman was deemed to have some magic power by people in the tribe.
那个老妇人被部落里的人认为具有某种魔力。

相关表达　近义词 regard

means [miːnz] ***n.*** **a way of doing or achieving something 方法，手段，财产，资力**

♥ He tried all means to get his new investment proposal approved by CEO.
他尝试了种种方法让他的投资建议得到总裁的批准。

♥ The central bank could have taken economic means to control inflation other than increasing interest rate.
中央银行本有提升利率以外的经济手段来控制通货膨胀。

词组拓展　a means to an end 达到目的的方法
by all means 一定；务必

相关表达　近义词 approach

记忆点拨　mean(想要) +s

hamper [ˈhæmpə] ***v.*** **to make it difficult for someone to do something 妨碍**

♥ Unfamiliarity of the new software hampered his ability to complete the project by deadline.
对新软件不熟悉妨碍了他按期完成项目。

♥ The sudden breakout of war hampered the recovery of economy.
突发的战争妨碍了经济的复苏。

相关表达 近义词 impede; get in the way of
反义词 facilitate

savannah [səˈvænə] ***n.*** **a large flat area of grassy land, especially in Africa** 大草原

♥ The beautiful Inner Mongolian savannah attracts thousands of tourists every year.
美丽的内蒙古大草原每年吸引成千上万的游客。

♥ The old man has been living on the savannah along for twenty years.
那个老人在大草原上孤独地生活了二十年。

juvenile [ˈdʒuːvinail] ***adj.*** **relating to young people who are not yet adults** 青少年

♥ Elvis Presley was the most popular rock star among the juvenile in 60's.
埃尔维斯·普莱斯利是六十年代年轻人里最流行的摇滚明星。

♥ Playing computer games was an important part of his juvenile life.
玩计算机游戏是他年轻时生活的重要部分。

相关表达 近义词 young; adolescent

记忆点拨 juven(年轻的) ＋ile（……的）

delinquency [diˈliŋkwənsi] ***n.*** **illegal or immoral behaviour or actions, especially by young people** 犯罪

♥ The new government increased budgets dramatically to prevent juvenile crime and delinquency.

新政府大量增加预算防止青少年犯罪。

♥ Many criminals have delinquency records during their youth.

很多罪犯在年轻时就有不良记录。

相关表达 近义词 misbehavior; wrongdoing

记忆点拨 delinquen [t](违法的) +cy(行为)

Lesson 34

adolescence [ˌædəʊˈlesəns] ***n.*** **the time, usually between the ages of 12 and 18, when a young person is developing into an adult** 青春期

♥ The education center has spent tremendous money on study of adolescence behavior.

那个教育中心在研究青春期行为方面花费很大。

♥ People experience dramatic emotional and physical changes during their adolescence.

人们在青春期时会经历很大生理心理上的变化。

记忆点拨 adolesc [e]（进入青春期）＋ence(名词后缀)

slur [sləː] ***n.*** **to criticize someone or something unfairly** 诋毁

♥ The slur upon the new city government did not make the major to back out his policy.

对新市政府的诋毁不能使市长收回他的政策。

♥ The artist can't accept any criticism on his works and think they are all slurs cast from his adversaries.

这个艺术家不能接受对他的作品的任何批评，认为这都是对手的诋毁。

相关表达 近义词 defame; insult

disloyalty [ˌdɪsˈlɔɪəltɪ] ***n.*** **doing or saying things that do not support your friends, your country, or the group you belong to** 不忠

♥ Disloyalty of employees has caused management to improve benefits dramatically.
雇员的不忠导致管理层大幅提高福利。

♥ The intelligent agency suspected the disloyalty of the ambassador and sent spy to monitor his activities.
情报机构怀疑大使的不忠，派了间谍监视他的行为。

记忆点拨 dis(不) ＋loyal(忠诚的) ＋ty(成为)

adolescent [ˌædəuˈlesnt] ***n.*** **a young person, usually between the ages of 12 and 18, who is developing into an adult** 青少年（**12～18** 岁）

♥ Adolescent psychology has been a hot topic among social scientists.
青少年心理学是社会学家的热门话题。

♥ A new adolescent center has been built for this community to improve the quality of education.
这个社区新建了青少年中心来提高教学水平。

记忆点拨 adolesc [e]（进入青春期）＋ ent （……人）

spiteful [ˈspaɪtful] ***adj.*** **deliberately nasty to someone in order to hurt or upset them** 恶意的，怀恨的

♥ The clerk gave his manager a spiteful look after he learned the layoff news.
那个职员听到解雇的消息后怨恨地看了经理一眼。

♥ The state governor continued his fiscal policy changes despite the spiteful attitude of people.
尽管人们怀有不满，州长还是继续他的财务政策改变。

相关表达 近义词 hostile; malicious

记忆点拨 spite(敌意) ＋ful(充满……的)

disillusionment [ˌdɪsɪˈljuːʒənmənt] *n.* 幻灭感

♥ The bad news of battlefield deepened people's disillusionment with the government.
来自战场的坏消息加深了人们对政府的幻灭感。

♥ 1997 was the year of disillusionment to people in Southeast Asia due to the economic crisis.
由于经济危机，1997 对于东南亚的人们来讲是希望破灭的一年。

相关表达 **disillusion** *vt.* 使觉醒；使幻灭

记忆点拨 dis(毁) ＋illusion(幻想) ＋ment(名词后缀)

evaluation [iˌvæljuˈeiʃən] *n.* **a judgment about how good, useful, or successful something is** 评价

♥ He got good performance evaluation from his manager at the end of year.
他在年底得到经理对他表现的好评。

♥ The new model of BMW got good evaluation from auto magazines.
新款的宝马获得汽车杂志的好评。

记忆点拨 evaluat [e](评价) ＋ion(行为)

infallibility [inˌfæləˈbiliti] *n.* 一贯正确

♥ The government tried all means to keep its image of infallibility even after the scandal came out.
即使在丑闻出现之后，政府还是尽全力维护一贯正确的形象。

♥ People were very disappointed after the infallibility of their leader was ruined by the bribery.

当领导的一贯正确形象被贪污行为破坏后人们很失望。

记忆点拨 infallibl [e](没有错误的) +ity(成为)

resent [ri'zent] ***v.*** **to feel angry or upset about a situation or about something that someone has done, especially because you think that it is not fair 怨恨**

♥ The shareholders resented the management of company very much after they learned the company could not meet the revenue forecast.

当股民得知公司不能达到预期收入后对公司的管理层极度怨恨。

♥ The new tax raise was resented by lots of middle class people.

很多中产阶级厌恶加税。

相关表达 近义词 hate

记忆点拨 re(又) +sent(感觉)

sincerity [sin'seriti] ***n.*** **when someone is sincere and really means what they are saying 诚挚**

♥ People believed in sincerity to the ability of the new government.

人们真诚地相信新政府的能力。

♥ With all the sincerity he donated all his fortune to philanthropy.

他诚挚地把所有财产捐给慈善事业。

相关表达 近义词 honesty; genuineness

记忆点拨 sincer [e](诚挚的) +ity(成为)

Victorian [vik'tɔːriən] ***adj.*** **morally strict in a way that was typical in the time of Queen Victoria 维多利亚式的**

♥ The Victorian style ornament in this building reminds people of the richness of the host.
这个建筑的维多利亚式装璜提醒人们它的主人的富裕。

♥ The small Victorian garden was her favorite place when she was young.
这个小维多利亚式花园是她小时候最喜欢的地方。

记忆点拨 Victoria(维多利亚）＋n（……式的）

retreat [riˈtriːt] ***v.*** **to move away from the enemy after being defeated in battle** 后退

♥ The army retreated after they ran out of ammunitions.
军队打光弹药后撤退了。

♥ He retreated from his position after people pointed out the calculation mistake.
当人们指出他的计算错误后他从原来的立场退缩了。

相关表达 近义词 recede; withdraw
反义词 advance

记忆点拨 re(向后）＋treat(对待）

unreasoning [ʌnˈriːzniŋ] ***adj.*** **an unreasoning feeling is not based on facts or good reasons** 不凭理智的

♥ The boy insisted his unreasoning trust to his friends even though he was cheated before.
那个小男孩坚持他对朋友非理智的信任，即使他被欺骗过。

♥ People kept unreasoning enthusiasm of stock market despite the bad earning reports.

尽管有不利的盈利报告，人们还是对股市保持非理智的热情。

记忆点拨 un(不) ＋ reason(理由) ＋ing

authoritarian [ɔːθɔriˈtɛəriən] *adj.* **strictly forcing people to obey a set of rules or laws, especially ones that are wrong or unfair** 专制的

♥ The authoritarian management style was hated by most employees in this company.

大多数雇员厌恶这家公司的专制管理风格。

♥ The authoritarian government issues lots of policy changes to restrict the freedom of people.

专制政府发布很多政策改变来限制人们的自由。

记忆点拨 authorit [y]（权威，权威人士）＋arian（形容词后缀）

cow [kau] *v.* **to frighten someone in order to make them do something** 吓唬

♥ The witness was too cowed to tell the truth to police.

目击者太害怕了，不敢对警方讲出事实真相。

♥ The girl was too cowed to say a word when she saw the car collision.

那个女孩看到车祸后怕得一句话也讲不出来。

Lesson 35

hub [hʌb] ***n.*** **the central and most important part of an area, system, activity etc., which all the other parts are connected to(活动的) 中心**

♥ Houston has become the commercial hub of the southern states in United States.

休斯敦成为了美国西部的一个商业中心。

♥ The computer lab has become the hub of boys who are enthusiastic about the games.

电脑房成为了喜欢玩游戏的男孩子的活动中心。

lunar [ˈljuːnə] ***adj.*** **relating to the moon or to travel to the moon 月球的**

♥ The lunar landscape is not a mystery anymore after people sent astronauts on moon.

在人类登月后，月球的表面景观就不再神秘了。

♥ Most western people are not familiar with Chinese lunar calendar.

大部分西方人不熟悉中国的阴历。

相关表达 反义词 solar *adj.* 太阳的

记忆点拨 luna(月) ＋r

oxygen [ˈɔksidʒən] ***n.*** **a gas that has no colour or smell, is present in air, and is necessary for most animals and plants to live 氧气**

- Man can't live without oxygen.
  人离开氧气无法生存。
- Oxygen and nitrogen are the two major components of air.
  氧气和氮气是空气的主要组成部分。

Apollo [ə'pɔləu] ***n.*** **in Greek and Roman mythology, the god of the sun, medicine, poetry, music, and prophecy** 阿波罗

- The Apollo program was designed to land humans on the Moon and bring them safely back to Earth.
  阿波罗项目是人类成功登陆月球并返回地面的。
- Apollo program was an outstanding example of how governmental agencies, industrial firms, and universities can work together to reach seemingly impossible goals.
  阿波罗项目是一个政府机构、工业界和大学一起合作来完成看似不可能的目标的成功典范。

accelerate [æk'seləreit] ***v.*** **if a process accelerates or if something accelerates it, it happens faster than usual or sooner than you expect** 加速

- The management urged employees to accelerate their assembly speed.
  管理层要求雇员们提高组装速度。
- The company decided to increase investment in China dramatically to accelerate their expansion in that market.
  公司决定大幅度加大在中国的投资来加快他们在此的市场扩充。

相关表达　近义词 hasten; hurry

反义词 decelerate; retard

记忆点拨　ac(到) +celerate(加急)

terrestrial　[tiˈrestriəl] ***adj.*** **relating to the Earth rather than to the moon or other planets** 地球的

♥ There was a good program about terrestrial wildlife on Discovery Channel last night.

昨晚探索频道播出了一部关于地球野生物的很棒的节目。

♥ There are lots of beautiful pictures of terrestrial national parks on National Geographic website.

国家地理的网站上有很多美丽的地球国家公园照片。

相关表达　反义词 Celestial *adj.* 天空的

记忆点拨　terre(土地) +strial（……的）

permanently　[ˈpɜːməntlɪ] ***adv.*** **always, or for a very long time** 永远地

♥ Some rare species disappear permanently from the earth due to the mistakes made by human being.

一些稀有品种因为人为的错误永远地从地球上消失了。

♥ The new treaty signed by the two countries in war was unlikely to solve the conflict between them permanently.

两国在交战中签的新条约看起来似乎不能永久解决他们之间的矛盾。

相关表达　反义词 temporarily

记忆点拨　permanent(永久的) +ly（……地）

fascination [fæsɪ'neɪʃ(ə)n] *n.* **something that interests you very much, or the quality of being very interesting 魅力**

♥ Fascination of movie stars like Hepburn would not change with time.
电影明星比如赫本的魅力是不会随着时间改变的。

♥ Expedition to deep caves has tremendous fascination to some explorers.
到深洞里去探索对于一些探险者来说充满魅力。

相关表达 近义词 attraction

记忆点拨 fascinat [e](使着迷) +ation(过程)

senior ['siːnjə] *adj.* **having a higher position, level, or rank 资历深的，年长的**

♥ Some senior people in this Indian tribe could tell you lots of stories about the mysterious treasure.
在这个印第安部落里有些老人能告诉你很多关于神秘财富的故事。

♥ He is the most senior person in this division and has been working for this company for thirty years.
他是这个部门资历最深的员工，已经在公司工作30年了。

记忆点拨 sen(老的，年长的) +ior

chasm ['kæzəm] *n.* **a very deep space between two areas of rock or ice, especially one that is dangerous 断层，裂口**

♥ The new CEO was able to bridge the chasm between consumers and the company by making significant improvement in product design.

新的总裁无法通过改进产品设计来填补顾客与公司间的裂痕。

♥ The explorers found a new gold deposit after months of search in chasms, caves and valleys of Rocky Mountains.
在经历数月在洛基山脉的断层、山洞和山谷搜寻之后，探险者终于发现了新的金矿。

canyon [ˈkænjən] ***n.*** **a deep valley with very steep sides of rock that usually has a river running through it 峡谷**

♥ Most people visiting Los Angeles from other countries would also take a trip to Grand Canyon if they have time.
如果有时间的话，大多数从他国去洛山矶旅行的人们都会去一趟大峡谷。

♥ The rangers in this canyon can tell you lots of stories about native Indian people living around.
这座山谷的护林员会告诉你很多关于附近的印第安人的故事。

Lesson 36

disunited [dɪsˈjuːnaitid] ***adj.*** **people who are disunited are in the same organization, country, or group but cannot agree or work with each other 分裂的**

♥ The union went disunited when people have different opinion of strike.
当人们对罢工有不同看法时，工会就分裂了。

♥ Ethnic issues are one of the major reasons for a nation to become disunited.
民族问题是国家分裂的一个主要原因。

记忆点拨 dis(不) ＋united(联合的，团结的)

correspondingly [ˌkɔrisˈpɔndiŋli] ***adv.*** **相应地**

♥ The company raised product price correspondingly after the inflation became serious.
在通货膨胀很严峻的情况下，公司也相应提高了产品价格。

♥ The foreign direct investment declined correspondingly after the government changed tax policy.
在政府改变税收政策后，外商直接投资也相应急剧下降了。

记忆点拨 cor（共同）＋ responding（相应的）＋ ly（副词后缀）

backward [ˈbækwəd] ***adj.*** **developing slowly and less successfully than most others 落后的**

♥ It is hard for this factory to improve profitability due to the backward equipment and lack of financial resource.

由于设备落后和资金短缺，工厂很难提高利润。

♥ The backward economy of this country could be changed soon after people found huge oil resources in it.

这个国家的经济落后可以由于人们找到了大量的石油资源而改变。

相关表达　反义词 ahead; forward

记忆点拨　back(后面的) ＋ward(向……)

incur　[inˈkəː] *v.* **if you incur a cost, debt, or a fine, you have to pay money because of something you have done, or you do not make money** 承担

♥ The tobacco company could not incur the huge cost of lawsuits and declared bankruptcy.

烟草公司不能承担诉讼的巨额费用而宣布破产。

♥ It is hard for a family to incur the cost of buying a house in this area as the real estate price soared these days.

在这个区域买房对家庭来说是很难承担的费用，因为房地产价格这些年飙升。

相关表达　**incurment** *n.* 承担

记忆点拨　in(不，非) ＋cur(跑)

administer　[ədˈministə] *v.* **to manage the work or money of a company or organization** 管理

♥ The asset left by the old man was administered by a trust company temporarily.

老人留下的资产暂时由一家信托公司管理。

♥ The manager was surprised to find out that no one took responsibility administering the IT system of that division.
经理发现没有人负责那段区域的信息系统管理时很吃惊。

相关表达 近义词 execute; manage

记忆点拨 ad(加强) +minister(服务)

administrative [əd'ministrətiv] ***adj.*** **relating to the work of managing a company or organization** 行政管理的

♥ The soaring administrative cost on earning report was complained by lots of shareholders.
收益报告上高速上涨的管理费用让股东们抱怨。

♥ The manager said he was very satisfied with the works of his administrative assistant.
经理说他非常满意他的行政助理的工作。

记忆点拨 administ [e] r(管理) +ative (……相关的)

analogous [ə'næləgəs] ***adj.*** **similar to another situation or thing so that a comparison can be made** 类似的

♥ By using analogous things in daily life, the teacher helped kids to accept math concepts easily.
通过运用日常生活中的类似事物，老师轻易地就让学生们理解了数学概念。

♥ Some critics used Vietnam as an analogous example when they commented on the situation in Iraq.
一些批评家在他们评论伊拉克形势时把越南作为一个类似的例子。

记忆点拨 ana(按照) +logous(比例)

overheads [ˈəuvəhedz] ***n.*** **money spent regularly on rent, insurance, electricity, and other things that are needed to keep a business operating** 一般费用

♥ The marketing overheads of this company were out of control before management paid attention to the problem.

在管理层注意这个问题以前，公司的市场费用就已经难以控制了。

♥ Some of the business overheads are tax-deductible in the company's expenses.

有一些商业费用对公司来说是可以免税的。

记忆点拨 over(在上) ＋head(头) ＋s

initiative [iˈniʃiətiv] ***n.*** **the ability to make decisions and take action without waiting for someone to tell you what to do** 主动，积极性

♥ No one took initiative to take on the project when the manger asked for volunteer in the meeting.

当经理呼吁志愿者时，没有人主动要求承担这个项目。

♥ The government took initiative to deal with the inflation issue by appointing a special committee.

政府主动通过任命特别委员会来对付通货膨胀。

词组拓展 on(one's)own initiative 自主的，没有他人的怂勇或指导的

记忆点拨 initiat [e](开始，发动) ＋ive（……性）

checker [ˈtʃekə] ***n.*** **someone who makes sure that something is written or done correctly** 检查人员

♥ Management blamed bad quality control to the negligence of checkers.

管理层把低劣的产品质量归咎于检查人员的疏忽。

♥ Human checkers were replaced by computers as part of modernization plan of this factory.

作为工厂现代化计划的一部分，人工检查员被电脑所代替。

记忆点拨 check(检查) ＋er(人)

foreman [ˈfɔːmən] ***n.*** **a worker who is in charge of a group of other workers, for example in a factory** 监工

♥ The wage of a foreman in that factory is not much difference from an assembly worker.

在那家工厂里，监工和装配工人的工资没什么区别。

♥ The company cut the number of foremen dramatically to reduce administrative overheads during recession.

经济衰退期时，工厂大幅度削减监工的数量来降低行政费用。

记忆点拨 fore(在前面) ＋man(雇工)

dividend [ˈdividend] ***n.*** **a part of a company's profit that is divided among the people with shares in the company** 红利

♥ Bush government cut dividend tax as part of his fiscal plan.

布什政府在财政年度里削减了利息税。

♥ That company has not issued dividend to shareholders for five years.

公司已经五年没有分红给股东了。

记忆点拨 divide(分配) ＋nd

unduly [ˈʌnˈdjuːli] ***adv.*** **more than is normal or reasonable** 过度地

♥ The unduly lenient sentence of the case caused rage of the public.

对案件过分宽大的审判引起了公众强烈的愤怒。

♥ The foreign investments shrank sharply due to the unduly restrictive tax policy.

由于过分严格的税收政策，外商投资严重减缩。

相关表达 近义词 excessively; immoderately:

记忆点拨 un(相反）＋duly(适时地）

Lesson 37

likelihood ['laiklihud] ***n.*** **the degree to which something can reasonably be expected to happen 可能性**

♥ The likelihood of economy recovery in near term is very small.

经济在近期复苏的可能性很小。

♥ Scientists suspect that too much fat in diet may increase the likelihood of heart disease.

科学家怀疑饮食过多的脂肪会导致心脏病。

相关表达　近义词 possibilities

记忆点拨　likely(很可能的) +hood(情形)

infant ['infənt] ***n.*** **a baby or very young child 婴儿**

♥ Infant mortality rate dropped steadily in developing countries due to improved access to medical treatment.

由于医疗条件的改善，发展中国家的婴儿死亡率稳步下降。

♥ The new book on how to raise an infant has been very popular among young mothers.

这本关于如何抚养婴儿的新书在年轻的母亲中很畅销。

记忆点拨　in(不) +fant(说话)

vulnerable ['vʌlnərəb(ə)l] ***adj.*** **someone who is vulnerable can be easily harmed or hurt 脆弱的**

♥ The shortage of oil reserves makes the country more vulnerable to price increase in world market.
由于石油资源的缺乏，国家就更受国际石油价格的上升影响了。

♥ Some species of wildlife are more vulnerable to climate changes.
有些野生动物品种受气候变化影响。

相关表达 近义词 exposed; susceptible

记忆点拨 vulner(伤) +able（……倾向的）

imperceptible [ˌimpəˈseptəbl] ***adj.*** **almost impossible to see or notice** 感觉不到的

♥ The quality difference between the two new cars, though imperceptible to most people, would become obvious after ten years of usage.
这两辆新车的质量区别虽然现在对大多数人来说都感觉不到，使用十年以后就会很明显了。

♥ There is an imperceptible smile on his face.
他脸上有一丝难以察觉的笑容。

相关表达 近义词 slight; vague
反义词 perceptible

记忆点拨 in(不) +perceptibilis(感觉到的)

steep [stiːp] ***adj.*** **involving a big increase or decrease** 急转直下

♥ The climate changes become so steep that it ruined harvest of this year completely.
气候变化如此剧烈，完全破坏了今年的丰收。

♥ The manager was worried about the steep decline of product sales this month.
经理对这个月产品销售的急剧下降很担忧。

相关表达　近义词 precipitous
反义词 gentle

ageing　[ˈeidʒiŋ] ***n.*** **the process of getting old 老化**

♥ Vitamin E is believed to be able to slow down the ageing process of man.
维生素 E 被认为可以延缓人的衰老。

♥ The ageing of population has become a serious social problem in some developed countries.
一些发达国家人口老化已经成为一个严重的社会问题。

记忆点拨　age(年龄) ＋ing（……过程）

odds　[ɔdz] ***n.*** **how likely it is that something will or will not happen 可能性**

♥ Almost no one gambled on the odds of that white horse to win the race.
几乎没有人投注赌白马会赢。

♥ Farmers could not count on the odds of rain in near term and applied loans to by irrigation equipment.
农民们不能依赖近期会下雨的可能性决定贷款购买灌溉工具。

词组拓展　at odds 争执不同意；意见冲突

记忆点拨　odd(奇数的，不固定的) ＋s

virtual　[ˈvəːtjuəl] ***adj.*** **very nearly a particular thing 实际上的**

♥ The Antarctic Circle becomes the virtual forbidden area to lots of explorer due to extreme weather.
由于那里极端的气候条件，北极圈实际上成了探险者的禁区。

♥ The man who could tell lots of interesting stories has become the virtual center of kids.
那个会讲很多故事的人实际上成为了孩子们的中心。

相关表达 近义词 actually; essentially

记忆点拨 virtu [e]（功效，效力）＋al（……相关的）

robust [rəˈbʌst] *adj.* **a robust person is strong and healthy** 强健的

♥ The robust recovery of sick boy made his parents very happy.
生病男孩强健的康复让他的父母很高兴。

♥ The economic growth in Asia-Pacific area is forecast to be robust this year.
预计今年亚太地区的经济增长会很强健。

相关表达 近义词 healthy; powerful
反义词 delicate

organism [ˈɔːgənizəm] *n.* **an animal, plant, human, or any other living thing** 有机体

♥ Scientist found some organism living under the extreme weather in Antarctica.
科学家发现有一些有机体在北极极端的气候条件下生存。

♥ Viruses are not typically considered to be organisms because they are not capable of independent reproduction or metabolism.
病毒一般不被看做是有机体，因为它们不能独立繁殖或者新陈代谢。

记忆点拨 organ（器官）＋ism（整体）

thermodynamics [ˈθəːməudaiˈnæmik] *n.* **the science that deals with the relationship between heat and other forms of energy** 热力学

♥ Thermodynamics is an elective class in mechanical engineering department.
热力学是工程系的一门选修课。

♥ There are still lots of theoretical problems remain to solve in thermodynamics.
在热力学里还存在很多理论问题需要解决。

记忆点拨 thermo(热，热电）＋dynamic(动力的，动力学的）＋s(说)

moot [muːt] *adj.* **something that has not yet been decided or agreed, and about which people have different opinions** 争论未决的

♥ There are still several moot points to be clarified after the judge made sentence.
在法官宣判以前还有几点争论的问题需要澄清。

♥ Gun control and ownership is still considered moot by the public even after the congress passed the law.
即使在国会通过法案后，枪支控制和拥有一直是公众争论的问题。

run-down [rʌndaun] *adj.* **a building or area that is run-down is in very bad condition** 破旧的

♥ The boy rewound the run-down toy dog and watched it moving again.
男孩子重新包好这个破旧的玩具狗，又看着它动起来。

♥ The run-down watch caused him big trouble as he lost time in the forest.
这个破旧的表给他带来大麻烦，让他在森林里不知道时间。

记忆点拨 run(趋向) ＋down(向下)

friction [ˈfrikʃən] ***n.*** **the natural force that prevents one surface from sliding easily over another surface 摩擦**

♥ The force known as friction may be defined as the resistance encountered by one body moving over another.
摩擦力又可定义为是一个物体对另一个所接触物体的阻力。

♥ If friction were absent, a car would move forward forever once it started.
如果没有摩擦力，那么一辆车开动后就永远停不了了。

Lesson 38

contamination [kənˌtæmiˈneiʃən] *n.* **the act or process of contaminating 污染**

♥ The factory was fined heavily due to the contamination it made to the river.
由于工厂对河流造成的污染，工厂被重罚了。

♥ The congress passed strict law to enforce contamination control.
国会通过严格的法案来执行污染控制。

词组拓展 contamination from(受……的污染)
近义词 pollution

记忆点拨 contaminat [e](污染) ＋ation(过程)

sanitation [sæniˈteiʃən] *n.* **the protection of public health by removing and treating waste, dirty water etc. 卫生，卫生设备**

♥ Improved water supply and sanitation is the main reason behind re-election of the mayor.
改进的水供应和卫生条件是市长再次当选的主要原因。

♥ FDA enforces strict control on food sanitation procedure and guideline.
联邦药品管理局严格执行对食品卫生程序和指导的控制。

词组拓展 environmental sanitation 环境卫生

记忆点拨 sanitat [e](使卫生) ＋ion(行为)

sewage ['sju(:)idʒ] *n.* **the mixture of waste from the human body and used water that is carried away from houses by pipes under the ground** 污水

♥ Thousand tons of untreated sewage water flows into coastal water every year.
每年数千吨的未处理污水流入海水中。

♥ Municipal government invested a lot on sewage treatment.
市政府投入大量资金治理污水。

记忆点拨 sew [er](排水沟) +age

leakage ['li:kidʒ] *n.* **when gas, water etc. leaks in or out, or the amount of it that has leaked** 泄漏

♥ Leakage of the important company merge news caused dramatic price fluctuation in stock market.
重要的公司合并消息的泄露使得股票价格剧烈波动。

♥ Leakage in kitchen was found when the real estate inspected the new house.
当房产检查新房子的时候，厨房的泄露被发现了。

记忆点拨 leak(漏) +age(名词后缀)

intermittent [ˌintə(:)'mitənt] *adj.* **stopping and starting often and for short periods** 间歇的，断断续续的

♥ Intermittent gunshots could still be heard after the truce between two sides.
两边休战以后还能在街上听见间歇的枪声。

♥ People could still find intermittent news about famine in the remote area.
人们间歇还能听见远方关于饥荒的消息。

相关表达　近义词 irregular; periodic
反义词 continuous

记忆点拨　intermit(中断) +tent(形容词后缀)

carbonated　[kɑːbəˈneɪtɪd] ***adj.*** **carbonated drinks contain small bubbles** 碳化的，碳酸的

♥ Archaeologist did a thorough study on carbonated tissue found in the ancient tomb.
考古学家对在古代坟墓里找到的碳化的组织进行了全面的研究。

♥ Carbonated drinks are the single biggest source of refined sugar in the American diet.
碳酸饮料是美国食物里人工糖分的最大来源。

记忆点拨　carbon 碳+ ate（……化）+（d……的）

acidic　[əˈsɪdɪk] ***adj.*** **very sour** 酸的，酸性的

♥ Some bacteria are adaptive to acidic environment.
一些细菌能适应酸性环境。

♥ Acidic industrial deposition is the major pollutant source in Norway.
酸性的工业废弃物是挪威的主要污染物质。

记忆点拨　acid(酸) +ic（……的）

alcohol　[ˈælkəhɔl] ***n.*** **drinks such as beer or wine that contain a substance which can make you drunk** 酒精

♥ The cop stopped the drunk driver and gave him an alcohol test.
警察截住喝醉的司机给他进行酒精测试。

♥ It is forbidden by law to sell alcohol drinks to people under 21 in United States.

在美国出售酒精饮料给未满 21 岁的人是违法的。

disinfectant [dɪsɪn'fekt(ə)nt] *n.* **a chemical or a cleaning product that destroys bacteria** 消毒剂

♥ Disinfectant was sprayed after the deadly contagious disease was found in this building.
在楼里发现了致命的传染病以后，洒上了消毒剂。

♥ Disinfectant was sold out after the SARS news came out.
SARS 的新闻发布后，消毒剂被买光了。

记忆点拨 dis(不) ＋infect(传染，感染) ＋ant(物)

sterilize ['sterilaiz] *v.* **to make something completely clean by killing any bacteria in it** 消毒

♥ The teacher asked the students to sterilize the equipment before they started the experiment.
老师告诉学生在实验开始前给仪器消毒。

♥ Hospitals sometimes use high amount of radiation to sterilize medical instruments.
医院有时用高强度的放射线来给医疗仪器杀毒。

相关表达 **disinfect**

记忆点拨 sterile(消过毒的) ＋ize(使……)

ethanol [iːθɔnəl] *n.* **technical ETHYL ALCOHOL** 乙醇

♥ Ethanol is a clear, colorless liquid with characteristic, agreeable odor.
乙醇是一种清洁的、无色的液体，有很独特的、愉悦的气味。

♥ Usage of petrol-ethanol car encouraged by government.

政府鼓励使用乙醇汽油做动力的汽车。

bactericidal [bækˌtɪərɪˈsaɪdəl] ***adj.*** 杀菌的

♥ Researchers found a new bactericidal material that could kill bacteria and other micro-organisms more efficiently.

研究人员发现新的杀菌材料可以更有效地消灭细菌和其他微生物。

♥ Bactericidal effect of the newly discovered chemical is still a mystery to scientists.

新发明的化学药品的杀菌效果对科学家来说还是神秘的。

记忆点拨 bacteri [a]（细菌）＋c（……的）＋idal（行为的）

negligible [ˈneglidʒəbl] ***adj.*** **too slight or unimportant to have any effect** 可以忽略的，微不足道的

♥ The side effect of this medicine is negligible as long as you take it no more than three weeks.

只要你服用不超过三个星期，这种药物的副作用就可以忽略不计。

♥ The cancellation of the contract has negligible effect to the company's earning this quarter.

对于公司这个季度的赢利来说，这份合同的取消可以忽略不计。

记忆点拨 neglig [ent]（疏忽的）＋ible

methylated [ˈmeθɪleɪtɪd] ***adj.*** **a type of alcohol that is burned in lamps, heaters etc.** 加入甲醇的

♥ Methylated alcohol is allowed for industrial usage only.

加有甲醇的酒精只被允许作为工业用途。

♥ The company started a new project to produce more methylated alcohol in Chinese market due to increasing demand.

由于需求增长，公司开始一个新项目来生产更多面向中国市场的甲醇酒精。

记忆点拨 methyl(甲基) ＋ated（……的）

Lesson 39

confess [kənˈfes] *v.* **to admit, especially to the police, that you have done something wrong or illegal 承认**

♥ It is extremely difficult for him to confess his mistakes in public.
对他来说公开承认错误是非常困难的。

♥ The marketing manager confessed that he had no idea about why the sales volumes declined dramatically last month.
市场经理承认他不知道为什么上个月的销售急剧下降。

相关表达　近义词 acknowledge; admit
反义词 conceal

记忆点拨　con(加强) ＋fess(坦白，供认)

inspiration [ˌinspəˈreiʃən] *n.* **a good idea about what you should do, write, say etc., especially one which you get suddenly 灵感**

♥ This great drawing was originated from the inspiration of artist when he visited Paris.
这幅伟大的作品来自于他在巴黎旅游时获得的灵感。

♥ Inspiration cannot replace hard work in scientific research.
在科学研究中，灵感不能代替努力工作。

词组拓展　get(draw)inspiration from 从……得到启示

记忆点拨 in(向内) +spiration[(拉丁) 呼吸]

interweave [ˌintə(ː)ˈwiːv] *v.* **if two things are interwoven, they are closely related or combined in a complicated way** 交织

♥ Different emotions were interwoven in his heart when he heard the bankruptcy news of the company.

当他听到公司破产的新闻时，各种不同的感情交织在他心中。

♥ He interwove the information coming from different sources and concluded that the enemy will attack again soon.

他把不同来源的信息汇合起来并总结出敌人很快会再袭击。

记忆点拨 inter(在……之间) +weave(织)

afresh [əˈfreʃ] *adv.* **if you do something afresh, you do it again from the beginning** 重新

♥ He started afresh in hope that he could pass the exam next time.

他开始重新希望他能够通过考试。

♥ The city afresh filed federal aid after the heavy storm.

市政府在大雨过后重新开始政府资助的申请。

相关表达 近义词 again

记忆点拨 a(加强) +fresh(新鲜的)

discern [diˈsəːn] *v.* **to notice or understand something by thinking about it carefully** 辨明，领悟

♥ People could hardly discern his southern accent from his speech.
人们很难从他说话里分辨出他的南方口音。

♥ No economists could discern the globalization of capital flow thoroughly.
没有经济学家可以完全分辨出资金流动全球化。

相关表达　近义词 detect; know

记忆点拨　dis(分) ＋cern(察觉)

indescribable　[ˌindiˈskraibəbl] ***adj.*** **something that is indescribable is so terrible, so good, so strange etc. that you cannot describe it, or it is too difficult to describe** 无法描述的

♥ The craziness of crowd was indescribable when the movie star showed on the stage.
当电影明星走上舞台时人群的疯狂是无法形容的。

♥ The beauty of the lake was indescribable in words.
湖水的美丽无法形容。

相关表达　近义词 exceptional; remarkable
反义词 describable

记忆点拨　in(不) ＋describ [e] (描写) ＋able(可……的)

blur　[bləː] ***v.*** **to become difficult to see or to make something difficult to see, because the edges are not clear** 使……模糊不清

♥ The heavy rain blurred the wind window of the car and the driver was forced to reduce speed.
暴雨模糊了车窗，司机被迫减低速度。

♥ Tears blurred her eyes when she saw her husband come back.
当她看到丈夫回来后，泪水模糊了她的眼睛。

相关表达　近义词 cloud; smear

yeast　[jiːst] *n.* **an agent of ferment or activity** 激动

♥ His heart was full of yeast when he learned the news that he was admitted by the school.
当他知道自己被学校录取了时，他的内心充满了激动。

♥ He could not hide his yeast when he heard the President mentioned his name in the meeting.
当他听到自己的名字在会议上被总统提及时，难以控制自己的激动。

fathom　[ˈfæðəm] *v.* **to understand what something means after thinking about it carefully** 领悟，彻底了解

♥ It is hard for a high school student to fathom the concept of calculus.
对高中生来说彻底了解微积分的概念是很困难的。

♥ Few people could fathom the intention of artist when they saw the drawing.
几乎没有人在第一次看到这幅画时就能领悟艺术家的意图。

相关表达　近义词 understand; comprehend

interminably　[inˈtəːminəbli] *adv.* **very long and boring** 没完没了地

♥ He boasted interminably about his venture to the remote island.
他没完没了地夸耀自己在荒岛上的探险。

♥ He could not wait interminably for her to change mind.
他无法没完没了地等待她回心转意。

相关表达　反义词 terminable

记忆点拨　in(无) ＋term(界限) ＋inable

winkle　[ˈwiŋkl] *v.* **to get information from someone who does not want to give it to you** 挖掘

- Journalists were enthusiastic at winkle the intention of Greenspan between his words.
  记者们热衷于挖掘格林斯潘言语间的含义。
- It is a waste of time to winkle the meaning of the manager's words as he always changes him mind quickly.
  挖掘经理话语的含义是浪费时间，因为他总是很快就改变主意。

incidentally　[ɪnsɪˈdentəlɪ] ***adv.*** **used to add more information to what you have just said, or to introduce a new subject that you have just thought of** 顺便说一下

- He visited his former advisor's home incidentally when he went to the city on a business trip.
  当他去那个城市出差时，他顺便拜访了自己以前的导师。
- The company's name was mentioned incidentally by the banker when he commented on the stock market.
  当那个银行家评价股市时，公司的名字被他顺便提及了。

记忆点拨　incidental(偶然的) ＋ly (……地)

pertinent　[ˈpəːtinənt] ***adj.*** **directly relating to something that is being considered** 中肯的

♥ The mayor made a pertinent speech about economic situation in election campaign.
市长在竞选中做了一个中肯的关于经济情况的演讲。

♥ The teacher revealed her pertinent view on the child when she met with his parents.
老师在和家长见面时表明了自己对这个孩子的中肯的看法。

相关表达　近义词 relevant

记忆点拨　per(强意) ＋ tinent[(拉丁) 持，握]

flirt　[flə:t] *v.* **to behave towards someone in a way that shows that you are sexually attracted to them, although you do not really want a relationship with them** 调情

♥ The girl's face turned red when she heard the flirting words of her boy friend.
女孩子听到她男朋友调情的话时，脸红了。

♥ She flirts with every handsome man she meets.
她和所遇到的每个美男子调情。

词组拓展　flirt with sb. 和……调情

inmost　['inməust] ***adj.*** **your inmost feelings, desires etc. are your most personal and secret ones** 内心深处

♥ He is an extreme introvert person and seldom discloses his inmost feeling.
他是一个非常内向的人，很少表露自己的内心感受。

♥ People could learn the inmost feeling of Beethoven from his symphony masterpieces.
人们可以通过贝多芬的交响乐作品来领略他的内心世界。

词组拓展　one's inmost feelings [thoughts] 内心深处的感情[思想]

相关表达　近义词 private; secret

记忆点拨　in(在……内) +most(最)

Lesson 40

signature [ˈsignitʃə] *n.* **your name written in the way you usually write it, for example at the end of a letter, or on a cheque etc. to show that you have written it** 签名，标记

♥ The application form requests a signature of the applicant at the bottom of the page.

申请表要求申请人在底部签名。

♥ An unexpected ending is the signature of O Henry's short novel.

一个意想不到的结局是欧·亨利短篇小说的特征。

词组拓展 over sb.'s signature 经某人签名

记忆点拨 sign(签名) ＋ature＝ure(名词后缀)

infinity [inˈfiniti] *n.* **a space or distance without limits or an end** 无穷

♥ We need to foster the children's curiosity toward the infinity of the universe.

我们应该培养孩子们对宇宙无限性的好奇心。

♥ It is hard to describe the concept of infinity in word.

用文字来解释无穷的概念很难。

词组拓展 to infinity 直到无限

记忆点拨 in(无) ＋finity(有限)

ray [rei] *n.* **a straight narrow beam of light from the sun or moon** 光线

♥ A ray of sunshine shone through the windows.
一缕阳光从窗外照进来。

♥ Two rays of car lights pierced the darkness.
两束车灯刺破黑暗。

相关表达 近义词 beam; gleam

energize ['enədʒaiz] *v.* **to make someone feel more determined and energetic** 给与……能量

♥ The success of the campaign is relevant to whether this candidate can energize the voters.
选举获胜的结果和竞选人能否鼓动选民相关。

♥ The coach kept on energizing the team members before the game began.
比赛开始前教练不断给队员鼓劲。

词组拓展 energize a person for work 激励某人从事工作

相关表达 energetic *adj.* 积极的

记忆点拨 energ [y](活力，能量) +ize(使有……)

rhythm ['riðəm] *n.* **a regular repeated pattern of sounds or movements** 节奏

♥ The gentle rhythm of the music can comfort people.
音乐柔和的节奏可以让人心情缓和。

♥ People are dancing around the bonfire to the exciting rhythms of drum music.
人们围着篝火随着激烈的鼓点跳舞。

词组拓展 the rhythm of dancing 跳舞的节拍

相关表达 近义词 beat; tempo

transmit [trænz'mit] *v.* **to send or pass something from one person, place or thing to another** 传送

♥ People used to have the bias that HIV can only be transmitted through sexual intercourse.
人们从前有偏见认为艾滋病只能通过性传染。

♥ Now people can use email to transmit information effectively worldwide.
现在人们通过电子邮件在全世界有效传送信息。

词组拓展 transmit-receive *adj*. 收发（两用）的
近义词 convey; send

相关表达 transmittable *adj*. 可传送的

记忆点拨 trans(转移) ＋mit(发送)

exquisite [ˈekskwizit] ***adj.*** **extremely beautiful and very delicately made** 高雅的

♥ The dress that you wore to the charity party was exquisite.
你在慈善晚会上穿的那件晚装很高雅。

♥ The musician played the violin with exquisite style.
音乐家优雅地拉着小提琴。

相关表达 近义词 delicate; marvelous; magnificent

记忆点拨 ex（……之外）＋quisite（寻找）

phenomena [fiˈnɔminə] ***n.*** **something that happens or exists in society, science or nature, especially something that is studied because it is difficult to understand** 现象

♥ Some natural phenomena still remain mysterious to human being such as mirage.
有些自然现象对人类来说还是神秘的，比如海市蜃楼。

♥ Child abuse, domestic violence are all social phenomena that needs public attention.

虐待儿童、家庭暴力都是需要公众关注的社会问题。

词组拓展 a social phenomenon 社会现象

the phenomenon of nature 自然现象

crest [krest] ***n.*** **the top or highest point of something such as a hill or a wave** 浪峰；顶峰

♥ He is trying to stay sailing on the crest of the wave.

他尽力在浪尖上滑滑水板。

♥ This mid-forty businessman is at the crest of his career.

这个四十中旬的生意人正处于事业的顶峰期。

词组拓展 crest of hill/wave 山/浪尖

相关表达 近义词 peak; summit

trough [ˈtrɔːf] ***n.*** **the hollow area between two waves** 波谷

♥ If you plan to have long-term investment in the stock market, you should not worry too much about the peak and trough.

如果你想在股市做长期投资，那你就不应该过多担心高峰和低谷期。

♥ People need encouragement at the trough of their life.

在生活低谷时，人都需要鼓励。

vertical [ˈvəːtikəl] ***adj.*** **pointing up in a line that forms an angle of 90° with a flat surface** 垂直的

♥ Please measure the wall carefully and keep the rule vertical.

测量墙壁请仔细并保持尺的水平。

♥ She looked over the cliff and found that she was standing at the edge of a vertical drop.
她俯视悬崖发现自己站在了一个峭壁的边缘。

相关表达 近义词 perpendicular
反义词 horizontal

记忆点拨 vertic(最高点）＋al

horizontal [ˌhɔriˈzɔntl] ***adj.*** **flat and level** 水平的

♥ The doctor asked the patient to lie down on the horizontal bed.
大夫要求患者平躺在水平的床上。

♥ The acrobatic is standing on a horizontal steel wire.
杂技演员站在水平的钢丝上。

相关表达 **horizon** ***n.*** 水平线

记忆点拨 horizon(水平线）＋tal

actuality [ˌæktjuˈæliti] ***n.*** **facts, rather than things that people believe or imagine** 现实

♥ When we grow up, we have to learn how to handle all the problems in actuality.
当我们长大成人，我们就必须学会如何处理现实中的各种问题。

♥ People may have different personality in the cyber world than in actuality.
在网络世界里人们可能拥有和现实中不一样的性格。

相关表达 近义词 reality

记忆点拨 actual(真实的）＋ity(使成为)

catastrophic [ˌkætəˈstrɔfɪk] ***adj.*** **a terrible event in which there is a lot of destruction, suffering, or death 大灾难的**

♥ The event of September 11th brought catastrophic impact on American people's life.

"九一一" 事件给美国人民的生活带来了灾难性的影响。

♥ The disclosure of the company's annual financial report brought catastrophic decline of its stock price.

公司的年度财政报告的披露给股票价格带来灾难性的下跌。

相关表达 catastrophe *n.* 大灾难

记忆点拨 catastroph [e](大灾难) +ic (……的)

particle [ˈpɑːtikl] ***n.*** **a very small piece of something 微粒**

♥ The motorcar is not working well, maybe because there are some dust particles inside.

汽车运行得不是很好，也许是因为有灰尘小颗粒进入了。

♥ We can't see most of the particles by naked eyes.

大多数微粒都无法用肉眼看见。

记忆点拨 part(部分) +cle(指小词)

maturity [məˈtjuəriti] ***n.*** **the quality of behaving in a sensible way like an adult 成熟**

♥ This job calls for a man with a great deal of maturity.

这项工作要求一个富有经验的人来干。

♥ As an adult, you are expected to have both intellectual and physical maturity.

作为成年人，你应该拥有心智和身体的成熟。

相关表达 mature *adj.* 成熟的

词组拓展 come to maturity 成熟

记忆点拨 matur [e](成熟的) +ity(使成为)

undulating [ˈʌndjuleitiŋ] *adj.* 波浪形的

♥ Our boat is floating on the undulating waves with leisure.
我们的小船在波浪上悠闲地漂浮着。

♥ Hiking on the undulating hills, we enjoyed a lot of beautiful scenery.
走在起伏的山路上，我们欣赏了很多美景。

记忆点拨 undulat [e](波动，起伏) +ing

tremor [ˈtremə] *n.* **a slight shaking movement in your body that you cannot control, especially because you are ill, weak, or upset** 震颤

♥ You can feel her nervous through the tremor in her voice.
你能通过她嗓音的颤抖感觉到她的紧张。

♥ The stroke caused him paralysis and uncontrollable tremor.
中风使得他瘫痪并无法控制地颤动。

相关表达 tremulous *adj.* 颤抖的
近义词 shaking; trembling

gravitational [ˌgræviˈteiʃənəl] *adj.* **related to or resulting from the force of gravity** 地心引力的

♥ Without the presence of the gravitational force, everything inside the spaceship needs to be fastened.

由于没有了地心引力，飞船里的东西都需要被固定住。

♥ Newton found out that apples fall into ground because of the gravitational force of the earth.
牛顿发现苹果掉到地上是因为地球引力。

相关表达 gravity *n.* 重力

记忆点拨 gravitat [e]（受引力作用）＋ion（过程）＋al（……的）

Unit 6

Lesson 41

technique [tek'niːk] ***n.*** **a special way of doing something 技术**

♥ The development of digital imagining technique totally transformed people's habit of taking photos.
数字成像技术的发展完全改变人们照相的习惯。

♥ The technique of human intelligence is still far from perfection.
人工智能技术离完美还差很远。

相关表达 technical *adj.* 技术的；technology *n.* 科技

tough [tʌf] ***adj.*** **difficult to do or deal with 强硬的**

♥ His tough attitude in the negotiation infuriated his client.
他在洽谈中强硬的态度惹怒了他的客户。

♥ The tough new traffic code is being introduced this week.
新的更严格的交通法规这星期实行。

相关表达 近义词 hard；firm

resentful [ri'zentful] ***adj.*** **feeling angry and upset about something that you think is unfair 忿恨不满的**

♥ She was resentful of anybody's attempt to interfere her work.
她对别人想干涉她工作的企图很忿恨不满。

♥ He is so narrow-minded. Once he had an argue with you, he would be resentful toward you forever.

他这人心胸狭窄。如果一旦有过争执，就会一直忿恨不平。

记忆点拨 resent(愤恨）＋ful(充满……的)

assign [ə'sain] ***v.*** **to give someone a particular job or make them responsible for a particular person or thing** 分配，指派

♥ The manager assigned the projects to different team members respectively in accordance with their skills.
经理根据组员的技能分别分配了不同的项目。

♥ The secretary was assigned to take notes for the meeting.
秘书被分派做会议记录。

相关表达 近义词 allocate; appoint

记忆点拨 as(朝，向……）＋sign(打上记号)

mahout [mə'haut] ***n.*** **someone who rides and trains elephants** 驯象人

♥ The mahout directed the elephant to move the lumber.
驯象人指挥大象运送木材。

♥ The mahouts have developed a harmonious relationship with their elephants.
驯象人跟他们的大象建立了和谐的关系。

calf [kɑːf] ***n.*** **the baby of a cow, or of some other large animals, such as an elephant** 幼仔

♥ Elephants usually received training when they are still calves.
大象通常从幼仔开始就接受训练。

♥ The adult elephant were taking care of the calf.
成年象在照顾小象仔。

pine [pain] ***v.* to wither or waste away from longing or grief** 消瘦

♥ The woman pined away after her beloved husband died in a car accident.
她丈夫在车祸去世后她迅速消瘦。

♥ You need to take care of yourself and stop pining away.
你需要好好照顾自己，别再瘦下去了。

underline [ˌʌndəˈlain] ***v.* to show that something is important** 着重说明，强调

♥ The speaker highlighted the figures in the power-point to underline their importance.
演说者加亮了幻灯片里面的数字部分来强调它们的重要性。

♥ The teacher raised his voice in talking with the students to underline his concern.
老师在和学生谈话的时候提高了声调来强调他的担心。

相关表达 近义词 emphasize; stress

记忆点拨 under(在……下) ＋line(线)

keep [kiːp] ***n.* the cost of providing food and a home for someone** 生计

♥ The college students begin to earn their keeps at the age of 18.
大学生们从十八岁开始自谋生计。

♥ Her father is the person who earns the keeps for the whole family.
她父亲要供养整个家庭。

subservient [sʌbˈsəːviənt] *adj.* **always obeying another person and doing everything they want you to do—used when someone seems too weak and powerless** 屈从的

♥ The government of the late Qing dynasty was subservient to the foreign invaders.
晚清政府屈服于外国侵略者。

♥ It is different to be courteous than to be subservient.
礼貌待人和卑躬屈膝是不同的。

词组拓展 be subservient to 追随，屈从

相关表达 subservience *n.* 屈服

记忆点拨 sub(在下)＋servient(从属的)

plunge [plʌndʒ] *v.* **to move, fall, or be thrown suddenly forwards or downwards** 向前冲

♥ The hunters plunged into the forest in pursuit of game.
猎人们冲入森林追捕猎物。

♥ The witness saw the aircraft plunged to the building and burst into flames.
目击者说飞机俯冲至大楼里后化为一团火焰。

tame [teim] *adj.* **a tame animal or bird is not wild any longer, because it has been trained to live with people** 养驯服了的

♥ His tame dog always stayed quiet in the backyard and never disturbed the neighbors.

他的温顺的狗总是安静地呆在后院，从不打扰邻居。

♥ It takes time to train the pet into a tame one.

把宠物训练成驯服的需要时间。

相关表达　近义词 gentle; obedient.

tether [ˈteðə] ***v.*** **to tie an animal to a post so that it can only move around within a limited area**(用绳）拴

♥ The infant was tethered to the baby crib in case that he may fall off during sleep.

为了防止睡觉时掉下来，这个婴儿被拴在了婴儿床上。

♥ The dog was tethered to the gate of the building for safety guard.

这只狗被拴在大门口守卫安全。

ticklish [ˈtikliʃ] ***adj.*** **a ticklish situation or problem is difficult and must be dealt with carefully, especially because you may upset people** 难对付的，棘手的

♥ I understand that fundraising is a ticklish matter.

我明白筹集资金是很棘手的工作。

♥ We need to discuss together who shall be assigned this ticklish project.

我们需要一起讨论由谁来完成这个难对付的工程。

记忆点拨　tickl [e]（搔，发痒）+ish

alarming [əˈlɑːmɪŋ] ***adj.*** **making you feel worried or frightened** 引起惊恐的

♥ The report on today's newspaper showed that there is an alarming rise in the use of alcohol by teenagers.

今天报纸上的报道说青少年酗酒率的上升让人不安。

♥ The alarming abuse of the narcotic has caused the concern of the medical field.
令人不安的滥用镇静剂行为已经引起了医学界的关注。

记忆点拨 alarm(警报，惊慌）＋ing

accompaniment [ə'kʌmpənimənt] ***n.*** **music that is played in the background at the same time as another instrument or singer that plays or sings the main tune** 伴奏，陪伴

♥ She sang to the accompaniment of the piano.
她由钢琴伴唱。

♥ The husband complained that his wife always request his accompaniment when go shopping.
丈夫抱怨说他妻子上街购物时总要求他陪伴。

词组拓展 play an accompaniment 伴奏
music accompaniment 音乐伴奏

记忆点拨 accompani [y](陪伴，伴奏）＋ment(行为）

soothe [suːð] ***v.*** **to make someone feel calmer and less anxious, upset, or angry** 镇定

♥ His gentle singing soothed the crying baby and made him falling into sleep smoothly.
他温和的歌唱安抚了哭泣的婴儿并让他平静地入睡了。

♥ A cup of ice tea soothed her nerve before the exam.
考试前的一杯冰茶安抚了他的紧张。

词组拓展 soothe sb.'s rage 平息某人的怒气

相关表达 近义词 calm; comfort

chant [tʃɑːnt] ***n.*** **a regularly repeated tune, often with many words sung on one note, especially used for religious prayers 单调的歌**

♥ The monotonous chant can easily make people drowsy.

单调的歌声容易让人变困。

♥ The fans on the stadium were singing the chant of the soccer game while they entered the field.

当足球队入场时，看台上的球迷们唱起了球队的队歌。

相关表达 近义词 ballad; prayer

reinforce [ˌriːinˈfɔːs] ***v.*** **to give support to an opinion, idea, or feeling, and make it stronger 加强**

♥ The on-site interview afterward reinforced his hope to get the job offer.

随后的当场面试加强了他得到这个工作的信心。

♥ The final technical report of the car accident reinforced the initial police report.

对车祸的最终技术调查加强了最初的警察报告。

相关表达 近义词 intensify; fortify

记忆点拨 re(重复) +inforce(enforce)(加强)

endearing [inˈdiəriŋ] ***adj.*** **making someone love or like you 惹人喜爱的**

♥ She appears very attractive because of the endearing smile.

由于她惹人喜爱的微笑，显得很吸引人。

♥ The candidate has an endearing charm for the voters.

这个竞选人对于选民有一种惹人喜爱的魅力。

记忆点拨 endear(使亲密) +ing

epithet [ˈepiθet] ***n.*** **a word or short phrase used to describe someone, especially when praising them or saying something unpleasant about them** 称呼

♥ These good friends made up different interesting epithets for one another.

这些好朋友互相取不同的有趣绰号。

♥ The baby will crawl toward his mother when she calls his epithet.

他母亲呼唤他的名字时，孩子就会向她爬过去。

susceptible [səˈseptəbl] ***adj.*** **a susceptible person is easily influenced or attracted by someone or something** 易受感动的

♥ She is susceptible to moving stories or songs.

她容易被感人的故事或者歌曲打动。

♥ To be a good lawyer, you can't be susceptible to the witness's testimony.

要想成为一个好律师，你不能轻易被证人的证词感动。

词组拓展 be susceptible 易受影响的

相关表达 近义词 impressionable; open

记忆点拨 suscept(感病体) +ible（……的）

blandishment [ˈblændɪʃmənt] ***n.*** 奉承

♥ You can't take his words seriously. It is just blandishment.

你别把他的话当真，只是奉承话而已。

♥ The customer was totally confused by the salesman's blandishment.

顾客完全被销售员的奉承话迷惑了。

记忆点拨 blandish(奉承) +ment

lash [læʃ] *v.* **if the wind, sea etc. lashes something, it hits it with violent force** 猛烈地甩

♥ The dog lashed its tails in front of his owner to show happiness.

狗在主人面前迅速地摆动着尾巴表示高兴。

♥ The rain lashes against the window.

大雨敲打窗户。

curl [kəːl] *v.* **to form a twisted or curved shape, or to make something do this** 使卷曲

♥ She went to the Salon to curl her hair.

她去发廊把头发弄卷。

♥ When you make the gift wrap, please remember to curl the ends of the ribbon.

当你包装礼品时，请记住把缎带的两端卷起来。

Lesson 42

earthquake [ˈəːθkweik] ***n.*** **a sudden shaking of the earth's surface that often causes a lot of damage 地震**

♥ 20 deaths have been confirmed after the earthquake.

地震后已经证实有20人死亡。

♥ All the buildings in Tang shan City completed after the 1976 earthquake are all quakeproof.

唐山市在1976地震后修建的建筑都是防震的。

记忆点拨 earth(地) +quake(震动)

slumber [ˈslʌmbə] ***v.*** **to sleep 睡眠**

♥ I can easily slumber even in a noisy environment.

即使在嘈杂的环境里我也能轻易睡着。

♥ He is just slumbered after one day's hard work.

经过一天辛苦劳动，他刚刚睡着。

相关表达 近义词 doze; nap

ninepin [ˈnainpinz] ***n.*** 九柱戏中的木柱

♥ Trees were going down like ninepins in the strong wind.

劲风中树木像九柱戏的木柱一样倒下。

♥ Ninepins was the most popular form of bowling in much of the United States from colonial times until the early nineteenth century.

九柱戏是美国从殖民时代到十九世纪早期的一种最流行的保龄球形式。

记忆点拨 nine(九）＋pin(栓）

rigid ['ridʒid] *adj.* **rigid methods, systems etc. are very strict and difficult to change** 坚硬的

♥ Since the wind is quite strong at night, we need a rigid support for our tents.
因为晚上风很大，我们需要一个坚硬的帐篷支柱。

♥ The judge is famous for his rigid adherence to rules.
这个法官以严格执行法规闻名。

相关表达 近义词 stiff; fixed

delicate ['delikit] *adj.* **needing to be dealt with carefully or sensitively in order to avoid problems or failure** 敏感的

♥ Our lab needs to purchase a delicate set of scales for the new experiments.
我们实验室为了新实验需要购置精密的刻度。

♥ A good writer needs to have delicate perception.
一个好的作家需要有敏锐的观察力。

相关表达 近义词 sensitive

记忆点拨 delica [cy]（微妙）＋te

seismometer [saiz'mɔmitə] *n.* **a detecting device that receives seismic impulses** 地震仪

♥ With the aid of seismometer, people can more accurate record the earthquake.
有了地震仪的帮助，人们能更精确地记录地震活动。

♥ The record of the seismometer is very comprehensive.
地震仪的记录非常全面。

记忆点拨 seismo(地震) +meter(计)

penholder [ˈpenˌhəʊldə(r)] *n.* **a rack or cup for holding a pen or pens** 笔架

♥ There are several nice-looking pens in the penholder.
在笔架里放着好几支很好看的钢笔。

♥ There is a book, a penholder and a laptop on his desk.
在他的书桌上摆着一本书，一个笔架和一个笔记本电脑。

记忆点拨 pen(钢笔) +holder(架)

legibly [ˈledʒəbli] *adv.* **written or printed clearly enough for you to read** 字迹清楚地

♥ You need to have a habit of writing legibly, otherwise your grade will be degraded in exam.
你应该养成书写清晰的好习惯，否则考试中会被扣分的。

♥ It is hard to writing legibly in a moving car.
在行进的车里很难写字清晰。

相关表达 近义词 clearly; readably

记忆点拨 legible(清晰的) +y

drum [drʌm] *n.* **a musical instrument made of skin stretched over a circular frame, played by hitting it with your hand or a stick** 鼓状物；鼓

♥ The film is rolled on a drum.
胶卷是卷在圆筒上的。

♥ They are dancing at the beat of the drum.
他们随着鼓点声跳舞。

wriggle [ˈrigl] *v.* **to twist your body from side to side with small quick movements 扭动**

♥ The tunnel was quite dark and narrow, but the rabbit managed to wriggle through it.
这个地道又黑又窄，不过这只兔子竟然扭动着钻过来了。

♥ The snake wriggled through the grass.
这条蛇在草里蜿蜒爬行。

词组拓展 wriggle out of 慢慢设法摆脱（困境）

相关表达 近义词 twist; wiggle

bluebottle [ˈbluːbɔt(ə)l] *n.* **a large blue fly 绿头苍蝇**

♥ This bluebottle in the room irritated me a lot.
屋里这只苍蝇让我很烦躁。

♥ The bluebottles flew over the garbage can.
苍蝇在垃圾箱上方飞来飞去。

记忆点拨 blue(蓝色) ＋bottle(瓶子)

graph [grɑːf] *n.* **a drawing that uses a line or lines to show how two or more sets of measurements are related to each other 图表**

♥ The graph of this season's sale record is very detailed.
这个季度的销售记录图表非常详细。

♥ They made a graph of the weather degree every day for a month.

他们画了一幅表示一个月内每天气温的曲线图。

相关表达 近义词 chart; diagram

graphic ['græfik] *adj.* **connected with or including drawing, printing, or designing** 图示的

♥ The graphic presentation is very impressive to the audience.

图表的演示让观众印象深刻。

♥ Graphic record is more vivid than a verbal one.

图表的记录比语言的更生动。

记忆点拨 graph(图表) ＋ic（……的）

longitudinal [lɔndʒi'tju:dinl] *adj.* **going from top to bottom, not across** 纵向的

♥ The navigator needs to make a longitudinal reckoning.

领航员需要进行经度的计算。

♥ The workers carefully made longitudinal measurement of the machine.

工人们仔细测量机身的长度。

记忆点拨 longitud [e]（经度，经线）＋inal

transverse ['trænzvə:s] *adj.* **lying or placed across something** 横向的

♥ The highway was cut by a transverse road.

高速公路被一条横穿的马路截断。

♥ There are many transverse bridges on Beijing's crossroad.

在北京的十字路口有很多横穿马路的天桥。

记忆点拨 trans(横) ＋verse(转)

Lesson 43

mercury [ˈməːkjuri] ***n.*** **the planet that is nearest the sun** 水星

♥ Mercury is the planet closest in distance to Sun, before Venus.
水星是离太阳距离最近的星球，其次是金星。

♥ Mercury has a sidereal period of revolution about the sun of 88.0 days.
水星围绕太阳公转所需的周期为88.0天。

hydrogen [ˈhaidrəudʒən] ***n.*** **a colourless gas that is the lightest of all gases, forms water when it combines with oxygen, and is used to produce ammonia and other chemicals** 氢气

♥ Hydrogen is the lightest gas which can combines with oxygen to form water.
氢气球是最轻的空气，可以和氧气混合形成水。

♥ That hydrogen-filled balloon is floating high above the sky.
那个充满了氢气的气球高高飘在空中。

prevailing [priˈveiliŋ] ***adj.*** **existing or accepted in a particular place or at a particular time** 普遍的

♥ The prevailing fashion trend of this spring is Chinese traditional dress.
今年春季的时装流行趋势是中国传统服装。

♥ The prevailing opinion of the community is to destruct this chemical factory.

社区的普遍意见是拆毁这座化工厂。

相关表达 近义词 prevalent; current

记忆点拨 prevail(流行，盛行) ＋ing

uniquely [juːˈniːkli] ***adv.*** 唯一地

♥ This artist is drawing pictures in his uniquely special posture.
这位艺术家正用自己独创的奇特姿势作画。

♥ She is the uniquely reasonable people in the family.
她是这家唯一理智的人了。

记忆点拨 unique(唯一的) ＋ly（……地）

rational [ˈræʃənl] ***adj.*** **rational thoughts, decisions etc. are based on reasons rather than emotions** 合理的

♥ You need to submit a rational proposal to persuade the committee.
你需要提交一份合理的计划书来说服委员会。

♥ You need to have rational action even in emergency.
即使在紧急情况下，你也需要理智行动。

相关表达 近义词 reasonable

记忆点拨 ration(定量) ＋al

radio frequency 无线电频率

♥ You need to adjust your two walkie-talkies into the same radio frequency to communicate.
你需要把你的两个步话机调整到同样的频率来通话。

♥ Every radio station has its own radio frequency.
每个广播电台都有自己专门的无线电频率。

cm *n.* 厘米

♥ His height is 178cm.
他身高 178 厘米。

♥ 1 meter is 100cm.
一米等于一百厘米。

emission [iˈmiʃən] *n.* **the act of sending out light, heat, gas etc.** 散发

♥ The city began implementing a more stringent standard of the car's emission.
这个城市开始实行更加严格的汽车尾气排放标准。

♥ The temperature of the room is quite high because of the emission of heat in a fire.
由于从火炉中发出的热，屋里的温度很高。

记忆点拨 emi [t](散发) ＋ssion(状态)

interstellar [ˈint(ə)ːˈstelə] *adj.* **happening or existing between the stars** 星际的

♥ The movie Star Wars is a fiction of the interstellar wars in the future.
电影星球大战是关于未来星际大战的科幻片。

♥ Interstellar travel is a remote possibility.
星际旅行是一种遥远的可能。

记忆点拨 inter(在……之间) ＋stellar(星的)

rendezvous [ˈrɔndivuː] *n.* **a place where two or more people have arranged to meet** 约会地点

♥ This park is a favorite rendezvous for lovers.
这个公园是情侣们最喜欢的约会地点。

♥ You need to clarify with him on the phone about the time and rendezvous of the date.
你需要和他在电话里说清楚约会的时间和地点。

相关表达　近义词 get-together; meeting

记忆点拨　来自法语 rendez-vous

Lesson 44

commonplace [ˈkɔmənpleis] *adj.* **happening or existing in many places, and therefore not special or unusual** 平凡的

♥ Some scientists believe that soon it will be commonplace for people to travel to the moon.

一些科学家相信，不用多久，人们到月球旅行会变成常见的事。

♥ It is now becoming more commonplace to have your own car in Beijing.

现在在北京拥有自己的私家车越来越普通了。

相关表达 近义词 ordinary

记忆点拨 common(普通的) ＋place(位置)

aberrant [æˈberənt] *adj.* **not usual or normal** 脱离常轨的，异常的

♥ Homosexual used to be regarded an aberrant sexuality.

同性恋曾被认为是异常的性特征。

♥ Genius usually had aberrant behavior in normal people's eyes.

在常人眼里，天才经常有异常的行为。

记忆点拨 ab(远离) ＋errant

trivial [ˈtriviəl] *adj.* **not serious, important, or valuable** 微不足道的，琐细的

♥ You need to give your priority to those important issues, not trivial one.

你需要优先考虑那些重要的事情，而不是无关紧要的。

♥ Don't argue with your mother over these trivial matters.

别和你母亲在小事上争论不休。

词组拓展 put the trivial above important 轻重倒置

相关表达 近义词 trifling; petty

记忆点拨 trivia(琐事) +l (……的)

predominant [pri'dɔminənt] ***adj.*** **more powerful, more common, or more easily noticed than others** 占优势的，起支配作用的

♥ The manager played a predominant role in the company's decision making.

经理在公司的决策中起着举足轻重的作用。

♥ The predominant feature of her character is aggressive.

她性格的主要特征是好强。

相关表达 近义词 superior; principal

记忆点拨 pre(前) +dominant(支配的)

manifest ['mænifest] ***v.*** **to show a feeling, attitude etc.** 表明

♥ *The Independent Declaration* manifested the desire to freedom among American people.

《独立宣言》表明了美国人民对自由的渴望。

♥ The unemployment rate manifested the severe economic situation.

失业率表明了严峻的经济形势。

pristine ['pristain] ***adj.*** **extremely fresh or clean** 纯洁的，质朴的

♥ The baby's smile is showing pristine innocence.
孩子的微笑表露出天真无邪。

♥ The national park of Yellowstone reserved the pristine natural view.
黄石国家公园保留了原始的自然景观。

stereotype ['stiəriəutaip] ***n.*** **a belief or idea of what a particular type of person or thing is like** 陈规

♥ It is a stereotype that Chinese are all good at mathematics.
中国人的数学都很好是一个陈规。

♥ It's wrong to stereotype people, as if they were all alike.
把人们看成都是一样的，这是错误的。

记忆点拨 stereo(立体) ＋type(铅字)

vernacular [və'nækjulə] ***n.*** **a form of a language that ordinary people use, especially one that is not the official language** 方言

♥ People in Taiwan and Fujian speak the same vernacular.
台湾和福建人民说同一种方言。

♥ Usually people who speak the same vernacular share the same custom.
一般来说，说同一种方言的人有共同的风俗。

相关表达 近义词 dialect

记忆点拨 verna(土生土长的奴隶) ＋cular

incumbent [in'kʌmbənt] ***adj.*** **if it is incumbent upon you to do something, it is your duty or responsibility to do it** 义不容辞的，有责任的

♥ I felt it was incumbent on us all to help our classmates in trouble.
我感到我们大家都来帮助有麻烦的同学是义不容辞的。

♥ It is incumbent on the parents to supervise their children before 18.
在孩子满十八周岁以前，父母有义务指导他们。

词组拓展 be incumbent upon sb. to do sth.
不容某人推辞（做某事的）责任

相关表达 近义词 responsible

记忆点拨 in(在……上) ＋cumbent(躺下)

preliminary [pri'liminəri] ***adj.*** **happening before something that is more important, often in order to prepare for it** 初步的

♥ To obtain doctoral candidacy, you need to pass the preliminary exam first.
要取得博士候选资格，你需要先通过初步考试。

♥ The recruiter decides to have a preliminary screening of the received resumes.
招聘人员决定把收到的简历先初步筛选一遍。

相关表达 近义词 initial
反义词 final

记忆点拨 pre(先于) ＋liminary(开头的)

proposition [ˌprɔpə'ziʃən] ***n.*** **a statement that consists of a carefully considered opinion or judgment** 主张

She is so stubbornly to reject the proposition of the mayor candidate on the urban planning.
她很顽固地拒绝市长候选人在城市规划上的主张。

The law students are fiercely debating the proposition "All Men Are Born Equal".
法学生们在激烈地辩论"人生来平等"的主张。

记忆点拨 propos [e](提议) ＋ition(名词后缀)

preferential [ˌprefəˈrenʃəl] ***adj.*** **preferential treatment, rates etc. are deliberately different in order to give an advantage to particular people** 优先的

US government announced to renew the Preferential Duties relationship with China.
美国政府宣布延续中国的关税最惠国待遇。

Diplomats are usually given preferential treatment in visa worldwide.
外交官基本能在全世界享受签证的优先待遇。

词组拓展 preferential duties 特惠关税

记忆点拨 prefer(更喜欢，宁愿) ＋ential

controversial [ˌkɔntrəˈvəːʃəl] ***adj.*** **causing a lot of disagreement, because many people have strong opinions about the subject being discussed** 引起争论的

"Hero" is a controversial movie of martial arts.
《英雄》是一部有争议的武打片。

It has been a controversial topic in scientists since the introduction of clone technology.
自从克隆技术的引进，它就成为了科学家间一个有争议的话题。

相关表达 **controversialism** *n.* 争论精神；争论癖

记忆点拨 controver[t](辩论)+sial(形容词后缀)

cactus ['kæktəs] ***n.*** **a desert plant with sharp points instead of leaves** 仙人掌

♥ Cactus can be easily found in desert.
在沙漠里很容易看见仙人掌。

♥ Be careful of the spine of the cactus.
小心仙人掌上的刺。

相关表达 复数 cactuses 或者 cacti

termite ['tə:mait] ***n.*** **an insect that eats and destroys wood from trees and buildings** 白蚁

♥ Termite is pest to houses made of wood.
白蚁对木头房子有害。

♥ It is wise to apply the termite-proof paint to the wood.
把木头刷上防白蚁的涂料是很明智的。

variant ['vɛəriənt] ***n.*** **something that is slightly different from the usual form of something** 不同的

♥ You can find variant fresh fruit in the supermarket.
你可以在超市里买到各种不同的新鲜水果。

♥ American and British English may have variant spellings for the same word.
同一个单词在美式英语和英式英语里可能有不同的拼法。

相关表达 近义词 different
反义词 identical

记忆点拨 var[y](改变,变化)+iant

barbarian [bɑːˈbɛəriən] *n.* **someone from a different tribe or land, who people believe to be wild and not civilized** 野蛮人

♥ Barbarian is a word only used by those who think their culture is superior.
野蛮人是那些自认自己的文化高人一等的人才使用的单词。

♥ It is so rude of you to call these farmers barbarians.
你称呼那些农民野蛮人是很没有礼貌的。

相关表达 近义词 savage

pagan [ˈpeigən] *n.* **one who is not a Christian, Moslem, or Jew; a heathen** 异教徒

♥ Pagans used to be prosecuted in the Muslim country.
在穆斯林国家异教徒曾被迫害。

♥ Pagans had their right to believe in their own religion.
异教徒有权信仰他们自己的宗教。

相关表达 **pagandom** *n.* 异教世界

记忆点拨 pag(农村) ＋an(人)

sophistication [səfɪstɪˈkeɪʃən] *n.* 老练

♥ Several years of legal profession bestowed him sophistication of handling cases.
数年的法律职业给予他办案的老练。

♥ Her sophistication can be seen from the way she dresses.
她的老练可以从穿着看出来。

相关表达　sophisticated *adj.* 诡辩的，久经世故的

记忆点拨　sophisticat［e］(究竟世故的）＋ion

premise　［'premis］ ***n.*** **a statement or idea that you accept as true and use as a base for developing other ideas** 前提

♥ If your premise is established, your conclusions are easily deducible.

如果你的前提成立，那么就很容易推断出你的结论了。

♥ When making an argument, you need to start from the premise and go forward.

当论述论点时，你需要从前提开始，再往前走。

词组拓展　on the premise of［that］……在……前提下

记忆点拨　pre(先于）＋mise(发送）

supernatural　［ˌsjuːpə'nætʃərəl］ ***adj.*** **impossible to explain by natural causes, and therefore seeming to involve the powers of gods or magic** 超自然的

♥ Ghosts and evil spirit are supernatural.

鬼怪和精灵都是超自然的。

♥ Harry Potter was said to have supernatural power at birth.

传说中哈利·波特从出生开始就有超自然的能力。

记忆点拨　super(超过）＋natural(自然的）

Lesson 45

dispute [dis'pjuːt] ***v.*** **to try to get control of something or win something** 争夺

♥ The two tribes disputed on the land of the border.
两个部落争夺边境上的土地。

♥ The two researchers are disputing over the copyright of this paper.
两个研究员争夺这篇论文的著作权。

记忆点拨 dis(分开) +pute(考虑，计算)

subdue [sʌb'djuː] ***v.*** **to defeat or control a person or group, especially using force** 征服

♥ The firefighters finally subdued the fire after two hours' burning.
大火在燃烧了两个小时后终于被消防员制服了。

♥ The flood was subdued to the dam.
洪水被大坝征服了。

记忆点拨 sub(离开……) +due(领导)

drainage *n.* the process or system by which water or waste liquid flows away 下水系统

♥ There are a lot of mice in the drainage of New York City.
纽约城的下水道里有很多老鼠。

♥ The city was flooded by the rain because of the jam of the drainage.
由于下水系统的堵塞，雨水把城市给淹没了。

记忆点拨 drain(排水) ＋age(名词后缀)

envision [in'viʒən] *v.* **to imagine something that you think might happen in the future, especially something that you think will be good** 预想

♥ It is such a pleasant to envision having our own house.
想像拥有我们自己的房子是多么令人高兴啊。

♥ The company envisioned recruiting one hundred more employees next year.
公司预想明年再招聘一百名员工。

记忆点拨 en(使) ＋vision(眼力，视)

latitude ['lætitjuːd] *n.* **the distance north or south of the equator**纬度

♥ Our position is latitude 20 degrees north.
我们的位置是北纬 20 度。

♥ The airplane's latitude is 40 degrees south.
飞机在南纬 40 度。

相关表达 反义词 longitude 经度

heretic ['herətik] *n.* **someone who is guilty of heresy** 异教徒，异端邪说

♥ It was said that Galileo was burned to death as a heretic.
据说伽利略是作为异教徒被烧死的。

♥ Heretic was deemed to be evil in the eyes of Holy Office.
在宗教审判厅的眼里，异端邪说是魔鬼。

conceive [kən'siːv] *v.* **to imagine a particular situation or to think about something in a particular way** 想像

♥ The chairman of the board conceived a plan to expand the company.
董事长构想了一个扩充公司的计划。

♥ The writer is conceiving the plot of an new novel.
作家在想像一本新小说的情节。

相关表达 conceiver *n.* 想象者；构想者

记忆点拨 con(一起) ＋ceive(取，拿) （原义是“把……拿来放在一起”）

suffice [sə'fais] *v.* **to be enough** 足够

♥ No words will suffice to convey my happiness.
没有言语能够表达我的喜悦之情。

♥ This food storage will suffice until next week.
这些储备食物能够支撑到下星期。

相关表达 sufficient *adj.* 足够的

记忆点拨 suf(sub)(下) ＋fice(做)

original [ə'ridʒənəl] *adj.* **completely new and different from anything that anyone has thought of before** 有独到见解的

♥ He is the most original student I have ever seen in my whole life of teaching.
在我毕生的教书生涯中，他是最有独特见解的学生。

♥ Poets have their own original words in writing.
诗人们写作时有他们自己独特的语言。

记忆点拨 origin(起源) ＋al

Lesson 46

gifted ['gɪftɪd] *adj.* **having a natural ability to do one or more things extremely well** 有天才的

♥ Beethoven is a gifted musician for centuries.
贝多芬是几个世纪来的天才音乐家。

♥ All are children are gifted in their parents' eyes.
在父母亲的眼里，每个孩子都是有天赋的。

记忆点拨 gift(天赋) ＋ed

psychologist [psaɪ'kɔlədʒɪst] *n.* **someone who is trained in psychology** 心理学家

♥ The psychologist was conducting a research on how people interact with computers.
这个心理学家在做人和电脑如何互动的研究。

♥ A qualified psychologist can successfully perform psychological research, testing, and therapy.
一个合格的心理学家能成功进行心理学研究、测试和诊断。

相关表达 psychiatric *adj.* 治疗精神病的
近义词 convulsion

记忆点拨 psycholog [y](心理学) ＋ist(专家)

spasm ['spæzəm] *n.* **a sudden strong feeling or reaction that you have for a short period of time** 一阵（感情）发作

♥ When she told her father that she was engaged, he was hit by a spasm of surprise.
当她告诉父亲她订婚时，他突然一阵惊讶。

♥ He felt just a spasm of guilt when he steal the old lady's purse, but soon forgot.
当他偷窃那个老太太的钱包时有那么一瞬间觉得内疚，不过很快就忘记了。

词组拓展 habit spasm 习惯性痉挛

相关表达 近义词 convulsion

futile [ˈfjuːtil] ***adj.*** **actions that are futile are useless because they have no chance of being successful** 无用的

♥ It is futile to cry over spilt milk.
为倒出的牛奶的哭泣是没有用的。

♥ It is never futile to learn a lesson and make up your mistakes.
吸取教训和弥补错误不是没有用的。

相关表达 近义词 useless; ineffective; unsuccessful

insinuate [inˈsinjueit] ***v.*** **to say something which seems to mean something unpleasant without saying it openly, especially suggesting that someone is being dishonest** 使潜入，暗示

♥ Over the year she insinuated her impact into her husband's career.
这么多年里她慢慢让自己的影响进入她丈夫的事业中。

♥ Are you insinuating that I am not capable to take this job?
你这是意味着我不够格做这份工作吗？

词组拓展 insinuate into sth. 使成为一部分

记忆点拨 in(内) ＋sinu [s](曲面) ＋ate

convulsive [kən'vʌlsiv] *adj.* **a convulsive movement or action is sudden, violent, and impossible to control** 起痉挛的

♥ When told that he has quit school, his father was struck by a convulsive rage.
当听说他退学了时，他父亲震怒不已。

♥ The basketball was posed because of one of the team members was hit by a convulsive movement of the muscles.
篮球比赛暂时中止，因为有一位队员突然肌肉痉挛。

记忆点拨 convuls [e]（使抽筋）＋ive

illumination [i,ljuːmi'neiʃən] *n.* **lighting provided by a lamp, light etc.** 启发，照明

♥ People believe that Newton's universal gravitation theory comes from illumination of apples' dropping from tree.
人们认为牛顿的万有引力理论是受到了苹果从树上掉下来的启发。

♥ The formation of quantum theory could be traced to illumination of discoveries in many fields of science.
量子理论的形成受到了很多科学领域的发现的启发。

词组拓展 illumination remark 启发人的言论

记忆点拨 illuminat [e]（照明，阐明）＋ion（过程）

undue ['ʌn'djuː] *adj.* **more than is reasonable, suitable, or necessary** 不适当的

♥ The company was caught by deep financial problem because of its undue debt/earning ratio.

由于不适当的债务/赢利比率，这个公司陷入了很深的财务问题。

♥ The newspaper criticized that the government made undue late aids to the people suffering famine.
报纸批评政府对受饥荒的群众的援助既不适当也不及时。

相关表达 近义词 improper

记忆点拨 un(不) ＋due(适当的)

grip [grip] *n.* 紧张

♥ She felt a grip when the car accelerated suddenly.
当车突然加速时她感到一阵紧张。

♥ Grip caught his heart when the interviewer asked a question he was unprepared.
当他被面试人问了一个未准备的问题时心里充满紧张。

recuperation [riˈkjuːpəreiʃən] *n.* **to get better again after an illness or injury** 休息

♥ He asked two weeks vacation because he needed some surgical recuperation.
因为手术后需要休息，所以他请了两星期假。

♥ That seashore resort is very popular for European people to spend recuperation time during weekend.
那个海滨胜地是欧洲人去度周末常去的地方。

相关表达 近义词 recovery

记忆点拨 recuperat [e](复原) ＋ion(状态，过程)

improvise [ˈimprəvaiz] *v.* **to do something without any preparation, because you are forced to do this by unexpected events** 临时作成

♥ He improvised a poem when the grandeur of palace caught his eyes.
当他被宫殿的宏伟吸引住时即时做了一首诗。

♥ Few people knew that the business plan of Southwest Airlines was improvised in a cafeteria.
很少有人知道西南航空公司的创业计划是在一个咖啡馆里即席完成的。

记忆点拨 im(不，没有）＋provise(预见的）

sedulously ['sedjuləsli] ***adv.*** **孜孜不倦地**

♥ The little boy studied sedulously on math and finally passed the makeup exam.
那小男孩不倦地学习终于通过了补考。

♥ The newly discovered physical phenomenon was studies sedulously by scientists around world.
新发现的物理现象被全世界的科学家不倦地研究。

记忆点拨 sedulous(坚韧不拔的）＋ly（……地）

vivify ['vivifai] ***v.*** **to give or bring life to; animate 使生气勃勃**

♥ The short rain vivified the wildlife in desert.
短暂的雨使沙漠充满生机。

♥ The funny question asked the little girl vivify the boring classroom.
小女孩的有趣提问使沉闷的教室充满生气。

相关表达 近义词 animate

记忆点拨 vivi（活的）＋fy(使……)

aggravate ['ægrəveit] ***vt.*** **to make a bad situation, an illness, or an injury worse 加剧**

♥ The economic crisis was aggravated by the heavy flood.
大洪水加剧了经济危机。

♥ The stress from work further aggravated his illness.
工作压力进一步加剧了他的疾病。

相关表达　近义词 exasperate; infuriate

记忆点拨　ag＝ad＝to＋gravis（"重"＝"使更严重"的意思）

trifling　[ˈtraɪflɪŋ] ***adj.*** **unimportant or of little value 微小的**

♥ They thought the labor shortage to be a trifling problem until time proved them wrong.
他们本以为劳力短缺是小问题，但时间证明他们是错误的。

♥ He was easily distracted by trifling matters on job.
他很容易被工作中的小事分散注意力。

相关表达　近义词 trivial

记忆点拨　trifl [e]（少量，小事）＋ing

gratify　[ˈgrætifai] ***v.*** **to make someone feel pleased and satisfied 使满意**

♥ Shareholders were very gratified by the earning this quarter and approved good compensation package to management.
股东对这个季度的盈利很满意，给了管理层很好的报酬。

♥ He was so picky about food that no restaurant in this area could gratify his taste.
他对食物很挑剔，这片地区的餐馆都不能满足他的口味。

相关表达 近义词 satisfy

记忆点拨 grati(高兴) +fy(使……)

caprice [kə'priːs] ***n.*** **a sudden and unreasonable change of mind or behaviour** 任性

♥ He decided to move to California because he didn't like the caprice of weather in this area.
他不喜欢这片地区的多变的天气，决定搬到加州住。

♥ The parents were angered by the caprice of the kid and published him with no new toys for a week.
孩子的父母被孩子的任性激怒了，罚他一个星期没有新玩具。

记忆点拨 (拉丁) cap(头) +rice(卷曲)

satiation [ˌseiʃi'eiʃən] ***n.*** 满足

♥ The guests exhibited great satiation of the food provided by the hostess.
客人们对女主人提供的食物很满意。

♥ It is hard to find a way to meet the boy's satiation of new knowledge.
这个男孩对新知识的欲望很难得到满足。

相关表达 近义词 satisfaction

frantically ['fræntikəli] ***adv.*** 狂乱地

♥ Many people watched on TV that the rescuers worked frantically to saved the beached whales.
很多人在电视上看到救援人员忙乱地抢救搁浅的鲸鱼。

♥ Lots of journalists looked frantically for the history of the new rising singer.

很多记者忙着搜寻歌坛新星的历史。

记忆点拨 frantical(狂乱的) +ly (……地)

avenge [ə'vendʒ] ***v.*** **to do something to hurt or punish someone because they have harmed or offended you** 替……报复

♥ The rebelling army avenged the attack of government by setting fires in villages.
叛军在村庄里放火作为对政府攻击的报复。

♥ The football team swore to avenge after they lost the game.
这个足球队输掉比赛后发誓要复仇。

词组拓展 be avenged on(upon)向……报仇，向……进行报复
avenge sb. on(upon)为某人向……报仇

记忆点拨 a(向) +venge(报复)

boredom ['bɔːdəm] ***n.*** **the feeling you have when you are bored, or the quality of being boring** 厌烦

♥ He finally made decision to resign because of the boredom of this job.
由于工作无聊，他作出了辞职的决定。

♥ The boredom of classroom was broken by a warm discussion of the recent football game.
教室的沉闷被一场关于最近足球赛的讨论打破了。

记忆点拨 bore(使厌烦) +dom(名词后缀)

clatter ['klætə] ***n.*** **if heavy hard objects clatter, or if you clatter them, they make a loud unpleasant noise** 喧闹的谈话

♥ The clatter in the meeting room stopped suddenly when the senior manager came in.

当高层经理走进来时会议室里的喧闹停止了。

♥ The clatter of that restaurant was complained a lot by the neighborhood.

这家饭馆的喧闹经常被邻居抱怨。

相关表达 近义词 noise

sustenance [ˈsʌstinəns] ***n.*** **food that people or animals need in order to live 生计**

♥ He did the job merely as a means of sustenance.

他只是为了生计做这个工作。

♥ He could hardly keep sustenance after three years unemployment.

失业三年后他很难维持生计。

相关表达 近义词 livelihood

记忆点拨 susten [ain](支撑，维持) +ance(名词后缀)

appetite [ˈæpitait] ***n.*** **a desire or liking for a particular activity 欲望**

♥ The professor kept a keen appetite for knowledge outside his research field.

这个教授对他研究领域之外的知识保持强烈的欲望。

♥ His insatiable appetite for money finally led him to commit crime.

他对金钱无法满足的欲望最终导致他犯罪。

词组拓展 have an appetite for 爱好

相关表达 近义词 craving; desire

记忆点拨 ap(ad)(临近) +petite(寻找，尝试)

grudge [grʌdʒ] ***v.*** **to do or give something very unwillingly 怨恨**

♥ The new mayor was grudged by lots of people as he made increases on sales tax.
新市长增加消费税后招致了很多人的怨恨。

♥ Employees grudged deeply against management and swore to strike if their salary requirement could not be met.
雇员对管理层怨恨很深，发誓如果他们的工资要求不被满足的话就罢工。

相关表达　近义词 dislike; ill will

absorbing　[əb'sɔːbɪŋ] ***adj.*** **enjoyable and interesting, and keeping your attention for a long time** 引人入胜的

♥ I found story in this book was absorbing and highly recommended you read it.
我认为这本书里的故事很吸引人，强烈推荐你读它。

♥ Yellowstone is considered to be one of the most absorbing resorts by Americans.
黄石公园被很多美国人认为是最吸引人的旅游胜地。

相关表达　近义词 interesting; attractive

记忆点拨　absorb(吸引) ＋ing

banish　['bæniʃ] ***v.*** **to try to stop thinking about something or someone** 排除，放弃

♥ You must banish your nervousness if you want to pass the exam.
你要想通过这次考试就必须消除紧张心理。

♥ Terms of racial discrimination in law was banished finally after people fought for years.
人们抗争多年后法律里种族歧视的条款最终被废除了。

相关表达　近义词 expel

反义词 receive

Lesson 47

assumption [əˈsʌmpʃən] ***n.*** **something that you think is true although you have no definite proof** 假定

♥ The manager made premature assumptions before he did a thorough research of the market.
这个经理在没对市场做仔细研究就过早地作出假定。

♥ The scientist failed to prove his previous assumption after the experiment result came out.
那个科学家在实验结果出来后不能证明他先前的假设。

记忆点拨 assum [e]（假定）＋ption（行为）

manoeuvre [məˈnuːvə] ***v.*** **to move or turn skilfully or to move or turn something skilfully, especially something large and heavy**（驱车）移动

♥ The army maneuvered secretly to the back of their enemy.
这伙军队悄悄地移动到敌人的后方去。

♥ It is hard for him to maneuver his big jeep in heavy traffic.
他很难在拥挤的交通中挪动他的大吉普。

myriad [ˈmiriəd] ***adj.*** **very many** 无数的

♥ Lots of beautifully storied were made by ancient people when they saw the myriad stars in the sky.

古代人看到天上无数的星星后编出了很多美丽的故事。

♥ Myriad lawsuits were filed against the company after the court determined the deficiencies of its product.

当法院判定产品的缺陷后这家公司受到很多起诉。

相关表达 近义词 many; numerous

paradox [ˈpærədɔks] *n.* **a situation that seems strange because it involves two ideas or qualities that are very different** 自相矛盾的

♥ His defense was weak and in paradox when new evidence was shown on court.

当证据被呈上法庭后，他的辩护变得虚弱并自相矛盾。

♥ The new theory was criticized by lots of people as they find many paradoxes in it.

因为人们发现这个新理论中很多自相矛盾的地方，所以受到很多人批评。

记忆点拨 para(半，类似) ＋dox(观点)

cynic [ˈsinik] *n.* **someone who is not willing to believe that people have good, honest, or sincere reasons for doing something** 愤世嫉俗者

♥ He became a cynic after his proposal was rejected by management for the third time.

当他的提议被管理层第三次拒绝后他变得愤世嫉俗。

♥ Many people like the ironic articles written by the cynic journalist.

很多人喜欢那个愤世嫉俗的记者写的讽刺文章。

sociologist *n.* 社会学家

♥ Some sociologists could get large amounts of sponsorship from the industry as their research result could be used to guide marketing campaigns.

有些社会学家受到工业界的大量资助，因为他们的研究成果可以被用于市场促销。

♥ There are many famous sociologists in that university.

那个大学有很多著名的社会学家。

记忆点拨 sociolog [y]（社会学）＋ist(专家)

shun [ʃʌn] ***v.*** **to deliberately avoid someone or something** 避开

♥ He was unable to shun the attack from the gangster and knocked down to the ground.

他没能避开匪徒的袭击被打倒在地。

♥ He tried vainly to shun the attention in public after the demotion news came out.

当降职的消息传出后他不能避开公众的注意。

相关表达 近义词 avoid; dodge

affluent [ˈæfluənt] ***adj.*** **having plenty of money, nice houses, expensive things etc.** 富有的

♥ The affluent dynasty was ruined by the invasion of nomads from the north.

这个富有的王朝被北方游牧部落的侵略毁掉了。

♥ The young man was born in an affluent family and received good education.

那个年轻人出生在富有的家庭，并受到良好的教育。

相关表达　近义词 abundant; ample

记忆点拨　af(ad)(朝向) +fluent(流动)

chambermaid　[ˈtʃeɪmbəmeɪd] *n.* **a female worker whose job is to clean and tidy bedrooms, especially in a hotel** 女招待员

♥ He left a good tip to the chambermaid in the hotel when he checked out.
当他在旅馆结账时，付给女招待员很多的小费。

♥ The pretty chambermaid has been working in this hotel for several years.
这个可爱的女招待员已经在这个旅馆工作了好几年了。

记忆点拨　chamber(会所) +maid(女仆)

boo　[buː] *n.* 呸的一声

♥ The beggar was angered when a pass-by said boo to him.
当行人对乞丐呸了一声后，他生气了。

♥ The boy booed his teacher in classroom when the teacher pointed out his mistake.
当老师指出他的错误时，这个男孩呸了一声。

maitre d'hotel　[metrədəuˈtel] *n.* [法语] 总管

♥ Less young people choose maitre d'hotel as their career these days.
现在越来越少的年轻人选择总管作为职业。

♥ You could ask that maitre d'hotel about the best red wine to pick for dinner.

你应该问那个主管哪种是晚餐最好的红酒。

snobbery ['snɔbəri] *n.* **behaviour or attitudes which show that you think you are better than other people, because you belong to a higher social class or know much more than they do—used to show disapproval** 势利

♥ The snobbery of the waiter angered the man with rural accent.

势利的侍者惹怒了那个带着乡村口音的男人。

♥ Snobbery has been favorite topic of literatures for many years.

"势利"多年来始终是文学的最喜欢的话题。

相关表达 snobbish *adj.* 势利的

hierarchy ['haiərɑːki] *n.* **a system of organization in which people or things are divided into levels of importance** 等级制度

♥ Strict hierarchy of social classes, known as caste system, still exists in some areas of India.

严格的等级制度，又称为世袭制度，至今仍然存在于印度的某些地方。

♥ The hierarchy of many high-tech companies is flat compared with traditional companies.

与传统公司相比，高科技公司的等级制度很浅。

相关表达 近义词 class

记忆点拨 hierarch(教主，掌权者) ＋y

entail [in'teil] *v.* **to involve something as a necessary part or result** 使成为必要

♥ The recent famine in East Africa entailed the help from United Nations.

最近的东非饥荒使得联合国的援助成为必要。

♥ The worsened ecological environment in this area entailed the attention from government.

这个地区变得更坏的生态环境使得政府的关注成为必要。

记忆点拨 en(使成为) +tail(尾巴)

inclement [inˈklemənt] ***adj.*** **inclement weather is unpleasantly cold, wet etc.** 险恶的

♥ The school kept the regular schedule in spite of inclement weather conditions.

尽管天气恶劣，学校还是维持了正常作息时间。

♥ The inclement weather makes the climbing more dangerous.

恶劣的天气使得登山更加危险。

相关表达 近义词 cold; cruel

记忆点拨 in(非) +clement(温暖的，温和的)

package tour 由旅行社安排一切的一揽子旅游

♥ The package tour offered by that travel agency was the best deal I had even seen.

旅行社提供的旅游计划是我见过的最实惠的了。

♥ He bought a five-day package tour which covered all major cities on East Coast.

他购买了一个五日游的计划，包括东海岸的所有大城市。

insularity [ˌɪnsjʊˈlærətɪ] ***n.*** 偏狭

♥ The insularity of people living on this island surprised explorers who were the first visitors from outside world.

住在岛上的人们的狭隘令第一批从外面世界来此拜访的探险者很吃惊。

♥ The insularity of the new fiscal policy scared away lots of foreign investors.
新的财政政策的狭隘吓跑了很多的外国投资者。

相关表达 **insular** *adj.* 海岛的；岛民的；岛特有的；孤立的；超然物外的

记忆点拨 insular(海岛的) ＋ity(性)

cater [ˈkeitə] ***v.* to provide a particular group of people with the things they need or want** 迎合

♥ He made special arrangement of schedule to cater the interests of the coming bankers.
他做出特殊的日程安排来迎合来访的银行家们。

♥ The young couple catered their guest with some good French wine.
这对年轻的夫妇用好的法国酒来招待客人。

相关表达 近义词 pamper; serve

exclusively [ɪkˈskluːsɪvlɪ] ***adv.*** 排他地

♥ Rooms on third floor were reserved exclusively for the coming high rank officials.
第三层的房间专门准备接待即将到来的高官们。

♥ The golf course is open exclusively to club members.
高尔夫课程是专门面对俱乐部会员的。

记忆点拨 exclusive(排外的) ＋ly（……地）

cosmopolitan [ˌkɔzməˈpɔlitən] ***adj.* a cosmopolitan place has people from many different parts of the world** 世界的

♥ New York is deemed to the cosmopolitan center of capital by the world.
纽约市被全世界认为是世界资本中心。

♥ Soccer, as a cosmopolitan sport has been well accepted in American recently.
足球，作为一项世界性的运动；已经逐渐开始被美国人接受。

词组拓展 a cosmopolitan city 国际都市

记忆点拨 cosmopolit [e](属于世界的) ＋an

preponderance [prɪˈpɔndərəns] ***n.*** **if there is a preponderance of people or things of a particular type in a group, there are more of that type than of any other** 优势

♥ Preponderance of evidence led to the innocence of the defendant.
证据上的优势使得被告宣判无罪。

♥ The preponderance of data paints a gloomy picture of economic recovery.
大部分数据显示出经济复苏迹象很不明朗。

记忆点拨 pre(先于) ＋ponderance(称体重)

overwhelmingly [ˌəuvəˈwelmiŋli] ***adv.*** 以压倒优势地，清一色地

♥ Our football teams won overwhelmingly during the second half of the game.
我们的足球队在下半场以明显优势取得了胜利。

♥ The congress overwhelmingly passed the act to provide additional financial aid to poor countries.
国会以压倒多数通过了向贫困国家提供经济援助的提案。

记忆点拨 over 在……之上 ＋ whelm 淹没 ＋ ing ＋ ly（……地）

patronage ['pætrənidʒ] ***n.*** **the support that you give a particular shop, restaurant etc. by buying their goods or using their services** 恩惠，惠顾

♥ The store owner appreciated the patronage of its customers by offering special holiday sales.
店主为了感谢顾客的惠顾而提供节日优惠。

♥ Student patronage to museum is encouraged by offering discounted tickets.
博物馆为了鼓励学生参观，推出了打折票。

记忆点拨 patron(保护人) ＋age(名词后缀)

sauerkraut ['sauəkraut] ***n.*** **a German food made from cabbage (＝a round green vegetable) that has been left in salt so that it tastes sour** 泡菜

♥ Sauerkraut is the favorite food to most Korean people.
泡菜是很多韩国人最喜欢的食品。

♥ He learned to make German sauerkraut when he visited Frankfurt last year.
去年他访问法兰克福时学会了做德国泡菜。

相关表达 近义词 Kimchi *n.* <朝鲜语>朝鲜泡菜

vie [vai] ***v.*** **to compete very hard with someone in order to get something** 竞争

♥ No substance could ever vie with diamonds in terms of hardiness.
没有哪种东西可以和钻石在硬度上竞争。

♥ He is the best athlete in our class and no one could vie with him on speed.
他是我们班最好的运动员，没人能跟他在速度上竞争。

相关表达 vier *n.* 竞争者
近义词 compete; rival

municipality [mjuːˌnisiˈpæliti] ***n.*** **a town, city, or other small area, which has its own government to make decisions about local affairs, or the officials in that government 市政当局**

♥ The corruption of municipality was not a secret to people any more after a major newspaper disclosed the scandal.
在一家大报纸详细披露了丑闻后，市政府的腐败对人们来说就不再是秘密了。

♥ Lots of complains were filed to municipality about the negligence of police department.
市政府收到了很多关于警察部门失职的抱怨。

记忆点拨 municipal(市政的) ＋lity(名词后缀)

itinerant [iˈtinərənt] ***n.*** **one who travels from place to place 巡回者**

♥ Gypsies have been itinerants on European continent for hundreds of years.
吉普赛人在欧洲大陆上到处流浪已经有上百年了。

♥ Itinerants in the forest area were paid special attention by the administrative agency as they often proved to be illegal hunters.
在森林里的游荡者引起了行政部门的特别关注，因为他们被发现经常是非法狩猎者。

记忆点拨 itiner [ary]((拉丁) 旅行) +ant(人)

heath [hi:θ] ***n.*** **an area of open land where grass, bushes, and other small plants grow, especially in Britain 荒地**

♥ He did little work on the heath of backyard as he was too busy doing his scientific research.
因为他太忙于科学研究，几乎没花什么工夫在后院的荒地上。

♥ Thousand acres of heath could be found in the remote north part of this country.
在这个国家遥远的北部能发现上千英亩的荒地。

alienate [ˈeiljəneit] ***v.*** **to do something that makes someone unfriendly or unwilling to support you 使疏远**

♥ His bad temper alienated himself from other colleagues in the office.
他的坏脾气使得他受到办公室同事的疏远。

♥ The company was alienated by most of its suppliers after they found the financial distress of it.
当供销商们发现公司的经济拮据时，就渐渐疏远了它。

相关表达 近义词 isolate

记忆点拨 alien(背道而驰) +ate(行为)

eternal [i(:)ˈtə:nl] ***adj.*** **continuing for ever and having no end 永久的**

♥ Ancient Egyptians believed that man's life would become eternal after their body was made into mummy.

古代埃及人相信当身体成为木乃伊后人的生命就能永久了。

♥ Eternal youth has been the dream of many people.
永葆青春是很多人的梦想。

相关表达

近义词 permanent; forever

反义词 momentary transient

Lesson 48

portfolio [pɔːtˈfəuljəu] *n.* **a group of stocks owned by a particular person or company** 投资组合

♥ Portfolio manager has been ideal job to many newly graduated MBAs in recent years.

近几年来对于新毕业的 MBA 学生来说，投资组合经理是很理想的工作。

♥ Complicated financial models were built by Wall Street Analysts to find out the best stock portfolios.

华尔街上的分析师们建立各种复杂的金融模型来寻找最佳的股票投资组合。

记忆点拨 port(携带) ＋folio(纸张)

tipster [ˈtipstə] *n.* **someone who gives information about which horse is likely to win a race**(以提供证券投机等内部消息为主的）情报贩子

♥ The incoming bankruptcy of the company was whispering among tipsters on Wall Street.

关于那家公司即将破产的消息在华尔街的情报人员中悄悄流传。

♥ It is hard to tell whether the information from a tipster on the street is true or not.

很难判断那些马路上的情报贩子提供的消息是否准确。

记忆点拨 tip(秘密消息) ＋s＋ter(人)

fritter [ˈfritə] *v.* **to waste time, money, or effort on something small or unimportant 挥霍，浪费**

♥ He frittered most of his inherited fortune in casinos.

他把大部分继承来的财产都挥霍在了赌场。

♥ The little boy was addicted to electronic games and frittered away lots of hours in front of computer.

小男孩沉迷于电脑游戏，在电脑前浪费了很多时间。

词组拓展 fritter away 浪费

相关表达 近义词 squander

reputable [ˈrepjutəbl] *n.* **respected for being honest or for doing good work 享有声望的**

♥ Warren Buffet is the most reputable investor ever in history and lots of people became rich by buying shares of his company.

沃伦·巴菲特是历史上最有名的投资家，很多人因为购买他公司的股票而致富。

♥ Almost every reputable scientist rejected his theory when Darwin published his research on evolution.

当达尔文发表他的进化论时，几乎所有著名的科学家都否定他的理论。

相关表达 近义词 honorable; respectable

反义词 infamous

记忆点拨 reput [e]（名誉，名声）＋able（……能力的）

broker [ˈbrəukə] *n.* **someone who buys and sells things such as shares in companies or foreign money for other people 经纪人**

♥ The brokers lowered their transaction fee significantly after people could buy stocks online.

当人们能够在网上购买股票时，经济人大幅度降低了交易费。

♥ Brokers from famous financial institution could offer valuable investment advice.

著名金融机构的经济人可以提供有价值的投资建议。

记忆点拨 broke(一文不名的) ＋r(人)

finance [faiˈnæns] *n.* **the money that an organization or person has, and the way that they manage it** 资金，财源

♥ Many small companies rely heavily on venture capitalist to manage their finance demands.

很多小公司非常依赖风险投资家来管理他们的金融需求。

♥ It is hard for a company to find adequate finance when rumors of bankruptcy spread out on the Street.

当公司破产的谣言流传在华尔街时，这家公司就很难找到资金来源。

词组拓展 the Minister of Finance 财政部部长

记忆点拨 fin(完，末尾) ＋ ance(该词原意“支付，还清借款”)

mortgage [ˈmɔːgidʒ] *n.* **a legal arrangement by which you borrow money from a bank or similar organization in order to buy a house, and pay back the money over a period of years** 抵押贷款

♥ He managed to get a ten year mortgage on his new house.

他用新房子拿到了十年的抵押贷款。

♥ The low interest on mortgage was the major drive for the soaring real estate price.

抵押贷款的低息是让房产价格飞速上升的主要原因。

记忆点拨 mort(死的) +gage(抵押)

pension [ˈpenʃən] ***n.*** **an amount of money paid regularly by the government or company to someone who does not work any more, for example because they have reached the age when people stop working or because they are ill** 养老金

♥ Many large companies still offer good pension plan for their retired employee.

很多大型公司会为他们的退休员工提供很好的养老金计划。

♥ Pension fund was a major source of capital to some companies.

养老金基金是很多公司的主要资金来源。

priority [praiˈɔriti] ***n.*** **the thing that you think is most important and that needs attention before anything else** 优先权

♥ He has difficulty managing priority of his tasks as all of them are emergent.

因为所有的任务都很紧急，他不知道该如何安排优先权。

♥ Priority of buying IPO stocks was usually given to large financial institutes.

购买上市股票的权利经常会给予大型的金融机构。

词组拓展 according to priority 依次

give(first)priority to 给……以（最）优先权

记忆点拨 prior(先，前) + ity(名词后缀)

gilt [gilt] *n.* **a stock or share that is gilt-edged 金边证券（高度可靠的证券）**

♥ He was an expert in trading options on gilt.
他做金边债券期权交易是个好手。

♥ Issuing gilt is an important financial instrument for government to finance public projects.
发行金边证券是政府给公共项目筹资的重要手段。

convertible [kən'və:təbl] *n.* **a convertible security 可换证券**

♥ You may minimize your investment risk by buying convertibles which could be exchange for company stock after specific term.
你可以购买可换证券来减小投资风险，它可以在若干时间后转化成公司股票。

♥ Issuing convertibles have become popular among large companies as the stock market fluctuated dramatically in recent years.
因为近几年股票市场的剧烈震荡，发行可换证券对很多大型公司来说变得越来越普遍。

记忆点拨 convert(转换）＋ible

sanguine ['sæŋgwin] *adj.* **happy and hopeful about the future 乐观的**

♥ It is hard to maintain a sanguine attitude during bear market when you watch the value of your portfolio going down rapidly.
在熊市时当你看见自己的股票急剧下跌时，很难保持乐观的态度。

♥ The crew was inspired by the sanguine speech made by the captain and fought harder with the storm.

水手们都被船长乐观的演讲所感染，决心更奋力地和暴风雨斗争。

相关表达　近义词 cheerful; optimistic

记忆点拨　sanguin(血液) ＋e(该词有“血红色的”的意思)

heady　['hedi] ***adj.*** **very exciting in a way that makes you feel as if you can do anything you want to 令人陶醉的**

♥ The artist was attracted by the heady landscape of the lake and decided to draw a picture on it.

艺术家被湖边令人陶醉的风景吸引了，决定为此画幅画。

♥ Hedge funds became the favorite investment choice among Wall Street bankers due to their heady return.

由于它们令人陶醉的回报，对冲基金成为了华尔街银行家最喜欢的投资选择。

记忆点拨　head(头脑) ＋y(形容词后缀)

alongside　[ə'lɔŋ'said] ***prep.*** **next to the side of something 在……旁边，和……一起**

♥ He sat quietly alongside the cheering crowd and paid no attention to the ongoing basketball game.

他安静地坐在狂呼的人群旁边，根本没注意看正在进行的篮球比赛。

♥ The quiet garden alongside the museum was completely ignored by people when the new exhibit went on.

当新展览进行时，这座在博物馆旁边的宁静的花园被完全忽略了。

记忆点拨　along(沿着) ＋side(旁边)

pedestrian　[pe'destriən] ***adj.*** **ordinary and uninteresting and without any imagination** 平淡无奇的，乏味的

♥ The pedestrian love story in his new book attracted little public attention.
他的新书中平淡无奇的爱情故事几乎没有引起公众注意。

♥ He was tired of pedestrian life in the small city and decided to move to New York City.
他厌倦了这座小城平淡无奇的生活，决定搬到纽约市去。

相关表达　近义词 ordinary

记忆点拨　pedestri(步行的) ＋an(该词原意"步行者，徒步的")